TIME KNEELS BETWEEN MOUNTAINS

Amra Pajalić

AMRA PAJALIĆ

MELBOURNE, AUSTRALIA

https://www.pishukinpress.com/

First Published 2025

Pishukin Press

Cover design: Created using Canva elements, cover image attribution Songquan Deng via @ Canva.com, image overlay 41199233@ DepositPhotos

For content and trigger warnings please go towww.amrapajalic.com/themes

Quality control: We care about producing error-free books. If you discover a typo or formatting issue, please contact admin@pishukinpress.com

Paperback Edition: 9781922871534

Author Note

Time Kneels Between Mountains was written as part of my PhD in Creative Writing at La Trobe University. While the novel draws on extensive research into the historical events surrounding the Srebrenica genocide, it is a work of fiction—specifically, a fictional crime novel.

The narrative, characters, and criminal investigations depicted in this book are entirely imagined. They do not reflect real individuals or actual crimes, and any resemblance to persons living or dead is purely coincidental. The only exceptions are real historical figures, who are named and listed in the Index of Characters.

This novel blends factual history with fictional storytelling to explore themes of justice, trauma, and complicity. It does not claim to represent specific real-world events or people but instead seeks to honour memory through a creative lens.

Index of characters

Torlak Family

Seka (Dževahira) Torlak, protagonist

Fadil Torlak, Seka's father, called Babo

Esma Torlak, Seka's mother, Mama

Emir Torlak, Seka's brother

Nuhanović Family

Behrudin, Seka's grandfather, called Dido

Habiba, Seka's grandmother, called Nana

Esma, Seka's mother, daughter of Behrudin,

Adna, Seka's aunt, daughter of Behrudin called Tetka Adna,

Mustafa, Seka's uncle, son of Behrudin, lives in Australia

Ibrahim, Seka's uncle, son of Behrudin

Paša, Seka's aunt, Ibrahim's wife

Imran, Seka's cousin, Ibrahim's six-year-old son

Minka, Seka's cousin, Ibrahim's four year-old-daughter

Nesiba, Seka's cousin, a one-year-old baby

Other children of Behrudin

Harun,

Ramiza, Harun's wife, Edina's sister

Muharemović Family
Ramo, Seka's beau
Omer, Ramo's father
Edina, Ramo's mother
Čazim, Ramo's brother
Hamdija, Ramo's brother
Orhan, Ramo's brother
Ramiza, Ramo's sister

Mihajlović Family
Belma, Seka's friend
Šerif, Belma's father
Aiša, Belma's mother
Four younger siblings

Hodžić Family
Kamila, Seka's friend
Harun, Kamila's father
Lebiba, Kamila's mother
Kinan, Kamila's brother

Softić Family
Nedjad, Belma's husband
Vahid, Nedjad's father
Dželila, Nedjad's wife,
Bilal, Nedjad's younger brother
Ismail, cousin

Đokić Family
Zora, Seka's childhood friend

Slobodan, Zora's father
Petra, Zora's mother

Other characters
Mrs Tanović, Seka's Grade 4 teacher
Zaim, interpreter at Potočari headquarters
Captain Luuk Van Dijk, DutchBat Captain at Potočari
headquarters
Boris, Fadil's Serb workmate and best friend, and his wife
Snežana

Real-life people
Alija Izetbegović-Bosnian President
Ratko Mladić-Serb Commander
Naser Orić-Bosnian Commander
General Philippe Morillon, commanded the United Na-
tions Forces in Bosnia

Pronunciation & Glossary

Pronunciation

A note on pronunciation:

Č č=Ch

Ć ć-a softer Ch sound

Đ đ=softer Dj sound

Š š-Sh sound

Ž ž-Dj sound

J-is pronounced as Y, so *ašikovanje* is pronounced *ashiko-vanye.*

Glossary

Ašikovanje, a flirting ritual indicating that a couple would be married

Balija (singular), *Balije* (plural)-derogatory Serb slur used against Bosnian Muslims

Alija- derogatory Serb slur used against Bosnian Muslims referencing the Bosnian President Alija Izetbegović

Babo-Father

Bosniak-Bosnian Muslims

Bosnian-A person from Bosnia

Chetniks-Serb Royalists

Šamija-headscarf

Džezva-coffee pot

Dimije-harem type pants worn by women in the village

Drina-famous river in Bosnia that runs through Serbia

Fildžan-demitasse coffee cup

Mama-Mum

Nana-Grandmother

Potočari-Industrial base seven kilometres away from Srebrenica

Rakija-a Balkan plum brandy,

Content Warnings

www.amrapajalic.com/themes.html

Prologue

"People know about the genocide, but not many remember the horror that we lived through in the three years that came before."
Srebrenica genocide survivor, as interviewed by journalist Alyssa Jones

1-Enemy

I threw open the front door and bolted out of the house, excitement at accompanying Mama and Edina as they went to town to make a phone call surging through my veins.

My mother's scream of terror stopped me dead in my tracks.

"What's wrong?" I returned to her side.

Mama was clutching the wall, her face white with terror. "You stupid girl!" She shook me by my shoulders. "A sniper will get you."

Srebrenica was surrounded by mountainous peaks, which provided a perfect vantage point for snipers. In the time it took them to shoot once, miss, and correct their target, an innocent bystander would only take one step.

"She'll be fine out the door, it's halfway down the street that they can sight you," my father said.

Since the war started, I hadn't been allowed to leave at all. Babo and Emir went to the black market together to exchange goods for food while I remained home. My parents used to tell me that the war would be over soon. They had stopped believing that. I could barely contain myself from hurtling out the door again. As if she could feel my restlessness, Mama took my hand, and we stepped out, her eyes fearfully scanning the hills.

"We have to continue with our lives. We can't stay in the house and live in fear." Babo squeezed my mother's shoulders as he reassured her.

Mama straightened her shoulders. Edina and Ramo followed us. They were refugees to our town, arriving from my grandparents and uncles and aunt when the Chetniks cleansed their village and forced them to evacuate.

Babo and Emir walked ahead of us because we couldn't all fit on the footpath together, my father and brother matching their long-legged strides to each other, as they were the same height now. Plastic sheets covered holes in roofs, and parts of houses were missing sections. I turned to look at our house as we walked. Babo and Emir repaired it between shellings. Even though two of our windows were covered with plastic sheets, and my bedroom window was boarded up as it faced the mountains, it still looked better than most houses on our street. Rubbish filled the street, the smell rancid and rotten in the summer heat.

Closer to town, the buildings were more and more damaged. The sidewalk was pockmarked with large craters from the homemade bombs filled with metal and nails that were dropped from aeroplanes. My excitement faded as terror took over.

"The Chetniks target the centre of town on purpose, so we admire their might." Emir turned around and held out his hand to encompass the surrounding destruction.

Fuck the Chetniks. Before the war, most faces in town would be familiar. Now, I mostly saw strangers. Since the villages around town were cleared, refugees flooded the town. The refugees were mostly peasants from the villages; the women were in *dimije*, the billowy fabric of the harem pants fluttering in the breeze as they walked, and the men wore dark berets. Those of us from Srebrenica wore our best finery. I was wearing my pink and white polka dot summer dress. I had grown in the past three months, and it was feeling tight around the chest and was above my knees, but it was still decent. Emir gave Ramo his clothes, even though Emir was slightly taller. The tracksuit pants and white t-shirt fitted Ramo well.

Mama and Edina stepped in and began talking while Emir, Babo, and Ramo walked together. Was this always going to be my fate now that Zora was gone, to be alone and friendless? I struggled to hold back tears as I thought of my best friend, who had to leave because she became a target as the enemy.

When we reached the black market, we broke away. Ramo and I followed my father and brother, while Mama and Edina continued to the centre of town, to the mall-yellow building with the huge aerial sticking out on the roof where the ham radio station was.

A long line stretched down the street in front of the building. The ham radio operator could manually operate the radio base to do a 'phone patch', which basically consisted of manually dialling a number to connect to the telephone network.

Mama was calling my uncle Mustafa, who lived in Australia. She'd done this trek many times and complained that she waited for up to three hours only to spend five minutes allocated by the man who operated the rickety army-green radio set, a ham radio, a relic in the time of telephones but a saviour in the time of war. Ramo's mother, Edina, was waiting to speak to her daughter, who lived in Sarajevo, which was also under siege.

The only difference between Sarajevo and us is that people seemed to care about Sarajevo. It received constant media attention with columns of newsprint and television reports while we were the forgotten second cousin, or at least that's what my father said when we listened to the radio broadcasts.

I followed my father and brother to the marketplace across the street from the Cultural Centre. As we approached, I heard the din, echoing voices, and the sounds of traditional folk music played with the rippling wave of a violin.

In the alleyway next to the market, we saw a man selling a UN ration bag to a woman, the two of them furtively exchanging the goods for money. My father hissed between his teeth. "Profiteers," and glared as we continued.

I shook his sleeve, and he looked at me. "He stole the UN rations and is selling them for profit."

My stomach lurched. I couldn't believe that in the midst of such deprivations, criminals were stealing for profit instead of ensuring that the rations were given to those of us who were starving.

We entered the market, shards of glass crunching beneath our feet from exploded windows and large chunks of plaster dislodged by shelling. I avoided the piles of horse dung from the villagers who walked down from the mountains to sell corn, potatoes, and eggs.

A seething mass of people congregated around the tables, some wearing blankets as they had no coats, with pieces of rug, sheets, or cow skin wrapped around their shoes with string to keep them tied together. I gawked at the food displayed on the tables, more than I had seen in months, and my mouth watered and stomach rumbled as I imagined scrambled eggs, baked potatoes, or corn on the cobb.

"Babo, buy some eggs." I tugged on his coat.

Babo approached the stall-holder with eggs in a basket at his feet. "How much for the eggs?"

"Ten Deutschmarks," the man said.

Babo frowned. "Ten Deutschmarks for ten eggs. That's very expensive." He took out his wallet and counted the money. Ever since the war began, regular life had ceased, including my parent's job at the factories in Potočari. The only money we had were the notes that my parents squirrelled away in the house before banks collapsed.

"That's for one egg," the man said.

"Ten Deutschmarks for one egg?" Babo was stupefied.

My stomach dropped, all my dreams of scrambled eggs disappearing.

Babo returned his money to his wallet.

"This is hell," I grumbled. "And why is everything in Deutschmarks?"

My father explained it was because of hyperinflation, but I'd lost interest.

"What about corn?" I urged, my rumbling stomach prompting me. I could almost taste the sweet juiciness of the corn in my mouth and the tang of salt. Then I remembered we had no salt. It felt like now that I was exposed to all this food, my senses were coming alive, and my brain was sending me memories of flavours I hadn't tasted in months.

Babo approached a woman with shucked corn in a bucket. "Ten Deutschmarks for a kilo."

Babo nodded and counted his money.

Emir and Ramo joined a group of young men, and they talked in the corner while I followed my father.

Babo talked to people he knew, asking about friends and family in the villages. I overheard everyone having conversations, trading news about the Chetniks' positions, and speculating about whether NATO would intervene or when the war would be over.

Babo waved me over. "Look who I found." He nodded towards a woman who was standing with her back to me.

I saw the wisps of dark hair slipping out of the headscarf and an hourglass figure in *dimije* from behind. The woman turned, and I gasped as I recognised Belma's green eyes and tanned face. Belma was my friend from my grandparent's village. We'd spent every summer together since I was a young child when we visited my mother's family.

"Belma," I shouted as I ran towards her.

She smiled at me and we hugged. She squeezed me back.

Her husband Nedjad was standing next to her, Belma's head reaching his shoulders as his tall and rangy frame loomed over her. Nedjad was brown-haired and blue-eyed. He had a scar cutting through his eyebrow, giving him a slightly sinister look that was completely at odds with his personality.

When my father introduced Ramo, Belma waggled her eyebrows at me. I shook my head and covered my face as I mimed vomiting by putting two fingers down my throat. We moved away from the crowd.

"I was hoping we would get to see you, but I didn't know your address," she said.

I quickly told her. "What about you?"

"We're living in a three-bedroom flat." She rattled off the address. It was on the other side of town.

"That's nice, having all that space to yourselves," I said.

Belma frowned. "No, we're all together. My parents, Nedjad's parents, my siblings, his brother."

"Oh." I took a moment to process. Belma had tried so hard to get away from her father and was now forced to live with him again. "How are you? What's the news?" I asked.

Her cheeks flushed, and she suddenly looked bashful.

"What is it?" I demanded, even though I suspected.

Belma touched her stomach and smiled. "I'm pregnant."

"Congratulations." I hugged her again.

"Come and visit me," she said. "Tell me all your news." She looked at Ramo and waggled her eyebrows meaningfully. "He's lovely to look at."

I glanced at Ramo, attempting to see him through Belma's eyes. I remembered the first time I saw him months ago when he'd arrived with my grandparents and aunts and uncles. Along with them were a woman and a boy. Blonde wisps of the woman's hair poked through her headscarf. His mother, Edina, had clutched him, even though he was head and shoulders taller than her, like he was her life buoy while she drowned in the ocean. Ramo had his mother's colouring—blonde hair and clear blue eyes—their pale skin translucent so that their veins were visible.

When my Uncle Ibrahim introduced me to after we exchanged greetings and hugs among family, Ramo had offered his hand. Despite the chaotic introduction, I was impressed that he adhered to our schooling by the Union of Pioneers of Yugoslavia and always offered a handshake. Ramo's callused palm scraped on my palm.

My pulse raced; it became harder to breathe. I glanced over at Zora. Her blue eyes were wide with curiosity as she glanced at Ramo.

"Tristan," I whispered in her ear.

She giggled. He looked like the hero in the romance novel we were reading.

Ramo offered his hand to Zora, but as my father introduced Zora's parents and her siblings, he winced as if he smelled dog shit, withdrawing his hand.

"Serbs," he said, looking at Zora's family like they were vermin.

"Slobodan is a family friend. They provided us with shelter when we were invaded. Now we are returning the favour," my father said.

Ramo kept his hand by his side but said nothing.

After Zora and her family left, I'd unleashed a death stare at Ramo. I couldn't believe I'd lusted after him. He was so ugly. Ramo had stared back at me balefully. Ever since then, I couldn't look at him the same way, and we had avoided speaking or talking to each other.

"Maybe he has a reason for being angry with Serbs," Belma said. "Did he lose family?"

I nodded grudgingly. The Chetniks stopped their bus and forcibly took his father and two older brothers off after they were evacuated from their village. We all knew their fate once they stepped off the bus, but no one spoke about it.

"Then you need to give him some leeway. He has every right to hate Serbs."

"But Zora and her family did nothing!" I exclaimed. "They were here, helping us." After the conflict broke out and Chetniks invaded Srebrenica, Zora's family hid us in their basement, and when Bosniak soldiers fought back and re-took the town, we hid them in ours.

"It's easy for you to separate between the good and bad Serbs. For those of us who lost our family homes, livelihoods and family, the Serbs are the enemy."

I glanced askance at Belma, noting the bitterness in her tone. I knew that things in the villages were different. The Serbs and Bosniaks did not mix as much because of the memories of WWII and the atrocities committed by the Chetniks, a Serbian nationalist and royalist paramilitary organisation active in Yugoslavia before and during World War II whose goals included the liberation of Serb-inhabited areas and the establishment of a Greater Serbia. However, I hadn't realised Belma's prejudice ran so deep. I used to talk to her about my friend with Zora before the war and she'd shared no xenophobic views then.

I squirmed internally. Maybe she was right? It was easy for me to be fair-minded when I still had my house, my family, and my community. For the refugees who were scrabbling to survive, their enmity would run much deeper.

We spoke a little more about people we knew—shared who passed away and who survived. "We have to go home. I have to prepare dinner," Belma said.

As we continued walking around the market, I couldn't stop thinking about Belma. She was sixteen years old, married, and with a baby on the way. In February, I had been envious of her entry into adulthood. Now, I shuddered with horror at the thought of having a baby during a war.

I glanced back and noticed that my father was engrossed in a conversation with other men. Now was the moment to implement my plan. "I'm going to find Mama," I told him.

"I don't want you going alone." He called Emir over, and Ramo came with him. "Take your sister to your mother."

"But I was going to be with my friends to the Cultural Centre." Emir pointed at the group.

"I'll take her," Ramo said.

"That's okay," I said. "No one needs to go with me."

"Then you can stay here," Babo said, and turned back to talk to his friends.

"Seka," Emir growled. "Don't ruin this for me."

"Okay, fine. Babo, I'll go with Ramo," I called out and walked. Ramo followed.

I glanced behind me and saw Ramo following a few steps behind. When we were away from the market, I stopped.

"You can go home now," I told him, still looking ahead and not at his face.

"I'm not leaving you alone."

I glanced at him. His jaw was determined.

"Where are you going?" he asked.

"To the high school to find books," I confessed.

He waved his hand, gesturing for me to lead the way.

When we reached the playground, we veered right, ran to the school, and abruptly stopped, my eyes taking in the destroyed school. The day before, a 'mosquito', a modified aeroplane, had flown into the city and dropped its destructive load onto the school. The mosquito had circled the town for half an hour, looking for a target. Usually, the improvised bombs, or boilers as we called them, fell onto the slopes, causing a tremendous crash and leaving a crater behind. But yesterday the bomb had landed on the school.

The two-storey school was now a mess of rubble. The bomb that had split it in two. All the windows had shattered, and the gaping holes reminded me of a screaming monster in a horror movie.

"Were they trying to hit the school?" I asked Ramo, the words coming unbidden to my lips.

"Yes, they were probably hoping there were students inside."

"Maybe the pilot was trying to hit the town and miscalculated?" I didn't want to believe that people could be so evil as to really want to kill children.

"Chetniks don't care if their targets are children or not. The only good *Balija* is a dead *Balija*," his voice coated with the same bitterness I had heard in Belma's tone.

As we looked at the destroyed school, I could understand Ramo's suspicion about the Chetniks' motives. He had witnessed their duplicity first-hand.

Now, as we wrestled with our courage to enter the school, I kept peering up at the sky fearfully. While the Jet planes that flew over the town at such high speed they broke the sound barrier—only to disappear as quickly as they had appeared—wreaked the most destruction, I hated the mosquitos the most. I could still hear the drone of the engine, the high-pitched sound imprinted into my brain, and now, even though the sky was bright blue and clear of any aeroplanes, I couldn't be sure if the noise was a figment of my imagination or a warning of real danger.

"We'd better get this done now," Ramo said.

I nodded. Since we had repelled the Četniks, life had become a series of monotonous moments of starvation and boredom, interspersed by shelling from the Četniks on the hills surrounding us and the bombs falling from the sky. They controlled the borders, and there was no aid coming in or out. I had become used to the cramps in my stomach, but my mind hungered for a respite from my life. My only escape was the pages of a book, and the only books were from the school library.

Before the bombing, Emir and his friends regularly raided the library and exchanged books. I was the recipient of his generosity, but I grew bored with reading his books. When I had planned my raid, I'd been excited about doing something daring, like my big brother. Now that I was standing in front of my former school, all I could think about was my life before the war. I wanted to scream at the stupid girl I used to be, the one who had spent hours counting down the minutes until the end of the school day. Now, what I wanted most in the world was to be an ordinary schoolgirl and have a regular, mundane day.

I carefully pulled myself over the broken window and stepped over shards of glass, all the time listening to the sky, barely breathing at every rustle. I crept through the corridors and classrooms, reaching the library. Part of the wall had collapsed, and the ceiling had caved in. Some books had been exposed to the elements and were pulpy from the dew, rendering them useless. However, there was a corner where they had remained protected. I crept to the corner, collecting books as I went.

"Come back," Ramo demanded as I reached the corner, but I remained undeterred.

Who knew when I could come back or even if there would be anything to come back to? We collected piles of books and carefully crept back out.

As I walked back with piles of books in an armful that reached my chin, Ramo picked up two from the ground. "Here, I'll help you carry them."

We divided the stack in half and walked back to the window we had arrived from. We passed by the classroom where I'd started grade seven before the war, before the darkness invaded my world. Zora and I sat in the back row together. Sometimes, we'd whisper under our breath, but we had to be careful not to be too obvious, or our teacher, Mrs Tanović, would punish us. Most of the time, we would pass notes to each other, starting with a sheet of paper that we would fill up to the end by the end of the day. I'd kept some sheets, and sometimes I'd be at home reading over them, remembering the days when my life was full of mundane details like complaints about the class, the content, the day outside and not being able to play, planning our games in the forest.

Ramo came beside me. "Bad memories?"

"I wonder where Zora is and what she's thinking," I said. My eyes were burning as I held the tears at bay.

"She's a Serb. She's probably only thinking about how she wants us dead." His tone was matter-of-fact.

"She's my friend and I don't want her dead. I hope she's alive and well. I hope she's living better than me," I spat heatedly, roughly wiping the tears seeping down my face.

Ramo opened his mouth like he wanted to say something, but he paused. "You have a good heart," he finally said. "You want to think the best of people. I hope that this war doesn't take that away from you."

I looked at him, saw the pain and sincerity in his eyes. I wondered what he was like before the war. If we had met then, would the attraction I felt developed unfettered by prejudice and anger? Would we have been something more? My eyes moved to his lips, and I noticed he'd caught me staring. I blushed, hurriedly moving away.

"Let's get going," I said, heading back to the window we'd entered.

He helped me get through, his hands gentle on my arms, making my skin tingle where he'd touched me.

"Look here," Ramo pointed at the concrete school playground as we walked past. "Emir told me that two Yugoslav fighter aeroplanes dropped bombs and hit a woman and child. They had to use a shovel to scrape off what was left of her."

"That's gross," I said, and sped up.

"Why? It's just what happens during war."

I turned to see Ramo's face. He was matter-of-fact, untouched by emotion as he spoke about the woman. I realised now what he'd meant when he said that he hoped I was untouched by war. He hoped I didn't become like him. I slowed and walked closer to him, so that our arms touched as we walked. We walked back to the yellow building.

Our mothers were still in line. Mama looked at the books I was holding and shook her head. She took a few from me and put them in the fabric bag she had on her. Ramo and I occupied ourselves, wandering through the lines and eavesdropping on conversations. A lot of refugees were in the lines, and they were attempting to find out information about neighbours and family members through the grapevine.

Mama's turn came, and I listened as she spoke to my uncle Mustafa in Australia. Usually it was my uncle Ibro who called, but since he was recovering from his wounds, it fell to my mother. I listened to her one-sided conversation.

"We're good. The parcels didn't come through.... Mama is struggling after losing Sumija... Our diet isn't helping her diabetes.... The Red Cross gave her medication.... We are all doing well.... Please send food parcels..."

"Your time is up," the man operating the ham radio said.

"I have to go," Mama told Mustafa. "We'll call again."

She stepped out, and Edina took her turn.

I glanced around, holding the books tighter against me. When I saw a tall blonde girl in the crowd, my heart skipped a beat, and I had to stop myself from calling out Zora's name. The girl turned, and I saw her face, my stomach sinking. It was Kamila Hodžić, a former classmate. I went to turn my head, but it was too late. We'd made eye contact. She waved and approached with a smile.

"Seka, I haven't seen you in months." She gave me a hug, and I had to fight from flinching away.

Kamila and I had been rivals for top student in class and she'd used the sharp edge of her tongue many times to put me down, always with a sweet smile, acting as if butter wouldn't melt in her mouth.

"Still a reader," she said.

I tensed, waiting for the insult to follow.

Her eyes were on the books in my arms. "*The Silence of the Lambs*," she said reverently, her hands caressing the book's spine. "Could I borrow it when you finish?" she asked, almost pleading.

I nodded jerkily, taken off guard.

Her mother, Lebiba, approached, her brown curly hair bouncing as she walked, still slightly plump. My mother greeted her, and they exchanged pleasantries.

Ramo appeared beside me. Someone nudged me from behind, causing a book to topple from my arms. Ramo quickly caught it and put it on his pile.

Kamila looked at him with admiration in her eyes. She nudged me and nodded, miming, 'Who is he?'

"Ramo, this is Kamila, my former schoolmate. Ramo and his mother are living with us," I added, not needing to explain that he was a refugee.

She smiled widely and coquettishly. A prick of anger overwhelmed me, and I shifted, stomping her foot.

"Ow," she exclaimed, shooting me a glare.

I glared back at her. "Sorry," she whispered. "He's yours."

I quickly glanced to see that Ramo hadn't heard her. I didn't want him to be mine—I just wanted her to keep her grubby hands to herself. Oh, no, I gasped, realising that my crush had returned full force.

We turned as we heard someone calling Mama's name. It was Emir and Babo returning from the black market.

"Three potatoes and a can of tomato," Babo said, holding open the bag that was over his shoulder.

Mama nodded, her face resigned. "We will make do."

"Lebiba, you need to do something about the crooks profiteering and selling UN rations," Babo said and shared what we'd seen.

Lebiba's eyes narrowed. "I'll take this to the Council and make sure it's our number one priority," she proclaimed, her voice ringing loudly so that those listening nearby would hear. Lebiba had been the principal of the high school before scoring a seat on our local Council. Her husband was a doctor, and the two of them were equivalent to Srebrenica royalty and the Yugoslav success story.

I caught Kamila's eye roll and stifled a smile. She caught it and smiled back, shrugging. "We can't pick our parents."

I could see it wasn't a lot of fun being the daughter of a politician and doctor. I'd seen her many times coming out of the school bathrooms red-eyed after getting a score that was lower than an A. Her parents probably placed a lot of demands on her.

I reached over, plucked the copy of *The Silence of the Lambs*, and handed it to her. "Here, you take it first and give it back when you read it."

Kamila's eyes widened with gratitude, and I glistened as if she was going to cry. "Thank you, Seka," she said huskily, squeezing my arm in gratitude.

Maybe it was time for me to start thinking about those still here, rather than longing for those left behind. I would never forget Zora, but I needed to focus on the here and now.

After we said our goodbyes, we left. The books felt heavier and heavier as we walked home. My strength was being depleted as food became scarce.

I heard a whistle. The world exploded. I felt myself being lifted off the ground, then slammed back onto the concrete. I got on all fours, trying to see through the dust as I coughed. My ears were ringing while everything was quiet and hushed. Images of others lying on the surrounding ground, their faces dazed, broke through the dust clouds. My hearing returned, screams piercing my eardrums.

2-Fracture

Mama screamed my name.

"I'm here, Mama!" I stood, walking towards her voice. I stepped on someone's leg. "Sorry." I looked down. My eyes travelled from the foot to the knee, the bloody tissue and cartilage hanging from the end of the torn limb. My stomach heaved. I walked on through a large red patch on the concrete, like spilled strawberry jam, glistening intestines in the middle. The red pulp was all that was left of a human being after the shell hit.

Mama reached me. "Seka, are you all right?" She examined me with her hands.

My hands and knees were grazed from landing on the ground, my ears ringing, and my whole body sore from the force of the shelling, but I was not wounded.

Mama's arm was bleeding. "You're hurt," I said.

Mama looked down. "It's just a scratch."

Ramo and Edina walked towards us. Edina was limping, a fragment hit her calf, blood trickling down her leg as Ramo helped her walk.

Mama headed towards a woman lying on the ground, her legs gone. She was holding her arms out for help, her mouth open in a scream of pain.

"No." Ramo pulled her back. "We have to move."

"I have to help her," Mama said.

"Not now." Ramo walked Edina to a building nearby. Mama hesitated, looking from the legless woman to me.

I heard the now familiar whizz of a shell again. Ramo pushed me and Edina against a building wall, crouching over us as he protected us with his body. The world exploded again. I clutched Ramo tightly, breathing in his scent, listening to his heartbeat, attempting to drown out the explosion.

We remained huddled. "Let's go," Ramo said, helping me up.

I stood dazedly, screaming for my mother. Mama dashed towards me through the dust. I looked to where the legless woman was. The dust cleared—all that was left now was an arm.

Ramo helped his mother onto a truck taking the wounded to hospital. "You two go home," Mama said. "I'll walk to the hospital and make sure Edina is alright."

Mama pivoted, heading towards the screams of those who were alive and needed help. She disappeared into the dust and melee.

I walked slowly home, ambulances and cars screeching past, Ramo walking beside me. A truck with legs hanging out, feet and stumps together, passed by, and I turned away as nausea hit me. They were transporting body parts and the wounded. Ramo helped me up. My legs felt weak like spaghetti. He kept his arm around my waist as we walked home, taking some of my weight.

When we entered the house I went to the bathroom, while he told my grandparents and uncle and aunt what happened. I had a flashback of the leg lying on the concrete, detached, the cartilage and bone visible and crouched down as my legs trembled.

Someone knocked. I opened it to find Ramo standing outside with a bucket of water. "Here, so you can wash yourself."

I nodded, taking the bucket. I washed the concrete particles in my hair and streaks of blood on my arm from a scratch, feeling my arm and leg, the warmth of flesh and blood. I took off the notebook pouch; there were bloodstains on it. The notebook inside was dotted with a few droplets but was otherwise relatively unscathed. I washed the pouch, tucking the notebook into my waistband. I'd promised Zora I would keep the notebook on me and write to her every day.

Afterwards, I told my grandparents I needed to rest and went to my parent's bedroom, onto the balcony, where I hung out the notebook pouch to dry.

The sky was a deep blue; the sun shining brightly, the roses in bloom in the garden below wafting their sweet scent. How could so much horror happen on such a beautiful day?

"*Today was not a good day,* I wrote to Zora. *There was shelling.*" I paused, chewing the top of my pencil. Should I write about what actually happened or protect her? We'd promised we would be completely honest with each other. I took a deep breath, scratching the pencil onto the page. "*I nearly died. It was so horrible.*" I paused, my hand holding the lead tip against the page. Horrible wasn't a strong enough word to describe the horror of what I had seen. The remnants of body parts littering the road. The screams of pain. I couldn't go back there and re-live it. I jumped ahead.

"If it wasn't for Ramo's quick thinking, I wouldn't be here now. I'd judged him so badly for how he viewed the Serbs who were attacking us, but he was the one who lived through the truth of what they were capable of."

I heard the shutter and peeked around the side of the house at the attic window. Ramo peered through. I waved at him to come over. He was a perfect sniper target in the window. He hesitated a moment before nodding.

"I think it's time that I make a new friend." I quickly returned the notebook to my waistband, opening the glass door behind me. Ramo was in the doorway. I waved at him again, more urgently. I put my finger against my mouth, warning him to be quiet. The floorboards creaked, and the living room was directly under us. Ramo tiptoed through the bedroom. I moved aside to let Ramo pass by me and rearranged the curtains, gently closing the door behind us again.

Ramo sat on the concrete beside me. The shelling became lethargic around midday. I imagined the Serbs napping under a tree after lunching, taking a break from their murderous exertions.

This was the first time we were alone since he arrived. Ramo leaned against the balcony wall next to me, his face upturned, eyes closed as the sun warmed his skin. His skin was still smooth, with no stubble, his eyelashes dark brown, thick and lush, resting on his sun-pinked cheeks. He had a dimple on his chin. It must be from his father; his mother didn't have a dimple.

"Thank you," I said.

He looked at me, his blue eyes so light in colour it was like I could see through them.

"For helping to save us from the second shell."

"It was nothing. Once you learn that Serbs have no humanity, it's fine."

I hesitated before speaking. He'd saved us after all, but I couldn't let this pass.

"Not all Serbs are like that."

Ramo looked at me like I was an interesting insect he was studying.

"My friend Zora isn't. When Srebrenica was attacked, her family took us in and protected us."

He hesitated, then looked away. "My experience was very different. My mother cries every night, murmuring the names of my father and brothers." He spoke as if he was talking about the weather.

"What were your brothers' names?" I asked.

He inhaled deeply. "Čazim, Hamdija, Orhan." He paused and continued speaking slowly. "Orhan was the closest in age to me. He was seventeen years old. We shared a bedroom together, and we loved going fishing on Drina. Everyone said Orhan and I looked alike and could have been twins. Čazim and Hamdija were 18 and 20. Hamdija wanted to go to the city and find a job, but our father needed him on the farm, so he kept putting it off. If he'd left, he would still be alive."

I reached down, grasping his hand. His fingers curled around my palm as he held tight. It was the first time I'd held hands with a boy—I forced myself to breathe evenly.

"Now they are all gone." He paused, swallowing as tears flowed down his cheeks. "We should never have gotten on the bus. They told us we wouldn't be harmed, but I should have known not to trust a Serb. We took only what we could carry. At the checkpoint, they ordered all the men to get out while the women and children stayed on the bus. I stood with my brothers, but Orhan pushed me back in the seat. A Serb looked at us. He's only sixteen, Orhan told him, and the Serb followed them out. My father and three older brothers, who were lined up in a meadow, faced twelve soldiers. Mama clutched me, trying to hide my face against her, but I fought her, staring out the window. One soldier looked at me through the bus window. He was the bus driver who used to drive me every day to school. As the bus lurched, I heard gunfire and saw my father fall."

He stopped speaking, his chest heaving with emotion. Emotion spent, he closed his eyes and leaned his head against my shoulder.

"That's why I hate them," he whispered.

I wondered if it was my family who was dead. Would I be able to still see humanity in Serbs, or would I be like Ramo, hollowed out with hate? Zora was a Serb. Would I hate her? She was different. Zora wasn't like the Serbs killing us. She was a Srebrenician—like me.

The sun was making me droopy too. I closed my eyes, leaning my head against his.

I heard the buzzing first, like an annoying mosquito that was pestering me. That's what I thought it was, and my hand fluttered beside my ear as I tried to kill the pesky insect.

"Seka." Ramo shook me. "Look."

I opened my eyes. Ramo was pointing at the sky. I stood beside him, looking at the plane flying towards the city. The pilot dropped, flying low over the roofs of the city. The international community banned flights across Bosnian airspace, so what was a plane doing flying here? As the plane passed our house, I saw the pilot's red Nike cap. The glass door behind us opened, and Babo and Emir stepped out onto the balcony. The plane was circling the town as if he was searching for something.

"What sort of plane is that?" Emir asked. "It's not a fighter bomber."

"That's a farming plane. It's used to spray insecticide on fields." Babo squinted as he looked up.

"What are they doing here? There're no fields here," I said.

The plane kept circling and flew low again, sounding like a buzzing mosquito.

"Did you see that?" Emir pointed at the plane's sides. "Those are machine guns attached to the plane."

Babo frowned. "We'd better leave before the Serbs shoot." He circled my shoulders with his arm and ushered me to the sliding door.

Flashes of light burst from the ground towards the planes.

"Our side is trying to shoot them down." Emir cheered. "Get the bastards."

I looked behind me.

"They shouldn't waste ammunition," Babo said. "A rifle can't shoot that far."

As he spoke, the sporadic shooting stopped as if the Bosniak soldiers had realised this and saved ammunition.

The plane swooped, and something fell. A bomb. It fell onto the slopes around the city with a tremendous bang. Dirt and dust flew up into the air. The shelling began again from the mountain tops, exploding roofs.

"Hurry, down to the basement now." Babo grabbed me by the arm, tugging me downstairs.

As we ran down the stairs, Babo called out to everyone in the kitchen. We descended into the dark basement, and Babo turned on the light. I huddled in a corner beside Mama with my family around me.

The bombs exploded above us, and then the whole house shook above us, dust falling from the rafters above, making us cough. My cousins screamed hysterically each time a shell exploded. Ibrahim and Paša held my two younger cousins. My father held the eldest Imran, tucking his blonde head against his side so he couldn't hear the bombing. My grandparents prayed, the Arabic rolling off their tongues fluently, their eyes closed. I tried closing my eyes too, but it just made the bombs scarier. In the darkness, I saw us shattering into a thousand pieces, the molten fire of the explosion burning us to charcoal. My eyes snapped open. I fearfully watched the ceiling, praying it wouldn't collapse on us.

The bombing lasted the entire afternoon—we waited an hour after that to be safe. Babo and Emir walked upstairs, peering through the windows before finally calling out the all-clear. Ramo and I snuck back upstairs to the balcony. Giant craters spread on the slopes above us like a giant pounding out his frustration. Smoke drifted from destroyed houses dotted around the ridges and in the centre of town.

"I believe the school was bombed," I said, noticing its red roof smouldering. I'd always thought that the war would finish soon and I would return to school, to my normal life. Zora would return, and the war would become a relic of the past. Now, I realised I would never be able to wash away the stains the war left behind.

"I'm sorry," Ramo said.

"It's okay," I turned away, hiding my wet cheeks. "It's just a building."

We watched the plumes of smoke drift into the sky. I couldn't pretend any longer. This was my normal. The Serbs would not be content until they overtook Srebrenica for themselves and forcibly expelled us like vermin.

A week later, Nana rushed into the house through the front door, calling my grandfather's name. Dido looked her over, checking for an injury. "Are you hurt?" he demanded.

Nana had no blood on her, but there was a possibility that she suffered an injury in a concealed area. I'd heard about a woman being hit by a shell fragment and dying instantly, but it had just looked like she was unconscious. When she was carried out of the bread truck to the hospital, a doctor examined her and pronounced her dead.

I peered out the front among the snow. Had a shell landed?

"A convoy is coming," Nana said, puffed out.

Our neighbour connected his radio to an accumulator and placed it on his window. People gathered below it to listen to the news. Nana enjoyed the opportunity to talk to the other women in the neighbourhood while she listened.

"It is?" Dido's voice changed to joy.

I called everyone, and we put on our coats and walked to the department store, scores of people leaving their houses to join us as they heard the news. Ramo and I ran ahead, and when we arrived at the department store, several white armoured military carriers were driving in front of about twenty trucks.

"We're saved." I took hold of Ramo's hand, trembling with joy. "The Blue Helmets will protect us. The Serbs can't shell us anymore."

Ramo squeezed my hand back, a broad smile on his face, his blue eyes sparkling with joy. I realised this was the first time I saw him so happy; he looked so young.

Two burly United Nations Protection Forces, UNPROFOR, soldiers wearing blue helmets with bushy moustaches sat atop the first vehicle, surveilling the city with squinty eyes. We joined hundreds of men, women and children who swarmed the trucks, everyone desperate to get food to take home. The street became blocked, causing the trucks to stop. I banged on the side of the truck. Why weren't they unloading?

An arm appeared through the window of the truck above me. One of the drivers threw a bag of sweets into the crowd. I dived into the mud and collected four pieces in my hand. I quickly tucked two in my pocket and handed one to Ramo. I unpeeled the brightly coloured wrapper and put it in my mouth. Children were still scrabbling in the mud when our Bosniak fighters appeared on foot and surrounded the truck, moving the crowd out of the way.

"They're moving on! They're moving on!' The crowd cried. I turned back to the convoy and saw the trucks passing by the department store, heading towards the upper part of the town.

"They're going to unload the food at the Petrica Warehouse in Klisa," I heard someone on my right say.

Ramo and I ran, joining the crowds of young people who were the only ones with the energy to run uphill.

"When we get there, say, *cigarette please*," I coached Ramo in English as we ran.

When we arrived, a soldier was throwing a packet of cigarettes into the crowd. A fight broke out as everyone jostled to get to the box.

Ramo was about to throw himself into the fray, but I yanked him. "Let's ask him."

I nodded to a soldier standing guard, watching the melee, his rifle at the ready, wearing a blue helmet and sunglasses. He wasn't much older than us, with a blonde goatee framing his lips.

"Cigarette please," we said in unison. Ramo held up his fingers in the universal sign of a cigarette.

The soldier looked, sizing us up. He smiled, took a packet out of his pocket, and offered us one each. I placed it in my mouth.

I mimed a cigarette lighter.

The soldier held up a stainless-steel lighter. As I leaned in for the light, I noticed a seal engraved on the side encircled by the words United States of America. The soldier blew on his hands after he returned the lighter to his pocket.

"Thank you." The nicotine hit my bloodstream. I was floating, carefree, and light in a way I hadn't felt for years. Ramo had a blissful look on his face.

A commotion began at the head of the convoy as the unloading began. The crowds from the department store reached us. I quickly inhaled the last of my cigarette and dropped the stub. The crowds tried to push in between me and Ramo. He threw his cigarette and held me tight against him. The crowds kept growing. The US soldier who gave us a cigarette scrutinised the crowd, holding his rifle tighter as the crowds surged towards him. People climbed on the trucks, and the soldier lifted his rifle as if he was going to shoot, but the soldier next to him tapped his arm, and they stepped back and away.

Bang, bang.

The sound of gunfire rent the air. I screamed, and Ramo crouched over me, attempting to provide some flimsy protection. Our soldiers broke through the crowds, roughly pushing people away. One of the Bosnian soldiers was holding his rifle aimed at the sky as he pulled the trigger.

"Get down," he shouted at those standing on top of the truck.

A man wearing a blue sweater, looking square from all the layers he was wearing beneath it, was holding a box he'd yanked from the truck. He climbed down, holding it in his hands.

"Leave that," the Bosnian soldier shouted.

The man looked at him defiantly, thrusting his lip out. The Bosnian soldier lifted his gun and aimed. Blue Sweater dropped the box sullenly. The Bosnian soldiers formed a cordon around the convoy, pushing the crowds back. The Blue Helmets joined them.

A few men in shirts and ties beneath their large woollen coats that reached their knees came to stand in front of the trucks. "We are from the Wartime Council," a man wearing a white shirt and black tie addressed the crowd. "All food will be unloaded and distributed fairly. Please remain calm and wait your turn." He held up his hands as if he were calming a wild animal.

"Maybe we should go?" I said to Ramo as the unloading continued.

He nodded, and we pushed through the crowd downhill. Blue Sweater was now standing beside us and grumbled, "I haven't eaten a proper meal in four months, and I have to wait."

"Look at that man. He hasn't gone hungry in months," a man beside me pointed at one of the local councillors who looked like a navy square cereal box in his woollen coat, his short chubby neck perched on the top with his fat-cheeks reddened from the cold.

Civilians jumped off one of the trucks beside us. "Who are they?" I nudged Ramo.

He shrugged.

"Journalists," one of our soldiers standing nearby answered me.

They all looked like they were wearing varying shades of camo colours. A man with olive cargo pants and a brown jacket held a large video camera on his shoulder. An Asian woman with straight black hair tied in a braid, wearing olive pants and an olive jacket, holding a microphone in her hand.

A shell burst nearby, the thunderous sound echoing off the hills and making the ground tremble. The journalists flinched, ducking down and covering their heads while we snickered. We'd learned the hard way that it wasn't the explosions that you heard that would kill you. The journalists looked at us with something resembling wonder. It seemed our inoculation to death had impressed them.

Behind them, the unloading was finished, and the trucks were now driving back down the hill to form a convoy and head back to Bratunac.

The black-haired woman approached us. Her tawny skin had a pink undertone with a smattering of freckles on her nose. Her hooded, deep-set black eyes were narrowed in concentration as she spat questions in our direction. I understood what she was saying in English, and even though her words were fast and furious, she pronounced words I knew differently from the American soldiers. Ramo and I stopped, frozen in place by their sudden attention.

Another woman with blonde hair translated with a Serbian accent. "Could you tell us how you manage here and how much longer you think you'll be able to hold out under such circumstances?"

"I—" I froze, wanting to answer in English but self-conscious about my pronunciation. During my indecision, Ramo jumped into the breach to answer, and the journalist angled the microphone towards him, and the Serb woman translated as he spoke.

"My family and I are on the edge here. We've been starving for months, and we'll die of starvation if someone doesn't help us," Ramo said into the microphone, and while the translator was whispering to the journalist, the crew turned its attention to something behind us.

Ramo and I looked over our shoulders. Naser Orić stood a few metres away, dressed in a camouflage shirt and cargo pants, balancing his M-84 machine gun, which the Serb soldiers called the "sower of death," against his shoulders. He perched his beret with the Bosnian emblem on his head, with a neatly trimmed black beard covering his face. Two fighters on either side of him looked almost exactly the same, with ammunition belts across their chests and hand grenades on their belts. Even though they weren't wearing any coats, they stood in the cold as if they couldn't feel it, their faces calm and emotionless.

The female journalist flocked to Naser. "How much longer can you hold out like this?" the Serbian translator said in Bosnian.

"We can continue like this for however long we have to." Naser's voice was resolute, his eyes cold as they flicked towards me and Ramo.

I clutched Ramo's arm tightly. Ramo looked at me with fear in his eyes.

"He's going to beat me with his machine gun," Ramo whispered under his breath. "What I said was treason. I'm making it easier for the Serbs to attack us."

Maybe he was right. Naser did look angry.

3-Witness

May 1992

"Let's go," I whispered. We scuttled around the crowds and away. As we ran down the hill, I had an idea. "You go home. I have to find my grandparents," I told Ramo.

"I'll come with you."

I shook my head. "It's better if you're at home."

"But what if the Serbs shell?" Ramo looked at the mountain peaks above us.

"They won't risk it with the journalists and UNPROFOR soldiers. Go, I'll be home soon." I waited until he'd turned the corner and returned to the warehouse.

Naser and his soldiers were gone. The journalist was talking to the Serbian translator. "No one will hurt you. See, they've given us a military escort." She pointed at a Bosnian soldier standing to the left of them.

The Serbian translator shook her head. "No, I agreed only if we had a military escort from UNPROFOR. I can't trust the Bosniaks."

"It's your job. I can't interview the locals without a translator," the journalist said.

"Excuse me," I interjected. The female journalist turned to me with a smile.

"Please, don't show what boy said." I pointed at the camera.

"You can speak English?" she said with surprise.

"Yes, I speak a little," I said, slowly enunciating my words. "Don't show footage. People be angry with boy."

"Not a problem," the journalist said. "I got my soundbite with Naser. He's the big story."

I knew she was saying something about Naser before the translation, but didn't understand the word soundbite.

"Do you want to earn money?" She put her hand in her pocket and took out a roll of Deutschmarks. "My translator is too afraid to come to the hospital. Would you do it?"

I couldn't tear my eyes away from the notes. My desperation mitigated any hesitation about my ability. We'd be able to buy a week's worth of food. "Yes, I will."

"Great." The woman gestured towards the cameraman behind her. "We're moving out. Where is the hospital?"

"Down this way." I walked downhill, and she picked up her backpack and tossed it over one shoulder and stepped in beside me.

"I'm Alyssa Jones. What's your name?"

"Seka Torlak."

She repeated my name, rolling her tongue on the R like a native.

"Where are you from?" I asked, not able to place her accent. She didn't sound like the actors in the American movies we watched, or like the British journalists we saw on the news.

"Australia."

I smiled. "My uncle Mustafa lives in Australia. I visit five years ago."

"Next time, call me, and we'll do coffee," Alyssa said.

I forced a smile, looking at the mountains looming around me, the buildings potholed by shells and artillery. I was a prisoner, and I didn't see a future where I would leave Srebrenica any time soon.

"You look different to other Australians," I said, pointing to her hair.

"My mother is Vietnamese. My father was an Australian soldier who fought in the war."

I nodded. I'd learned a little about the Vietnam War from school, where the US victimised a country and its people to stop communism, but I hadn't known Australians also fought in the war.

As we approached the hospital, my dread built.

"That's the hospital." I pointed up the hill. As we approached, the bandages drying outside fluttered in the breeze, and we heard screaming.

"Get it from this angle." Alyssa nodded to the cameraman, who filmed around the hospital while she filmed her introduction. "Cut," she said when she finished, and the cameraman turned it off. "I'm guessing it's stenchy?"

I looked at her blankly.

"Stinky," she clarified, waving in front of her nose.

"Yes, very stinky. I vomit," I told her.

Alyssa yanked her backpack to her front as she walked. She rifled through and pulled out a tin. After lifting the lid, she rubbed her finger inside and coated it into some thick ointment that she rubbed under her nose. She passed the tin to the cameraman, who did the same.

"Vicks Vapo Rub." She passed me the tin. "It helps with the smell."

I tentatively rubbed a dab of ointment under my nose, the menthol smell filling my nostrils and the ointment cooling my skin. Alyssa returned the tin to her backpack. I explained to the security guard that Alyssa was a journalist, and he called one of the nurses, who told us that the doctor was amputating.

"I'd love to film that," Alyssa said eagerly.

I hadn't signed up to watch a live amputation. I just wanted to earn some money to buy food. The nurse went to ask permission, and I edged towards the door.

"I'll need you to translate," Alyssa said. "I'll double the pay."

My feet stopped moving. Double the pay! The nurse returned and rushed us into a large room just inside the hospital entrance. A bare-chested man was lying on a low cot. After the introductions, the doctor told Alyssa about the patient.

"His comrades brought in this soldier from the battlefield with a large wound to his arm from an anti-aircraft gun. The soldiers who brought him didn't know first aid and didn't use a tourniquet to stanch the bleeding." The doctor used his scalpel, making incisions as he spoke, and I translated. "It's all right, you're doing well," he said encouragingly to the young man.

I stumbled on the word tourniquet and mimed tying something around the arm.

"That's why he is pale. I need to finish the amputation before he goes into shock." The doctor's hand was steady as blood seeped on the table and onto the floor, dripping slowly, a pool gathering by our feet. "Hold on."

The patient's skin was white and clammy. His eyes were closed, and he was panting shallowly. The young man moaned but didn't move. The doctor continued cutting through the flesh and sinew of the arm. "Could you please stop for a moment?," the young man asked. The doctor paused, holding the scalpel, watching and waiting as the young men took a few deep breaths. The young man nodded.

The doctor continued cutting into the flesh. "I administered some pain-numbing medication, but I think it has lost its efficacy because it was in the sun too long." He paused, and the nurse wiped the sweat off his forehead. "Sterilise."

The nurse got a bottle, tipped some liquid on a bandage, and rubbed it on the skin.

"How do you sterilise?" Alyssa asked.

"We found hydrogen peroxide in the abandoned battery factory. We dilute it with water in fifty litre vats we used to distil plum brandy. A three per cent solution oxidises bacteria to death without harming human tissue. We call hydrogen peroxide Bosnia's greatest war hero."

He used a scalpel to cut through tendon and sinew, the blood pooling around the incision, the white of bone and pink flesh appearing. My head floated like it was separating from my body. Alyssa hugged me and pulled me away from the operating table. She handed me her water bottle to drink. "If you can't do this, you can leave." She was unaffected by the blood, the smells, the moans of pain.

"How do you do it?" I asked.

"Because someone has to. If I do this story, then people will know how desperately you need medicine, and the international community will help. That's how my mother's people in Vietnam received help."

I gripped the water bottle as I breathed in shallowly. I wanted to run home to my mother and hide, but I couldn't. Alyssa was right. I had to push through. She knew from first-hand experience how important it was to be a witness. I had to take this opportunity to get help for my family and my people.

Alyssa rifled through her backpack and pulled out two biscuits wrapped in a cellophane wrapper. My mouth watered. She ripped open the cellophane and handed it to me. I jammed it into my mouth and closed my eyes in ecstasy as the crumbly biscuit melted. Alyssa handed me the other one. I hesitated. I wanted to save it for Ramo.

"You need to eat now to get through this. I need you," Alyssa whispered.

I took the second biscuit and ate it. I took another few sips of water and felt my stomach settle.

"Are you ready?" Alyssa asked.

I nodded, and we returned to the surgery. "I have isolated the nerves and now need to shorten them." The doctor pointed to the long sinews of flesh joining the nearly severed arm to the rest of the shoulder. He touched a nerve. The patient jumped on the cot as if an electric shock jolted him.

"We're going to have to hold you down now," the doctor said. With closed eyes, the young man nodded, his entire face showing intense concentration. As the nurse advanced, she held his shoulders down while a technician leaned across his chest. The surgeon cut through the remaining nerves at once.

The man on the table lurches upward, a groan of pain escaping from his clenched lips.

"It's done now." The doctor patted the young man's shoulder. "I just have to do sutures." He used a needle to suture the wound closed. The man stayed motionless as the doctor sutured his skin closed. "Normally, we keep contaminated war wounds open to drain and avoid infection and are closed a few days later. I'm going to close the wound with sutures now. I don't want him to go through another painful procedure in a few days. The body can take only so much."

Night was approaching, and a single bulb wavered and flickered. A homemade hydroelectric power generator built on the stream that ran through town powered the light. It was the only light in the hospital. A nurse placed pieces of oil-soaked cotton to smoulder in coffee cups and a medicine bottle on the surrounding tables, which gave off a smoky light.

"When darkness falls, the lice that have infested the hospital will stir and bite, scurrying across the skin of patients and doctors." The nurse beside us lifted her sleeve and showed her red-spotted skin where bugs had nipped her.

My skin tingled like tiny legs were crawling on me. I scratched my head. Beside me, Alyssa was calm and interested, as if we were on a picnic and not in a war hospital operating under medieval conditions.

"Take him to a bed," the doctor said as he cut the thread. He winced as he straightened from bending over the patient. Two men entered the room and began transferring the man onto a cot to carry him to the ward. The man barely moved. He was unconscious now and immune to the pain for a few blessed moments.

Somehow, over the hours I'd watched the surgery, I became inured to the smell. Now, it coated the back of my throat, threatening to make me gag. "Vicks," I asked, looking at Alyssa.

She shook her head, jerking back to the doctor. If the doctor could endure the stench, then so could we. I breathed in shallowly, tamping down the rising nausea.

We passed a stretcher in the corridor, the man on it unmoving, patches of blue liquid on the sheet. "Is he..." Alyssa pointed at the man.

The doctor touched the man's neck and nodded. "Yes. We won't be able to move the bodies of the patients who die until morning."

I shuddered as I realised the dead would lie among those who were gasping for life.

"What happened to him?" Alyssa asked.

The doctor lifted the sheet and showed her the blue blood that oozed from his wound and dried on his skin. "We suspect the Serbs are using chemical weapons. Some patients stop breathing as if paralysed while their heart continues beating. We attempted to give him atropine to block the nerve receptors that were overstimulated by the chemical agent. It has helped some of our patients, but not this one."

He lifted the sheet and covered the man's face.

A blue helmet appeared at the hospital doorway and called for Alyssa. Her translator stood next to him, rapidly speaking in English and outlining, with a voice filled with hysteria, all the ways she could be murdered in the dark.

We walked out of there, and Alyssa handed me the money underhanded as she shook hands with me. "I'll see you again," she promised.

I nodded, knowing she was lying. No sane person would ever voluntarily return to Srebrenica. But what if she did?

"Please, stop," I followed her outside the hospital entrance. "My friend Zora Đokić is in Australia."

"Zora, that's a Serb name," the translator said in English.

Alyssa opened her notebook and wrote Zora's name.

"Please find her for me. Tell her I'm okay."

Alyssa nodded. "I will. I'll find her," she shouted as UN soldiers herded her to the truck.

The hospital doors opened behind me, and the doctor who did the amputation was standing behind me.

"You did well, kid," the doctor patted my shoulder. "We might need you to translate. Give your details to the nurse."

I wrote my name and address on the piece of paper the nurse held out.

As I walked out, I saw a small figure climbing the hill, a basket hanging off her arm. As she got closer, I recognised the blonde hair of Kamila and called her name. She looked up at me with concern. "Is everything all right?"

I nodded, quickly filling her in on my translating job.

"That's great. I wish I'd learned English. Instead, I studied German." She shook her head with frustration.

"What are you doing here?" I asked her.

"Bringing dad dinner. He doesn't have time to come home, so I'm the courier." She lifted the basket.

I peered in but couldn't see what was in it because there was a tea towel covering the top.

"Have you read *Silence of the Lambs*?" I asked.

She shook her head.

"Oh, I was hoping for it back. I lost the other books in an explosion." I knew it was terrible to grieve the lost books when people had lost their lives in the shelling, and yet I couldn't help myself.

"Do you have other books?" she asked.

"Read them all," I said despondently, "twice." I lifted my fingers up for emphasis.

Kamila hesitated and then added, "Why don't you bring your books, and we can swap? I've re-read my books too and am sick of them."

I brightened. We talked through the titles we each had and made sure I didn't bring any duplicates to exchange for something she had in her library. After settling on a day and time, she told me her address. I'd pretended I didn't know where she lived, even though we all knew that the three-storey white rendered house and balconies jutting out of each bedroom was the one belonging to the doctor and the principal.

I walked home in the clear night, my breath forming into vapour before me. I enjoyed seeing the steam. It told me I was alive.

When I entered the house, Ramo met me in the hallway. "I was looking for you."

"I helped a journalist translate at the hospital." I took out the roll of Deutschmarks out of my pocket.

Ramo looked at the roll with awe.

"You don't have to worry about the footage she took of you. She won't show it on TV."

"Really?" Ramo smiled with relief. "But Naser is still angry with me."

"Yes, but since he doesn't know who you are and won't have any reason to search for you, you'll be fine."

Mama walked into the hallway and demanded to know where I'd been. I handed her the roll of money and told her everything I saw.

"Where are Minka and Imran?" Hearing their names, my cousins tumbled into the hallway. "Here." I took out the two hard lollies I'd snatched from the ground and gave them one each. They screeched in ecstasy as they ripped off the wrapping.

The next day, Mama went to the department store and received our rations: two and a half kilograms of food per person and half-kilogram packs of feta cheese to share between four. My mother and aunt divided the cheese into eight portions to make it last for two days. Half a litre of oil, and a few kilograms of wheat flour each. Mama made bread for the first time in months. The soft bread melted in my mouth. It was a good day.

4-Ravenous

September 1992

I trudged down the streets and to Kamila's house, my legs struggling, climbing uphill after months of deprivations. In the four months since Srebrenica had been under siege, the Serbs had made food scarce and were not allowing any humanitarian aid to enter, even when UN convoys were allowed through, life was not much better. I had learned to push through my malaise, and this excursion was going to cost me dearly.

I carried my dog-eared copy of *White Fang*, excited about exchanging it with Kamila's copy of *The Secret Diary of Adrian Mole*, our regular routine.

When I knocked on her door, there was a delay, and she appeared, opening the door just enough to peer through. When she saw it was me, she let me through, her jeans looking immaculate, wearing a t-shirt featuring Michael Jackson. I sighed ruefully and looked down at my scuffed and worn jeans, so thin from numerous washes that they were fraying. I shouldn't have been able to fit into them, not with the inches that I'd gained, but the war diet was keeping my hips sharp and my stomach hollow.

I followed her, admiring the leather couches and paintings hanging on the walls. While my parents had good jobs and our house displayed our good fortune, Kamila's house was like something out of a magazine, even now in the war.

"Here," she handed me the book she lifted from the black marble coffee table.

"Kamila," her mother called out, appearing in the doorway to the living room, holding a *tacna* in her hands, the smell of beef filling the air. I gasped as I inhaled the delicious smell, which awakened my stomach, making it rumble and gurgle. I inched closer, peering into the tacna and seeing *tirit* pita - a traditional Bosnian dish made with diced meat cooked in a rich, flavourful sauce and served over pieces of bread.

"Beef," I gasped, my eyes widening in wonder.

"A patient of Babo's gave him some beef as payment for his services," Kamila interjected.

Her mother quietly left, walking into what I knew was the dining room. My feet were stuck to the ground, fighting the urge to tackle her mother to the ground and wrestling the tray of food from her hands.

"Anyway, you take your time reading that," Kamila said, tapping the book in my hands.

I looked down, bewildered, remembering that was what I came for. Kamila's hands were on my back, propelling me to the front door as she ushered me out, the door slamming loudly behind me.

I trudged back home, feeling bereft and angry. I knew that in this war, there was no place for hospitality etiquette. Pre-war, it would have been scandalous to refuse a visitor food. Now, it was a survival instinct. Still, the unfairness bit me like a wasp. It was luck of the draw that her father was a doctor, and his services were in high demand during a war, and yet I cursed my father and his engineering bias.

When I returned home, I found my parents in the living room, preparing for the trek to the surrounding villages to exchange our jewellery with the villagers who could still work in the fields and had produce to sell.

"This is all we have." Babo laid out on the coffee table mother's wedding ring, Paša's necklace, and Nana's bracelet that she received as a wedding present from her parents forty years before. Ramo tried to add Edina's wedding ring, but my father returned it. It was too cruel to take the only memento she had of her husband.

When my mother sent me out of the kitchen while preparing meals, I was relieved. But then I noticed the hushed whispers in the kitchen, and the meals became smaller and smaller. My young cousins were the only ones who didn't notice. Their portions were tiny, so we all sacrificed some of our food so they would get full rations.

"I want to come." I wanted to do something.

"It's too dangerous," Babo said.

"She needs to know where the villages are located. She might have to go by herself one day," Emir said.

My excitement dulled. Emir wanted me to know how to get to the villages in case something happened to him and my father. Shells were constantly dropping. Since the first attack by the mosquito aeroplanes, their buzzing was a regular feature, followed by the thunderous explosion from the boilers, the homemade bombs that they dropped. Jet planes also flew over the town at high speed, breaking the sound barrier, dropping bombs on their next pass, disappearing as quickly as they appeared, leaving behind demolished buildings, shredded bodies, and enormous craters.

"I'll come too," Ramo said from the doorway.

Babo nodded.

"We'll leave at two in the morning, under the cover of night." Babo glanced at the clock. It was five o'clock in the afternoon. "We'd better sleep after dinner."

Mama served watery soup with tiny chunks of beef from a tin received in the humanitarian aid parcel. We each got a small piece of bread. I bit into it, the bitter taste of ground hazel-bush making my throat sore. We'd used up all the white flour, then the mills began grinding wholemeal, then maize flour, and now hazel-bush.

After dinner, I lay on the couch reading, losing myself in the world of *The Secret Diary of Adrian Mole*. As I imagined myself in a normal life like Adrian, where his only concern was getting pimples, the gnawing pain in my stomach faded away. I floated out of the hell that had become my hometown.

I was halfway through my book when I heard loud voices outside. I moved to the window to watch. People stood on the street in the early evening, talking about the news they'd heard, hoping for a reprieve. Everyone's clothes hung off them, their skin sallow and pale from lack of nutrients.

"This is a death camp," one woman shrieked. "They are killing us."

When we were still at school, I had read *Anne Frank's Diary* and watched the movie *The Attic* based on the book. Death camps had barbed wire fences, watchtowers and armed guards that prevented people from attempting to escape.

Although we didn't have any of that, we were prisoners nonetheless. We had no way to hide and nowhere to run. We were on display for snipers to pick us off, for shells to turn us into minced meat, and aeroplane bombs to vaporise us.

"Naser Orić is planning an action," a man said. "He will link Srebrenica with the free territory of government-held towns of Čerska and Konjević Polje to the northwest. Srebrenica will finally stretch out and touch hands with government-held central Bosnia. Serbs won't be able to touch us then."

"If we don't starve to death before that," the woman said; everyone else nodded in agreement.

For months now, I'd wondered why the Serbs were not attacking us and finishing us. Now I knew. They were waiting until we were dead of starvation. I wiped a tear, putting my book away.

We went to sleep, Emir and I lying on our sponge mattresses on my parent's bedroom floor. Later, my father sat up in bed, his feet beside my face waking me. We dressed in the semi-darkness. The windows were shattered from the shelling and were covered by plastic sheets, making it a perfect invitation for a sniper to test his aim. I went downstairs with my family; a few minutes later, my Uncle Ibrahim and Ramo followed. My Aunt Paša was staying home with her children, as were my grandparents, Aunt Adna and Edina.

We walked down the street in darkness. We arrived at the villages surrounding the enclave as dawn broke the sky. Seeing the lush, fertile fields stretching around the houses, my spirits lifted.

A man wearing a blue mantel and black pants walked out of his house and to the barn, carrying a milk bucket. Babo waved at him. Babo held up my mother's wedding ring. The diamond sparkled in the bright sun. The man's eyes gleamed as he took it in hand and examined it.

"I'll give you two kilos of capsicum," the man said.

"That's a diamond ring worth at least 500 Deutschmarks."

"You can walk on and see if you can get a better price." The man returned the wedding ring and picked up his bucket.

"Please. We're starving, and you have all this." Ibrahim held his arms out towards the green fields of corn beside us. I felt my mouth water as I eyed a husk within arm's reach.

"Why didn't you fight and stop the Serbs?" the man said.

Emir's hands formed into fists. Babo quickly grabbed him, yanking him back while Ibrahim continued negotiating. Emir pulled himself free from Babo's grasp, walking down the road to wait for us. The villager agreed to the trade; he returned to his house to get the capsicum while we waited.

Beside me, Ramo watched the corn blow in the breeze, the leaves shushing in the breeze. Birds trilled in the trees, and cows mooed as they waited to be milked. It had been so long since I'd heard the sounds of nature.

"Are you alright?" I nudged Ramo's arm.

Ramo nodded. "He's right. We should have fought when they first attacked."

Ibrahim stiffened. "With what?" he demanded.

Babo yanked my uncle away. I took Ramo by the arm and led him down towards Emir.

"Those arrogant peasants," Emir muttered. "Do they think they are untouchable? I'm going to take some corn with me." Emir stepped towards the field.

"No, Emir. We're not thieves," I urged him back.

"It's not theft when you're starving." Emir walked into the field just as the man we had negotiated with came out of the house with two younger boys about Emir's age, probably his sons. They were carrying rifles. They stopped ten metres away from Babo and Ibrahim while their father walked on, exchanging the capsicum and cheese that they had negotiated for.

"Stop! They have guns." I pointed.

Emir swore under his breath. Ibrahim and Babo walked to us; we all walked back the way we came.

"They're profiteering," Babo said. "Let's see if their money does them any good when the war reaches them."

The walk back was harder. We wore improvised rucksacks that were made of common sacks that Mama had sewn belts on to use as straps. The sacks were huge. Once they held 20 kg of flour or potatoes, now they were our only way to transport food. Babo had the largest belt. The stronger the belt, the more you could carry. I'd dreamed of bags of food that would last us for days. Now, the empty rucksacks were mocking us.

As we returned to town, we crouched, ducking and weaving behind cars and buildings so we wouldn't be a sniper's target. We entered the house, and Mama ran out to greet us.

"What did you get?" Mama smiled widely with hope as Babo took off his backpack.

"We got a little of cheese and a couple of kilos of peppers for your wedding ring."

Mama's face collapsed, but she rallied and forced a smile. "I'll make stuffed capsicum with the cheese."

By the end of the week, we were ravenous. Hunger was a constant companion; we were down to one meal a day. My cousins were crying, begging their mother for food. I found my eldest cousin Imran in the kitchen one day, licking his fingers and running them on the shelves, collecting crumbs and granules of leftover food.

We were sitting in the living room, slowly eating the watery stew Mama had prepared.

"People are walking to villages in the Drina Valley to find food in the empty houses," Emir told us. "I want to go."

"It's too dangerous," Babo said. "You have to walk through the woods and across Serb lines to reach the Valley."

My parents argued with Emir but soon gave up. We had to make the dangerous trek worth it and bring back as much food as possible. Babo decided we'd leave as soon as dark fell.

After eating, I washed the dishes and wiped down the sink. The adults were in the living room drinking coffee made from baked rice and smoking homemade cigarettes, the acrid smell filling the room. In desperation, Babo picked quince leaves from our tree in the backyard during the night. He dried them on the stove, then crumbled the dry but still green leaves onto a page of a newspaper before rolling them to make cigarettes.

I went upstairs and sat at my mother's vanity table. Sun pierced through the nylon sheet, lighting up the room. In the mirror, a stranger stared back at me. She had my brown eyes, but they looked enlarged in her bloodless wan face.

I opened my mother's drawers and found her pink lipstick, dabbing a tiny dot on my lips and rubbing it in so my lips were pink. I had to be stealthy with my makeup application. It wouldn't do for my parents to notice my transformation. I gently brushed the blush into the apple of my cheeks and used the eyeliner under my eyes. I almost looked like a normal teenage girl.

I stood and looked at my headless body in the mirror. I was wearing my jeans and t-shirt. The jeans hung on me, so my mother punched another hole in the belt, making it thick and ungainly as it wrapped around me twice. I lifted out my favourite cherry-patterned summer dress from the wardrobe. I looked in the mirror again, smiling with delight. The belt cinched and snugly hugged my waist while the skirt rested on my thighs. I looked womanly. I lifted out my necklace, the silver coin resting in the tiny valley that was my cleavage. Swiftly, I threw on a robe and stealthily descended the stairs into the basement.

Mama instructed Ramo and me to bring down cushions and blankets to the basement so we were comfortable when we retreated from the shelling. We'd rigged a sheet to hang off the back of the stairs and tucked into cushions so that we weren't visible to anyone walking downstairs. When I tiptoed down, Ramo was waiting for me. His eyes skimmed over my dress. My cheeks warmed as I saw the pleasure on his face.

I crawled into the fort, and he arranged the sheet behind me.

"I can't believe we're going to go into Serb territory," I whispered, my voice breaking with excitement. I imagined myself as a ninja spy sneaking among the trenches while the Serbs were nearby.

"More likely they will kill us." Ramo was leaning against the wall, looking at the back of the stairs. "We have nothing to protect ourselves with to fight back, and we will be like bottles on a wall for them to practice their target shooting."

My excitement tamped down. He was right. This was really dangerous. Someone could be hurt, or killed. I looked at Ramo beside me and remembered his father and brother dying. I could lose my parents or my brother.

"We might not make it back," Ramo said. His blue eyes were watching me with a look I couldn't interpret. He lifted his hand, tucked my hair behind my ear, and leaned forward slowly, giving me time to move away.

I closed my eyes as his lips gently brushed against mine, once, twice. I leaned forward and placed my hands on his shoulders while his hands moved down to my waist. As we kissed, something stirred within me, a different kind of excitement that was centred between my thighs. I was warm and wanted to get closer. His hands grasped my waist, and something hard pushed into my hip. I broke away.

Ramo's cheeks flushed, and his lips glistened from our kiss. He sat back against the wall, and I leaned against him. We hugged quietly, waiting for our emotions to subside.

"I've got a present for you," Ramo said.

I sat up and watched eagerly as he reached into the wall and lifted out a brick. He took out a handkerchief and revealed a cigarette.

"I picked apple tree leaves and dried them in the attic. I used the newspaper to make them." He lit the end with a lighter, inhaling deeply, coughing once, and then passed it to me. I inhaled, the acrid smoke bit my lungs, and a faint hint of apple filled my nose. As the smoke filled my lungs, my stomach pangs faded.

"That was great." I lay back against his chest.

"I've tied a bunch of leaves and left them hanging off a hook behind the chest in the corner of the attic."

My happiness evaporated. He was telling me in case he didn't return tonight. I pulled him in for a kiss. I tasted the cigarette on his lips, and I liked it.

"Seka," my mother shouted from upstairs.

I fought through the curtain hiding us. I'd left my robe on the stairs and quickly shrugged it on, finger-combing my hair. Slowly, I took my book out of my pocket and opened the basement door. No one was in the kitchen. I stepped out and found Mama near the back door.

"Where were you?" Mama demanded.

"Reading," I held up my book.

"Let's lie down while we can."

I nodded and followed her upstairs. I ducked into the toilet and changed back into my tracksuit and t-shirt, which were hidden under the sink. My hand moved towards my notebook.

"Dear Zora,

This might be the last time I write to you. Tonight, we have to leave the enclave and search for food in the nearby villages. It's so dangerous, but we don't have a choice anymore. The Serbs want to starve us, and if we stay here, that's exactly what will happen. I'm terrified of what might happen out there, but doing nothing scares me even more.

I miss you so much, Zora. Sometimes, it feels like my chest aches from how much I wish you were here. But then I think about it and feel relieved that you're not. I hope, wherever you are, you have enough to eat and don't spend every day wondering if it will be your last. If I don't make it back, all I can hope is that this notebook somehow finds its way to you, someday, somewhere."

When I returned, Ramo was on the stairs to the attic. He reached out his hand, and I placed my hand in his. He looked so handsome; his cheeks brightened with colour, and his blue eyes sparkled.

"I have something to show you," I said, lifting my top and showing him the pouch I placed Zora's notebook in. "If anything happens to me, please take this. Keep it safe and try to get it to my friend Zora."

I debated whether to leave the notebook at home or take it with me. If the house were to be shelled while we were gone, the notebook would be destroyed, and if anything were to happen to me, it could also be destroyed. In the end, I decided to always keep it with me.

"Nothing will happen to you." Ramo cupped my cheeks with his hands and kissed me quickly on the lips, risking discovery in such an open space. "I will make sure of it." He pressed his forehead on mine. He reluctantly let me go up the stairs, his blue eyes on me.

I lay down on the sponge mattress at the foot of my parent's bed and distracted myself from the fear that was rising by rubbing my tingling lips and reliving Ramo's kiss.

Later that night, I walked out of the house behind my father and saw our neighbours off to gather food like us. Our first stop was Podloznik where we would meet Bosnian soldiers who would be our scouts, and then walk to the villages in the Drina Valley. We walked through the forest, stepping on uneven ground, the moon hidden by clouds and the darkness smothering us. I stumbled and fell onto a fallen tree trunk, scraping my hands against the bark.

Ramo helped me up. "Are you all right?"

"Yes, thanks," I whispered huskily, my cheeks heating.

Ramo stepped in behind me, and when I nearly fell a second time, he caught me. He walked gracefully through the dark while I stumbled like a heifer, ungraceful and heavy.

"Here." He took my hand, and we walked side by side.

I nodded ahead at my parents.

"They can't see," Ramo said.

I was grateful for Ramo's sure-footedness. Bosnian soldiers escorted us, and a scout showed us the way. We walked through the forest for hours. The scout waved his arm in the pre-arranged signal to let us know that we'd reached the Serb line. He signalled five to run across. When it was our turn, I sprinted, slipping by the Serb bunkers from which I heard snoring.

When I thought I couldn't walk another step, we reached the village. The village had roofs caved in and some houses destroyed due to shelling. The wall of sheds painted with the words, "Muslim house," caught our attention, as those who had left marked it to protect their houses from being set on fire. Roaming refugees expelled from their homes were known to set Serb houses on fire as revenge.

We divided up the houses. Ramo and I entered a house and opened the kitchen cupboards. We put sugar and flour into our rucksacks.

"There's corn in the field," Emir said.

Ramo and I went to the basement. The shelves of preserves had already been pilfered, but a few jars still remained. As I lifted my rucksack, I groaned. "I don't know how I'm going to make the trek back."

Ramo was holding a jar. "Close your eyes."

I closed my eyes, my stomach fluttering with butterflies. Something wet and soft touched my lips. I opened my mouth, and an explosion of sweetness hit my tongue, making me moan from pleasure.

We used our fingers to pluck out thin slivers of peaches, licking the juice off our fingers. It had been so long since I ate something sweet that a surge of energy pumped through my veins. As we finished the jar, we were giggling with happiness. I stepped on my tiptoes, kissing Ramo on the lips.

Emir called my name as his footsteps pounded on the stairs to the basement. "We have to get going."

Ramo and I quickly stepped away from each other as Emir reached the bottom of the stairs. "What did you find?"

"Two jars of peaches." Ramo held the empty jar we'd finished behind him.

"And flour and sugar," I added.

"Woo hoo," Emir whooped. "I've got a whole backpack of corn."

We climbed up the stairs and outside to join our parents and the scout. The scout set a fast pace. We had to make it past the Serb front line while it was dark out. We reached the demarcation line when the shooting started. Bright flashes of light lit up in the night as Serbs shot at us. Screams rent the sky. A loud explosion burst in my eardrums.

"They're using rocket launchers," Emir shouted beside me over the noise and din.

"Run!" Ramo urged me.

I crouched down, running between the trees. People fell to the ground as they screamed. I tripped and fell. A young girl was lying on the ground under me, her stomach ripped open from an explosion and her intestines glistening under the flashes of light from the rockets, her blank eyes staring at the sky.

Ramo grabbed my arm and lifted me up. I stumbled away before stopping and retching, the peaches I'd eaten tasting bitter as I vomited.

Time slowed, and it seemed as if I was in a strange twilight as we ran, stumbling and crouching through the darkness. I looked behind me and saw Mama and Babo, bright lights chasing them. Ahead of me, my Uncle Ibrahim jerked and fell, like a doll dropping to the ground.

Uncle Ibrahim lay on the ground, screaming, holding his arm, which was bleeding. My parents helped him stand, taking one shoulder each. They walked jerkily, slowly, as bullets and shells exploded around us.

Ramo and Emir took over carrying my uncle. After a few hundred metres, Emir's knees gave out, and he dropped to the ground. He tried to stand again, but Ibrahim pushed him away.

"Leave me," Ibrahim said.

Bullets whizzed around us. Ibrahim's eyes were glistening with tears. His face looked sallow and strained from pain. A grenade exploded a few metres away, and dirt landed on us. I coughed and spluttered as I wiped the dirt from my eyes.

Ibrahim twisted his hand and handed Mama something. She took it, grabbed Emir's and my hands, and tugged us along.

Babo bent and helped Ibrahim up. "The rest of you run!" he shouted.

I twisted around and saw the two of them staggering as the night lit up around them in strobe flashing lights. I went to turn back, but Mama firmly tugged me forward, forward, as they disappeared in the foliage behind us.

We were out of breath when we slowed. The shooting was now a distance away, and the grenades couldn't reach us. We were in Bosnian territory.

Mama placed my uncle's wedding ring on her index finger. We looked behind us, peering through the foliage, hoping to see them. An hour passed, and the sun rose in the sky, but they didn't appear.

Mama transferred our food supplies to Ramo's rucksack, urging him to return home. I refused to leave with him.

My mother and brother huddled on each side of me as the sun rose. Some who passed asked questions, and others could see by our faces that we were holding onto hope, even though it was being strangled by the passing of time.

Three men appeared, weaving like they were drunk. "It's them," Mama shouted and ran.

When we reached my father and uncle, dirt covered them. My father was shirtless. He'd used it to wrap around my uncle's arm, his bare chest peeking through the coat he had on. Ibrahim looked pale, his eyes glassy and staring out into the distance. A stranger was the third man. He had stumbled across my father and uncle as he was making his way back home.

"Thank you," Babo said to the man.

The man nodded and trudged home, his face gaunt and tired from the exertion, his backpack swinging on his back. Emir took his place and held my uncle up.

Mama hugged my father, who was weaving from exhaustion. He wilted against her and fell to his knees.

"We need to get him to a hospital." Mama and Emir took a shoulder each and walked with my uncle while my father forced himself to his feet.

I ran ahead down Marshall Tito Street to the hospital perched on the hill above me. The hospital was surrounded by row upon row of washing lines, where bandages hung out to dry. The bandages, used, reused, and washed repeatedly, formed a yellowish wall around the hospital. I walked up the hospital's steep driveway. The hospital, which had three storeys and a white-washed exterior, was built on a slope. The top floor was covered in coffee-coloured tiles. The once white render of the hospital was stained, and the gutters were chipped and damaged.

I climbed the stairs on the side of the building to the entrance, shielded by a jutting roof that was rotted and stained. The screams from inside pierced my ears. The doctors had run out of anaesthetic and had to perform operations on conscious patients. As soon as I stepped inside, the foul air made me gag; the hospital reeked of dead tissue and everything that comes out of a human body—urine, faeces, pus, and sweat. The smell coated my nose, invaded my throat, and made my empty stomach rise up as I vomited. I was thankful I had no food in my stomach.

A guard inside the hospital stopped me from entering.

"Please, we need help," I forced myself to speak as I dry-retched. "My uncle, he's injured. Can't walk."

The guard nodded and called out into the foyer. Two men came out with a stretcher and met my family.

As I passed the guard again, I nodded my thanks. Behind us was a group of people who didn't look injured. They were obviously from the villages; the women wearing *dimije* and headscarves, the men in plaid shirts. The guard stopped them from entering.

"Please, we need food. Anything," a woman begged with her outstretched hand.

"No food here. Move on your way."

"Please, we're starving," the woman wailed.

I looked behind my shoulder and saw she was grabbing the guard's shirt, practically holding onto him.

The guard roughly pulled her away. "Go away," he said tersely, speaking like she was a mongrel dog.

The group left, the wailing woman's mouth open in despair. I turned and followed my parents inside. I had visited the hospital a few years ago when Zora's mother gave birth. Then, the long, narrow hallways echoed with the cries of women in childbirth. Now, the long, narrow hallways were filled with the moans of the injured and dying. Then the beds accommodated patients suffering from illnesses; now, the rooms were occupied with six or more young men injured on the front lines, with women, children, and the elderly, and even a few babies among them, their piercing screams rising above the din. Flesh shredded by weapons of war: by shell fragments that sliced them, mines that exploded them or bullets that shattered them.

When I visited the last time, I saw a few familiar faces, people I had known since Srebrenica was small. Now, all the faces were strangers, refugees who were displaced by war and had run head-long to Srebrenica seeking shelter and instead ended up trapped in a Serb-made prison.

The men carrying my uncle bustled into a large room just inside the hospital entrance and placed him on a low cot with a black foam covering and white-painted metal legs that served as an operating table. Through the closing door, I saw the medical staff leaning over him.

I glimpsed the doctor as he passed us. The doctor entered the room where my uncle was and returned a few minutes later. "Are you the wife?" He had a broad face with high cheekbones, and a cleft chin.

"Sister," Mama said, between bloodless lips.

"I need to amputate. It's the only way to save him." He patted my mother's arm absent-mindedly. "I'll see you when it's done."

Mama covered her mouth, and she cried as the doctor left. "Seka, go home and tell your aunt and your grandparents."

I nodded wearily and left the hospital. I trudged home, my feet knowing their way even though I could barely stand. I'd just walked onto the main road when arms enveloped me.

"Seka, Seka, are you all right?" I heard Ramo's words like I was in a dream and coming back to consciousness.

He took out a cloth and unwrapped a cob of corn, charred and blackened from a fire. The smell overwhelmed me, and my knees buckled. I took it from him and shoved the cob into my mouth, chomping on it like a hungry dog with a bone. I chewed all the way around, eating all the kernels, and then grazed my teeth along the cobb, attempting to collect all the tiny pieces left. As Ramo walked me home, I caught him up. At home, Ramo lay me on the couch, taking off my boots and layering blankets on me as he told my grandparents and aunt about Ibrahim's prognosis. I fell asleep, and when I awoke, it was night. I stirred from the couch and found Ramo sitting beside me. "Ibrahim?" I asked.

"He survived the surgery; now he just needs to survive the night," Ramo said.

5-Battleground

January 1993

I felt movement and opened my eyes, the fog of sleep clearing. Nana slept on the couch; Dido was up and kneeling next to her as he gently placed his blanket over her, kissing her on the cheek. She stirred, smiling briefly, her hand clasping his, her eyes closed. Dido kissed Nana every time he left her side. He'd once told me he wanted her to remember their goodbye in case it was the last time they ever saw each other.

Dido jerked his head towards the blanket we strung up at the entrance leading to the corridor. I nodded, sitting up on my mattress. Ramo was sleeping near my feet, his mother on his other side. I arched my feet, gently touching him with my toes. His eyes opened. He eased out of the blanket so as not to disturb his mother. Dressing wasn't necessary. We were all wearing heavy layers to keep warm. We'd lifted the beautiful golden parquet my father had so carefully laid throughout the house, using it as firewood when we all retreated to sleep in the living room to survive winter.

During the night, the sound of cracking pipes in the ceiling woke me up as the water that remained after the Serbs mined the water supply system had frozen, which turned out to be a blessing in disguise because I was awake to put another log on the fire. The day before the fire died out, I fetched embers from our neighbour. It reminded me of a Flintstone's episode, with pre-historic Fred and Thelma living with the dinosaurs. I gave no thought to matches or lighter fluid for lighters before the war. The need to continuously feed the fire or borrow fire from neighbours consumed our whole life, as we risked freezing to death otherwise.

The dying embers of the fireplace provided enough light to illuminate the shapes on the floor, which were my sleeping aunt and uncle and their three children lying between them to create a heat cocoon. My Uncle Ibrahim couldn't help us with the back-breaking task of collecting firewood. Without his arm, he didn't have the strength, while my parents and brother were at the front. So, it was up to the three of us to trek into the woods.

While we were all emaciated and pale from lack of nutrition, Babo and Emir truly looked like concentration camp prisoners after being on the front. They'd shaved their hair because they had no opportunity to wash it; Babo's face was covered with a thick beard, while Emir's face was covered with thinner tufts that formed a beard. Mama heard how they had no hot food, no help with mending clothes. The only thing that the army provided were cigarette packs as payment, which were used as currency in the enclave because they helped stave off hunger pangs. Babo told her some wives and mothers were on the front, helping the soldiers, and so she decided to go.

I tiptoed to the blanket-curtain. With bated breath, I stood still as Dido lifted the blanket, and we ventured into the freezing corridor, my socked feet scrunching beneath me. I donned my winter boots with relief. As I put on my winter coat, the cold receded when I added my woollen hat and scarf, securing it around my neck in a knot to protect my chest and neck. I called my scarf my pneumonia protector. After taking turns sparingly using a bucket of water in the downstairs bathroom for our morning ablutions, Dido got the axe and rope from the utility closet under the stairs. He handed me the rope and locked the front behind us. Every day, refugees streamed into the township as the front lines encroached on their doorsteps. They went from door to door, attempting to turn handles until they found an empty house or a sparsely occupied one.

My lungs ached as I breathed in the cold air. It was seven in the morning and still dark. Sunrise came late during winter; it wouldn't be light for another hour. The snipers weren't out when it was dark. As we trudged down the road, the snow crunching under our feet, I saw a large shell hole left behind by the shells during the night, dark splotches of dirt interspersed between the pristine snow. The house roofs had holes pierced through them, and we steered clear of the debris of brick and mortar on the road. The Serbs shelled all night in full force. It was New Year, and to celebrate, they'd attempted to wipe us from existence. I couldn't help but feel it was a bad omen to the year 1993, which began with the booming sound of explosions. My head ached from a restless sleep, but I had no respite. We'd burned through the last of our wood last night and faced frostbite today if we didn't get more.

We walked past a destroyed house, snow gathered on the shattered walls. The roof of the house had collapsed, filling the shell with snow, and a chimney rose above the rubble.

Abandoned cars filled the streets, covered with snow and looking like sad sculptures. Once, they were a symbol of prosperity and wealth; now, they were useless without petrol or a place to drive to. Mangy dogs weaved between piles of trash, their panting breath condensing in front of them, their concave stomachs showing the desperation of hunger.

Even though it was barely daylight, people stirred around us, their faces and hands stained black. So many were homeless, camping out on the roads, setting quick-burning plastic crates afire as they huddled around like penguins in a herd, desperately seeking warmth. They had nowhere to go, nothing to do, so they wandered aimlessly to keep warm. Serbs had pursued them from their villages and these refugees had arrived in Srebrenica with the clothes on their backs using any mode of transport they had. Some pulled rough wooden sledges, leading horses, pushing wheelbarrows and sleigh-bottomed carts—searching for a place to live.

They'd left their homes in summer and didn't have coats, so some wore layers of sweaters. The women's *dimije* were mud-covered, most held bundles of what seemed to be rags, but were precious babies, bundled in cloth to keep them warm. Some children wore socks but no shoes, their tiny feet crunching through the snow.

On the radio, a refugee worker called the sight of the thousands in the streets "Dickensian." I remembered reading *David Copperfield* by Charles Dickens, where poor people lived in terrible poverty with large families sometimes living in one room, not having enough to eat. Even though it was another country and another century, it truly was a perfect description of Srebrenica.

We climbed up the bare hills. Each day, we climbed higher to find firewood because the woods closest to town had been chopped down. As we didn't have the luxury of time to dry and season the wood before burning it, we actively searched for dead trees that could be used immediately to burn in a fire. The sun rose; daylight broke across the valley, sparkling like diamonds, making me squint. I signalled to Dido to stop, lifting my thumb to my mouth to indicate I needed water. He passed me the canteen bottle from his shoulder.

As I drank, I saw Srebrenica spread out before me from halfway up the hill, coated with a thick winter fog. Snow dusted the hills surrounding us, hugging the town in its icy embrace. Conifer trees dotted the hills, their branches looking muted from the snow covering them. Snow covered all the roofs in the valley, giving everything a white and still appearance. We felt frozen in time, abandoned and forsaken, which was a true reflection of our internal state.

"The government should create a new tourism campaign. Srebrenica, the place where time kneels between mountains." Ramo waved his hands out to the terrain before us.

After we got our breath back from laughing, I passed the bottle to him. My cheeks flushed as he placed his lips over the spout where my lips had been. He finished drinking and handed me the bottle. Our fingers touched, sparks flying.

I returned the bottle to Ramo, and we continued climbing. As the hill got steeper, I removed my gloves to grasp at shrubs. We clambered with our hands and knees, the cold, wet sticks biting into my palms. We finally reached the top of the cliffs and a small meadow. Dido approached the first tree we came across and nodded. Ramo arched his arm back, hitting it with the axe, the sound of steel hitting bark echoing across the valley. When the tree weakened, he and Dido pushed it, and it fell onto the hard ground, bouncing a few times, its branches breaking with a crackling sound that rended the air. Ramo cleaved off a few branches and tied a rope around the log. I put my gloves back on, and we all stood in line, tugging on the rope and pulling the tree to the edge of the cliff. Ramo untied the rope, and we pushed the tree off the edge, watching as it arched through the air and jabbed into the ground.

To our left passed another two men who were throwing their log. They nodded at us. "We'd better hurry," Ramo said.

"I'll catch up." Dido waved his hand.

We briskly clambered down the steep edges and followed goat tracks, trying not to hurtle off the edge. The men were behind us. We'd heard stories about logs being stolen. Everyone was desperate. We reached the log, tied our rope around it, and dragged it behind us slowly. As the two men passed by, I tensed, but they continued on. The walk home was much longer and more gruelling as we slowly dragged the log.

As we reached the bottom of the hill, the biting cold of the winter day seemed to seep into my bones, leaving me weary and drained. Someone called my name, and I lifted my head to see Kamila with her father, Harun, and their blonde locks escaping from the woollen caps they wore. A dark-haired young man trudged behind them, his hulking height matching that of his father. As they reached us, I realised it was her older brother, Kemal.

"You did well," Harun exclaimed jovially, his breath visible in the crisp air.

Dido nodded. "We started at dawn because we had to climb so far up."

Harun's smile faded. "How far up?" As Dido explained the paths we took and how bare they were, Harun's visage changed to one of consternation. He took off his cap to reveal his receding hairline and ruffled the hair he had left, a gesture of concern.

"We need to find some wood today..." He didn't finish his sentence, the weight of their situation evident in his voice.

I was too tired to engage in small talk with Kamila, the long journey home weighing heavily on me.

"We can spare a few logs," Dido said, stepping in. "I can get the boy to bring some over."

Harun's face brightened. "Of course, we'd appreciate that."

I glared at Dido, a surge of rage burning within me. We had worked so hard for the wood, and now he was just handing it out without a second thought.

"And I'd be happy to help your family out," Harun added gratefully.

Dido nodded. "Of course, doctor. We'd better get going," he said, gesturing for Ramo to continue dragging the log.

As they walked away, I couldn't contain my frustration. "Why did you do that?" I snapped at Dido.

"It doesn't hurt to have a doctor owe us a favour," Dido muttered. "And it's too late for them to find anything now."

I knew Dido was right, but the thought still rankled. In an enclave with no other access to medical care, Harun's services were a hot commodity, but I couldn't help but feel that we had given away something valuable too easily.

When we got home, Ramo chopped the log, so we had firewood for the day. We took the rest to the basement to dry out until we had the strength to chop it. I trudged inside, taking off my boots and jacket with relief and sitting on the sofa. Once again, we transformed the living room by stacking the mattresses and bedding against a wall.

Nana and Aunt Paša came in carrying bowls and cornbread that they put before us. I peered in, seeing watery stew. I picked up the cornbread and hesitated, my mouth already drying.

"Any salt?" Dido asked.

Nana shook her head.

Nana told us that the Serbs were keeping salt out of the enclave on purpose. The people of Srebrenica had the nickname of the goitre people. For centuries we'd suffered from iodine deficiencies leading to an enlarged thyroid. As a child, Nana used to see people with large lumps on their throats bigger than fists. Some struggled to speak or swallow because it pressed on their oesophagus, while others suffocated as it cut off their breathing. My grandmother said that in her time people believed it was because of the river contamination from silver mining.

Mama told her it was preposterous Serbs were stopping salt from coming in, as it would take years for a thyroid to develop. "They don't know that," Nana said.

I took a spoonful of stew and tore off a piece of cornbread with my fingers, putting it into my mouth. I kept my eyes closed as I chewed and swallowed. It did not taste good, but at least I'd got it into my empty stomach. We ate slowly, drawing the process out of necessity to fool our bodies into thinking the food was palatable.

After eating, I curled up to snooze on the couch. It was a hard morning, and I was exhausted. I woke up, still feeling heavy and lethargic. This was nothing new. Not eating enough slowed a person down and made them too weak to move.

My grandmother was sitting on the couch across from me. "How are you feeling?"

"All right." I stretched as I sat up. "Tired." I went to the bathroom, and when I came out, my grandmother was standing outside the door.

"I thought perhaps you needed some rags?" Nana held out her hand with cut-up pieces of cloth.

We had no pads and used rags for menstruation, which were then hand-washed, the water and blood coating my hands and leaving me self-conscious for days about the smell.

I shook my head.

"You have used none for months now," Nana said, her voice tinged with suspicion.

I cocked my head, attempting to remember. I realised she was right; it was months since I had my period.

Nana gasped. "Oh God, are you pregnant?"

"Why would you think that?" I asked.

"When you're pregnant, your menses stop?"

I felt slightly queasy. I hadn't known that you lost your period when you were pregnant.

"I'm not pregnant," I said.

"I saw you sneaking around with that boy." Nana gripped my hand hard. "The two of you have been going up to your mother's bedroom and getting intimate."

"No, we didn't... I'm not..." My stomach dropped.

Nana left me in the bathroom. I wished I could speak to Belma and talk to her about the loss of my menses, but she'd just had a baby a few weeks ago. When I'd visited, she was exhausted. I needed my mother. She was the one person I could talk to about things. I missed her so much it was becoming a physical ache. Yesterday I went to her wardrobe and wore one of her sweaters, just so I could smell her on me.

When I returned to the living room, Uncle Ibrahim was sitting on the couch, smoking his cigarette slowly, dread etched on his face, a backpack of supplies by his side.

My grandparents were sitting on the couch opposite.

"I want to go with you," I told him. "I want to see Mama."

"It's too dangerous," Dido said. "Children can't go to the front."

When he used that voice, I knew better than to argue with Dido. I left the living room and put on my boots and coat, stomping out the backdoor, slamming it shut behind me. I would not let them stop me.

The backdoor opened, and Ramo came out. "What's going on?"

"I'm going to follow Uncle Ibrahim to the front."

"I'm coming with you."

We tiptoed around the house and into the garden bed of what was once Zora's house. The rose bushes her mother loved and tended to carefully poked through the snow, the branches bedraggled and wild, starved of tenderness.

Finally, after ten minutes of waiting and stomping our feet to keep warm, the front door opened. We stilled, ducking behind the sparse winter bushes, hearing the crunching of snow as Ibrahim walked past. We gave him a head start, waiting to show ourselves until it was too late for him to send us back.

After two hours of walking, we broke through the woods to find a rag-tag mob of men and women. When I thought of the frontline, I'd conjured up images from World War I and II movies where soldiers were holding their position in bunkers dug into the ground. Instead, everyone appeared to be in a mad scramble.

Mama was quickly hauling down a tarpaulin folded over a rope held up by two trees, creating a makeshift tent. Ramo and I hurried over to her. Mama saw me, holding out her arms. As I hugged her, I felt how much thinner she was. She pulled and stroked my face, but then her eyes drifted to her red hand, and she quickly lifted it away.

"Just a moment." Mama stepped to a bucket, poured water on a rag and used it to scrub her hand.

"Is that blood?" I asked.

Mama hesitated before nodding. "A young boy had a wound in the stomach. I had to help hold him together before they took him to the hospital." She looked down the hill and towards the rooftops, peeking through the trees at the town. "I hope he made it."

Mama had changed so much. When I'd hurt myself on barbed wire last year, she'd nearly fainted, yet now she talked of holding a boy's intestines as if she were talking about baking a pita.

"Where are Emir and Babo?" I looked around.

Mama peered towards the north of the campsite. "They should be back soon."

Ramo took off his backpack, handing Mama the humanitarian aid packets we received: shiny packets of orange juice powder, a big tin of oil, and packets of pasta and rice.

"Salt?" Mama asked.

I shook my head.

Mama sighed heavily. She stacked the plastic packets in a footlocker that was among the trees.

"Mama, I need to talk to you." I bit my lip as I looked at Ramo and Ibrahim. "In private."

Mama nodded. We walked away into the woods, and when we were out of earshot, I told her I hadn't had my period in months.

"Don't worry, my love." Mama cupped my cheek with her hand. "A lot of women have lost their menses because of lack of nutrition."

I sighed with relief.

We returned to the camp.

Soon, men appeared among the trees. Most of the men were wearing civilian clothes and carrying guns, a white piece of cloth tied around their one arm. Our side didn't have any uniforms; the cloth was the only way to identify them as Bosnian soldiers.

A few minutes later, Emir appeared, trudging up the hill slowly, a rifle hanging off his shoulder. In the two months since I saw him, Emir had aged. A beard covered his face; he no longer looked like a carefree eighteen-year-old. Lines I didn't remember marked his hardened face. Even his eyes looked different, smaller, more suspicious, as if all the squinting he did shooting his enemy permanently marked a change. I was wary of approaching this stranger who resembled my brother. He smiled when he saw me, and for a moment, I saw a glimmer of the brother I knew.

I ran, throwing myself into his arms. As he hugged me tight, relief surged within me. He was still there. The brother I loved was still there.

"Where is Babo?"

"He'll be back soon."

Mama stepped forward and took Emir's rifle. She checked that the safety was on, then leaned it against the tree trunk, her eyes scanning Emir's body, looking for injuries.

A column of soldiers came from the woods, led by a brown-haired man in his twenties, his uniform tight across his wide shoulders. I gulped, tugging on Ramo's sleeve as I pointed. It was Naser Orić. Our saviour. Notwithstanding his run-in with Ramo and the media crews, Naser was the only person that represented hope. Emir saluted Naser as he passed. He was beloved by his soldiers because he was always the first one running into battle.

Naser turned to me, and I found myself captivated by the sway of his green eyes flecked with gold. Cat eyes.

I looked for Ramo; he was hiding behind a tree until Naser passed, still mindful of his gaffe with the journalist a few months ago.

Emir's friend Harun appeared, his eyes following Naser like a sunflower. After Emir performed introductions, I demanded titbits about Naser.

"You should have heard what happened during his last action," Emir said.

"Are you sure you should tell the children?" Harun teased.

"What happened?" I demanded, shaking Emir's arm like a puppy shaking a slipper.

We watched Emir with wide eyes as if we were children waiting for a bedtime fairytale. In the enclave, life was hard and brutal. We'd long given up on the international community saving us from starvation, or the corrupt officials in our local Council doing the right thing by distributing international aid fairly. It was Naser we turned to for salvation. He was fighting to join Srebrenica with the rest of Bosnia so that we had access to food and ammunition to survive.

"Naser and his men attacked Zalazje," Emir said. "Everyone who could carry a rifle set off for the village. They entered the ground floor of a house and walked from room to room, fingers on the trigger, ready to shoot Serbs. They cleared the ground floor. Naser placed his foot on the bottom step. A hand grenade rolled down, metal tinging on wood as it bounced off each step. It landed between his legs. Naser threw himself backwards towards the entrance, rolling away, while the grenade exploded, scattering hundreds of tiny metal balls. Naser led his men upstairs, where they shot all the Serbs. If it was a larger grenade or he had hesitated, he would have died."

"Wow," I sighed. Naser was a super soldier. In our rag-tag army, where most men had never fired a gun, he was the real deal. He was the bogeyman keeping the Serbs at bay.

"I want to marry him," I sighed.

Ramo shot me a look but said nothing. This wasn't just any man; this was Naser, after all.

"So do I," Harun was sitting to the left of Emir, cleaning his rifle.

"Aren't you already married?" Emir teased.

"My wife would understand," Harun said.

"Your wife would beat you to the punch," Emir said.

"True." Harun nodded.

"And what did you name your son?" Emir asked.

"The only true manly name in Bosnia. Naser," Harun said.

"And what about you, Tarik?" Emir called out to another soldier across the encampment who was lying against a tree, his hat over his face. "What did you name your son?"

"Naser," Tarik said.

Emir turned to us, laughing. "The only male name given by Bosnian soldiers."

In this time of hopelessness, we all pinned our hopes on Naser's broad shoulders. In an enclave starved of entertainment and news, we all recycled and enlarged tales of Naser's heroics.

Babo walked into the camp, his back straight and his shoulders set. He walked with purpose now, as if he had somewhere to go and not much time.

When Babo saw me, he smiled. I ran to him, and as he hugged me, I laughed. It had been so long. Mama was cooking in a makeshift wooden stove used for camping before the war.

"Emir, tell him the story about Naser," I demanded, smiling at my brother.

"Babo doesn't want to hear stories about Naser," Emir said.

"Why not?" I looked at Babo in confusion.

"Don't believe the fairytales, my child. Naser is not our saviour. He is just a man, and he is as corrupt as any man," Babo held my chin as he spoke, forcing me to look into his eyes. Emir's were full of light and hope when he spoke of Naser, while Babo's were dark with suspicion.

"That doesn't mean that he's not serving our army," Emir argued.

"Yes, but he's serving himself first," Babo said.

This was an argument that they hashed and rehashed. People said Naser was involved in black market profiteering, but I didn't want to believe it.

"Let's leave this talk for another time. Dinner is ready," Mama said.

Mama served beans on small tin plates. The beans were tasteless, barely edible, with no salt to add flavour. I chewed quickly, avoiding having them in my mouth for long. They hit my stomach like a fist.

"Tell Seka about the boy," Mama urged, staving off a reprisal of their argument.

Babo sighed before slurping up the last of his beans and passing her the tin dish. "One day, a young boy was walking towards our line. He was about ten years old, and he was calling for his Babo. He came to our side and looked at us with surprise. *Where is Babo? I brought him lunch*, he said, holding up a bucket in his hand. *What's your father's name?* We asked him. *Miroslav.*

"We realised he was a Serb boy who had gotten lost and came to our side instead. His father's name was called, and we informed him that we had his son. We heard thudding footsteps through the forest. *Please take me,* a man's voice called out. *Don't take my son.*"

Babo took another sip of beans, slurping as he spooned it into his mouth.

"*We don't want either of you,* we told him and urged the boy out. *The boy is coming, call his name*," he continued when he'd swallowed. "We heard the boy's footsteps as he ran to his father, and then, *Thank you, a million thank you's*, Miroslav shouted, his voice thick with tears."

"The next morning, the boy called out to us and came back to our side. *Babo told me to give you this*, he said, holding up a bottle of rakija. *But first, I have to do this.* He took off the lid and sipped, his face screwing up with disgust before he handed us the bottle. He returned to his side of the battle-ground." Babo paused, looking pensive as he stared into the fire. "These are the moments when I think we have not lost our humanity."

"We haven't lost ours. But we're not the ones returning mutilated corpses when we exchange prisoners," Emir said.

"Mutilated?" I asked.

"Emir, stop," Babo warned.

"The Serbs return our soldiers with their heads or penises chopped off. Sometimes both," Emir continued, speaking over our father. He kicked the fire and walked off.

Babo and Mama looked at each other with concern as they watched him retreating.

"We'd better get going." Ibrahim looked at the setting sun.

"Just a moment." Mama moved away with Babo, who shot me a look, his face full of consternation. My toes curled with embarrassment, and I stopped breathing. Did she tell my father about my period?

"I'll be coming back with you." Mama put on her coat. She hugged Emir and Babo, and we walked out of camp together, holding hands. I should have been happy. I had my mother back, yet I couldn't help but feel that Emir needed her more. As my brother's hate grew, it hollowed him out from within, changing him into someone unrecognisable from the brother I knew.

When we got home, after Mama greeted the family, she insisted on having a bath before night fell, and it was too dark to move around the house without electricity. She said she hadn't washed properly for two months.

I sat on my parent's bed and wrote to Zora.

"I wonder what will be left of us when this war is finally over. Surviving takes everything we have, and it feels like it's stealing our humanity too. Once, we were all the same people, but now we see each other as less than human. I could never see you as anything but my Zora, but I'm scared. If this war drags on much longer, I might change too. I might turn into someone I don't even recognise—like my brother."

A few minutes later, Mama called me from the bathroom, breathless and annoyed. I hid my notebook under the mattress. When I opened the door, she was sitting on the edge of the bathtub, her face red. "I can't get these boots off." She'd unlaced them but couldn't tug them off her feet.

I knelt and tugged. They were stuck hard. I pulled and pulled, Mama wincing with pain, finally yanking one off and then the other. Mama took off her socks. I gasped in horror when I saw her feet. Her feet looked as if someone had boiled them in a washtub.

"What happened?"

"I haven't taken my boots off in two months." Mama removed the rest of her clothes. "You have to be ready to run at a moment's notice."

She stood nude before me, her ribs poking through her ribcage, the flesh of her arms hanging loose from her bone. She sank into the bathtub with a sigh.

6-Parachute

I sat on the hillside, holding a torch, staring up at the stars in the sky, waiting for the sound of an American C-130 cargo plane. The soft half-melted snow at my feet signalled the end of a long winter. Ramo sat next to me. The icy wind on the bluff was strong and cut through me like knives on this frosty night, and I was grateful to feel the warmth of his body next to mine. Under the cover of darkness, he took my hand in his, and we smiled at each other. Our gloves had practically disintegrated under the duress of a long winter fetching wood and scaling the mountain. Now, we tucked our icy hands into each other, feeling our skin slowly warm to the touch.

In the last few months, the local Council entreated the UN to ensure the Serbs did not stop food convoys, but nothing happened. It was only when Sarajevo refused to receive any further aid that the US arranged for aid packets to be parachuted into Srebrenica.

My grandfather and Uncle Ibrahim were nearby, talking to a few men. Since my father was still at the front, they had shouldered collecting the food drops for the past few days, and this was the first time they had invited me and Ramo to join.

"Early in the week, they delivered only flour and beans," one man said. "We didn't even get any little packets of Tabasco to spice up the food."

"Last week was a gift," another man said. "We got M&Ms. We burned the plastic wrappings as fuel."

"Did you hear that?" I slapped Ramo's arm. "They're delivering chocolate." I salivated. I hadn't tasted chocolate since the war began nearly a year ago.

"Who cares about chocolate? I want food." Ramo shrugged.

"Seriously, you'd rather have flour and beans."

"I'm a growing boy. I need my protein." He flexed his arm and arched his eyebrow at me.

I laughed because it was true. He was still growing. Even though the deprivations we were going through thinned him out, he still maintained the tall and wide stature and tan he had when he first arrived in Srebrenica. He was wearing Babo's jacket and pants. Mama scrounged through Babo's wardrobe, giving Ramo two pairs of pants and two jumpers to alternate as they washed.

"Do you hear anything?" I shivered in my coat. Although really it was Mama's special red woollen coat for going to the city in winter. She used to wear knee-high black high-heeled boots and a red beret perched on her head to match the slash of lipstick on her lips. She used to walk tall and proud as she drew attention from men and women alike in the eye-catching colour. Now, her special red coat had been reduced to the most basic of its parts—I wore it because it was the warmest coat Mama owned, and it reached down to my calves.

The wind buffeted the refugees like scarecrows in a field. They huddled in summer clothes, still wearing what they had on when running from the onslaught of Serbs last summer. I'd heard talk of refugees freezing to death during the harsh winter. The cold slithered like an eel in the spaces where the coat buttonholes were and on my ankles.

Ramo shook his head. He always heard the planes before I did. I sighed with frustration.

My ears pricked, and I tuned back into the conversation the men were having.

".... and I took home a parachute that my wife made into shirts and pants. See." The man stood and turned.

I turned on my torch and saw the shiny fabric of his pants.

"Look at that." I pointed the torch back at the man in the parachute pants. "Maybe Mama could make a dress for me."

"Maybe," he said.

The men were now talking about the Vance-Owen peace plan, the newest brainwave of some bureaucrat, about how to arrange peace.

"Do you think the Serbs will accept the peace plan?" one man asked.

"No chance," Dido said, his usually slicked-back hair flying in every direction. "The Serbs will not compromise. They want all Srebrenica's riches. And revenge for the Muslims holding all the important positions during Tito's era."

"Europe won't let this war go on," Ibrahim said. "They will intervene and stop the Serbs' killing."

"You're kidding yourself. The only reason the cargo planes are here is because the Sarajevo government stopped receiving food aid until we did. They shamed the UN. Europe doesn't care. They'd rather that the winner is a cross worshipper than a Muslim," Dido said.

"They should stop wasting their breath," Ramo muttered. "The Serbs don't want peace, so it will never happen." He stared straight ahead.

Last night, I'd heard him moaning from his mattress as night terrors gripped him. His moans had been faint, his fists clenched in front of him, before his mother hugged him to her, singing to him gently. I'd heard him shifting afterwards, trying to find a comfortable position, until he finally stared at the ceiling. I'd lifted my head, and our eyes met briefly before he closed his, pretending to sleep. I fell asleep, still aware of him wide awake a few metres away, his brain churning with images of death.

"You didn't sleep well," I said, not sure how to broach the topic.

He stiffened beside me, glancing at me sideways. "Did you hear?"

I nodded, taking his arm between mine, leaning against him and not caring who saw us. "Were you dreaming about your brothers and father?"

He nodded. He was about to speak when a bright torch hit us, making my eyes wince from the brightness. Dido aimed the torch. His eyes narrowed suspiciously.

I moved away from Ramo. "We'll meet later today," I muttered under my breath. I paced to keep myself warm. "Are they coming?" I stared at the dark sky. We'd waited for hours.

"They will be here soon," my Uncle Ibrahim said.

"We hope. Last night the drop was here, but I got nothing. A group of men with guns surrounded the pallet and threatened everyone who came close," said the man my uncle was talking to.

I glanced around fearfully, looking for men with guns. Ramo straightened and paced the perimeter while Dido and Uncle Ibrahim took position as lookouts, scanning in opposite directions.

"Didn't the army stop them?" I asked.

When the food drops were first announced with leaflets fluttering from the sky, Naser Orić barred civilians from the drop zone and ordered work brigades to recover the sacks of wheat flour and other supplies from the parachuted pallets and transport them to the department store for distribution. Naser had announced that each person would receive enough food for one meal a day. Work brigades had climbed the mountainsides above town every night and lit fires in the snow to direct planes where to drop their cargo. Some food made it to the department store, but never enough. Rumours circled about workers hiding food in the snowbanks and returning under the cover of darkness to take sacks of flour to their houses. Fist fights erupted outside the department store when supplies ran out before each civilian received their fair share. Men brought weapons and used them to threaten to collect food. After seven days, Naser stopped the work brigades, and it was each man, woman and child for themselves.

"How many of you?" a man asked my grandfather.

Dido pointed at me and Ramo. "Ah, you've got a sturdy boy. He'll be able to carry a lot. And the girl is young. She can do her share."

I stood straight, happy to have this adult responsibility. The first few nights, Ibrahim and Dido came alone, and didn't get to carry much for the rest of the family.

"Be careful. Last night, they failed to open and crushed a 15-year-old boy to death when it landed on him. Stay out of the way until the pallet lands," he told us loudly.

"Stay close to me. I'll hear them coming," Ramo told me.

I nodded.

"Where is my wife?" A male voice called out in the dark. "Derviša. Derviša."

"You've lost your wife, Mujo," another man said. "Who knows what she's doing in the dark?"

"Next time, she'll stay home," Mujo said. Laughter broke out among the group, and I smiled too. Sometimes, humour was the only way to deal with the threat of falling pallets or sniper fire from Serbs.

"It's coming." Ramo cocked his ear.

I listened for a moment but heard nothing. "Are you sure—"

There was the unmistakable sound of the cargo plane, its jet engines thundering in the sky above us. Lights appeared, and then the shape of the aeroplane appeared against the dark, inky sky.

"Turn on your torches!" someone shouted.

We all turned on our torches and pointed up. I waited with bated breath as the plane ducked. The engine's sound changed.

"It's dropped," Ramo said.

I heard a whistling sound from above, something coming down with quick force. I strained my eyes to see in the dark and could see the faint outline of a pallet with a parachute attached, dropping.

"Come on, run." He took my hand, and we ran full pelt.

Ibrahim and Dido lacked the vigour to run fast. It was speed that decided who got the most food. A bang ahead and a rush of people joined the hunt, pushing and ducking and weaving. When we reached the pallet, I took out the knife tucked into my knapsack and cut through the plastic in a quick, decisive strike. Inside were packs and cardboard boxes. I took a cardboard box and hunched myself over, protecting it from sight. Quick hands grabbed and tried to snatch it from me, but Ramo appeared at my side and pushed a boy younger than me away, holding his knife up with an angry look in his eye. The boy ducked around us and went to find his own goods. Ramo and I hurried away. He was hauling three boxes.

I glanced behind me and saw the pallet was nearly empty. "I want the parachute."

Ramo took the box from me. "Go."

I ducked back among the people. Everyone was consumed with picking food off the pallet, and the parachute remained tangled on the side. I used my knife to tear off the string attaching it to the pallet, folded it up and ran back to Ramo with it tucked awkwardly tucked under my arm. My uncle and grandfather had joined us—

Bang, bang. We could hear a gunshot echoing from beyond the hill. I saw the red flash of the muzzle a few metres away.

"Is it Serbs?" I asked, ducking down.

"No." Ibrahim shook his head.

A man standing next to a pallet, holding a gun aloft. On the ground was a man, dead, a dark stain spreading on his chest. All the people who had huddled to get food off the pallet stepped back. The man collected boxes calmly, as much as he could carry in one arm, and walked away. Once he had disappeared, people swarmed the pallet again, unfazed, stepping over the dead man to get food.

We were like ants teeming on the hill, snatching bread-crumbs to prolong starvation for another day. The dead man was someone's father, someone's son, someone's brother, but in these times of desperation, he was just a speed bump we had to step over.

Ramo stepped closer, his eyes closing in anguish.

"Do you know him?" I asked.

Ramo turned away and nodded. "Derviš. He was a neigh-bour in my village."

"That crazy Bešić shot him," a man to our left said, pointing to the man who was now calmly walking downhill.

Ramo's face hardened, and he turned away. "Perhaps he was the lucky one. After all, a bullet was a more efficient way of dying," he said as we walked downhill.

We returned home just before dawn. Ramo was panting by the time we got to the front door, overloaded with supplies. Ibrahim shuffled along slowly, holding a sack with boxes over his back, and Dido was to my left, a heavy sheen of perspi-ration coating his face as he walked. The rest of the family greeted us like gladiators. While the four of us curled up on the sponge mattresses to rest, Mama and my aunt spent the morning in the kitchen.

The smell of beans filled my nose. Mama handed me a bowl, and I ate like a sleepwalker, little pops of flavour from the Tabasco sauce like an explosion on my tongue after eating bland and tasteless food for so long. I took out my notebook and wrote: *"Tonight was wild. It was risky going up the mountain for food, but it felt so good to be doing something that actually matters. At least one good thing about this war is I'm not stuck just doing boring girl stuff anymore. Now, I'm actually helping my family survive."*

The next morning, the town lay quiet under a blanket of snow, the chill of winter settling deep into the bones of its inhabitants. Ramo was still quiet as we ventured out into the cold, the crunch of snow under our boots the only sound breaking the silence.

I tugged on my mother's coat, caressing the soft fabric against my skin, and followed Ramo to the side of the house, where we could speak freely. "You're thinking about your neighbour," I stated, placing my hand on his shoulder, seeking to comfort him.

He nodded, taking my hand and kissing it gently before pulling me into a tight hug. "It's not right. Life is hard enough now without us being murdered by our own."

"Then we should do something," I said, determination creeping into my voice.

A wry smile tugged at the corners of Ramo's lips. "What?"

I rubbed my lip, considering our options. In times of peace, reporting a crime to the police would have been the obvious choice. But the nearest police station was now in Bratunac, held by the Serbs.

"The army," I finally said. They were the closest thing to an authority now.

"We're just going to show up at the army headquarters to tell them there was a murder committed?" Ramo asked sceptically.

"Why not?" I replied, trying to sound more confident than I felt.

Ramo sighed. "Lead the way."

We walked into town. The snow crunched under our boots as we made our way to the bustling post office, now commandeered as command headquarters. Soldiers in mismatched uniforms hurried about, their breath visible in the cold air.

"We're here to report a murder," I told the officer who stopped us at the entrance.

"Are you for real?" he demanded. "There's a murder every day in Srebrenica. The Chetniks are slaughtering us."

"But this was a Bosniak man killing another Bosniak," I burst out, desperation creeping into my voice as I recounted the details.

"I'm sorry to hear that, but we don't have the manpower or authority to deal with civilian matters," the officer said brusquely, ushering us out.

"This is bullshit," I muttered, seething as we walked along the footpath. I glanced at Ramo, but he seemed lost in thought.

"Are you all right to get home?" Ramo asked, gesturing towards the Civic Centre where refugees sought shelter and services.

"Why?" I asked.

"I'm going to find Derviš's family and tell them what happened to him," Ramo replied quietly.

I bit back my questions and nodded, watching him disappear into the crowd. He returned hours later after we had all settled into our beds for the night. His mother stirred, asking him where he had been, and he told her he was visiting friends.

The next morning we met in secret on the balcony, the snow-covered mountains looming in the distance. Ramo was subdued, his eyes dark with burden.

"What happened?" I asked, taking his hands in mine and tucking them under my jumper to warm them.

"I found Derviš's brother. He had already recovered his brother's body and buried him. I told him Bešić killed him. He insisted we go search for him so he could beat him up, and I had to come with him because I knew what he looked like. It didn't take long to find Bešić. He was in one of the high-rise flats by the school. Derviš's brother knocked on the door, lying that he wanted to buy food. When I confirmed the murderer's identity, he stabbed Bešić in the gut. He said that he had fulfilled his blood oath and left the man to die in his wife's arms."

I held Ramo's hands tightly, the weight of his words sinking in. The concepts of blood oaths and revenge killings were not unfamiliar to me, but it was chilling to hear them play out in our own town.

"You didn't know that would happen," I said, trying to reassure him.

Ramo remained silent, lost in his thoughts. "Is it really wrong to kill a cold-blooded murderer?" he asked after a while. "Shouldn't we seek some justice somewhere?"

I didn't know what to say, so I said nothing. We sat quietly, watching the snow-covered mountains around us, a stark reminder of the harsh reality of our world.

Vahida, the nurse, told me they needed my services as I popped into the hospital the next day, seeking some time away from Ramo.

"Oh," I asked. It would be good to be busy, and any work would lead to food I could take home to my family.

"This is Dr Tonel. He's a general practitioner who wants to help the refugees in the Srebrenica schoolhouse."

I fought hard not to flinch. Hundreds of displaced persons packed the schoolhouse, and the overwhelming stench of human refuse filled my nostrils during the few times I passed. Since they shut off the water, it became even worse.

"Hello Seka," the doctor said in English with a French accent.

"Hello Dr Tonel. You want to go to the schoolhouse?" I asked. "I'm here to help you translate."

"Good, good," the doctor nodded. "Let's get medication." We walked upstairs to the storeroom, which was full of boxes that were haphazardly stacked in the storeroom. Dr Tonel zipped his backpack full of medicine.

Vahida walked ahead with the doctor as we headed down the main road towards the school. When we arrived, Vahida told the children to ask the adults to gather. "This is Dr Tonel," she told them. "He is here to treat all of you."

The doctor put on gloves, walked over to three children, and took hold of a boy's arm. Painful-looking red bumps covered the boy's skin.

"These are scabies," the doctor said in English.

I didn't know what the word was in Bosnian.

"We call them *šuga*," Vahida said. She had her gloves on and was opening a box of ointment. She poured it onto the boy's hand and told him to smear it on. More and more children came closer, all of them with red painful skin. Vahida and the doctor handed out ointment.

"We need to do more than this," the doctor said. "We need to stop this happening." He walked into the schoolhouse, and we followed.

Now, the classrooms I remembered were filled with desks pushed together, topped with blankets and clothes. The refugees were using them as beds to sleep on. Children had covered the green chalkboards in writing and drawing that reached the top of my head. People leaning against them have used up the chalk and rubbed out the chalkboards. Above the chalkboards were photos of Tito. I felt nostalgic for a moment. So many public spaces had removed Tito's photos, and I hadn't even realised. Seeing the photo in the classroom reminded me of what our life was like when we were Yugoslavs and before the war that tore us all apart.

The classrooms were filthy, and the smell was rancid. The toilets were backed up because the water had been shut off, causing the refugees to go into the forest at the back of the school to defecate.

One refugee was telling the doctor that since the Serbs had taken over the water plant and cut off running water to Srebrenica, diarrhoea had spread through the school. I fought to keep my face neutral as I translated.

The doctor took a group of refugees into the bathrooms, and they started cleaning, using hospital disinfectant. The doctor went back to the hospital with a few men and returned with boxes. He opened them up, hung up water bladders, and explained to the refugees how they could use them to have a shower.

"It is very important that you practice good hygiene," the doctor instructed. "Because you are in such close proximity, disease spreads quickly."

I translated the doctor's instructions about the importance of hygiene to ensure that they remain in good health. A woman in the crowd called out, "that's all well and good for those of you who have water." She stared hard at me, my shiny hair a taunt to her.

I turned away, feeling guilty that I had the benefit of my house and the luxury of indoor plumbing.

"They're very pale," the doctor murmured. He approached a little girl and looked at the pale pallor of her skin, and then at her mother. He held up the girl's hand and looked at the nails, which were brittle and broken. "Are you experiencing dizziness, fatigue, and light-headedness?" the doctor asked, and I translated.

"Yes, yes," the woman said, nodding. "I thought it was because we don't have enough food. My daughter has eaten dirt."

"Yes, that is a symptom of anaemia," the doctor said.

This time I didn't have to look at Vahida for the translation. It was said the same in both languages, just with a slight pronunciation difference.

Vahida handed Dr Tonil medication. I translated his instructions about taking a tablet once a day.

At the end of the long day, I trudged back to the war hospital, my footsteps echoing in the dimly lit corridor. The only source of light came from flickering candles, casting long shadows that danced on the walls. The air was heavy with the stench of sweat, blood, and antiseptic, a constant reminder of the harsh reality of our situation. When I reached the storeroom, I encountered a shocking sight—empty shelves where there had once been rows of neatly stacked boxes.

"What happened to all the medication?" I asked Vahida, my voice echoing slightly in the empty room.

I left the hospital with my head spinning, the chill of the night air biting at my skin. As I stepped outside, a figure emerged from the shadows, stepping into the circle of light cast by the generators. I gasped, my heart racing until I recognised Ramo.

"Everything okay?" he asked, stepping closer and instinctively arranging my scarf around my neck to shield me from the cold.

I told him about the missing medications, and he let out a bitter bark of laughter. "The corrupt bastards took them to sell on the black market before they were all given away to the needy people."

"No, they couldn't," I gasped, a sense of disbelief and betrayal washing over me.

Ramo gave me a sidelong glance, his expression sombre, and I sighed, the truth settling heavily upon me. They could, and they did. I tucked my arm into his elbow, seeking comfort and solidarity as we rushed through the dark and cold night, the snow crunching under our boots with each step.

7-Promise

12 March 1993

I was reading *The Famous Five* by Enid Blyton wishing myself in the tranquil English countryside when Ramo shouted my name.

"Seka, Seka, did you hear?"

"Hear what?" I asked.

Ramo's chest heaved as he said, "General Morillon is in Srebrenica." Morillon commanded the United Nations Forces in Bosnia.

I ran to the door and put my boots on. Dido followed.

"Run, run!" Dido said, waving at us. "I'll catch up."

We reached the centre of town to see several dozen green trucks and white cars in a convoy slowly driving down the main road. The white cars were the size of a mini tank and looked like they were from the movie *Back to the Future* with the letters UN on them.

"Those are Armoured Personnel Carriers," Ramo said in response to my question. "They're used by the United Nations to transport people so they don't get injured."

"How do you know?" I asked, looking closer. The APCs only had tiny little windows at the front that were at a 45-degree angle. I could see how they would keep soldiers safe from injury.

"I asked the soldiers." He pointed to the Bosnian soldiers who were standing by the side of the road, mostly in civilian clothes, a gun over their shoulder. A red and white flag undulated in the wind, hanging off the flagpole on the trucks and APCs. It was a flag I hadn't seen before.

Ramo saw my look of confusion. "Those are Canadian soldiers."

The convoy stopped and the soldiers threw back the hatches on top of the APC. Soldiers in baggy uniforms and blue helmets emerged from the trucks and APCs. They surrounded a man with white hair under his blue helmet.

"That's Morillon," Ramo said, pointing.

Morillon had a long face and was wearing glasses. He looked like an ordinary man, not like a soldier, but was being treated with deference. The Council President, his deputy and the chief of staff greeted him. A crowd gathered and everybody wanted to touch the soldiers. I held out my hand and shuffled closer to the Canadian soldier, gently touching his uniform, feeling the fabric. It was as if I was waking from a nightmare and needed to feel proof the soldiers were not a figment of my imagination. I thought the camouflage would be tough, but it was soft to touch, like cotton. Now that I was closer, I could see the armband that the soldiers wore that showed their national symbol, a red leaf against a white background, framed by two red panels on either side.

Ramo and I followed Morillon and the soldiers as they attempted to walk through town, but every street that the General entered was a squat. The refugees who were lucky crowded into basements between charred walls and public buildings like the school gym and town hall. But those who arrived last slept on cardboard and plastic that they lay on a square of the street. A woman in *dimije* fanned an open fire in the middle of the street, roasting the leg of a cow. So many of the refugees fled with their livestock, not wanting to leave them behind to be slaughtered and eaten by the Serbs, only to arrive at the town proper and realise there was no space to tether or feed them.

Morillon stopped to converse with the woman through a translator. She told him about her village being attacked by Serbs, about escaping through the countryside while being shelled and shot at; that she was living on the street in a lean-to made of wood and plastic. As I stopped, I could feel my boots slipping on something slick. I looked down and saw I was in a patch of blood. As the surrounding crowd shifted, I saw the edge of the road and the cow head perched on a box like a trophy. A cow that desperate refugees had brought with them when they ran and was now being slaughtered because of necessity. It seemed the lifeless eyes were following me. I quickly shifted so that I couldn't see it anymore.

After a couple of hours of walking and talking to the populace, reassuring them he would report back to the UN and bring help, Morillon returned to the post office. He disappeared inside with the bureaucrats, and the crowd thinned.

Ramo and I crouched behind the post office. A group of people gathered around an open window. Morillon was in a room with the President. They were talking about the Serb offensive. They offered Morillon a slice of hazel-bush bread. He took a hearty bite and chewed. His face screwed up at the bitterness. He forced himself to continue chewing, attempting to hide his revulsion. He finished the bite and said, a little embarrassed, "Healthy food, good for the digestion."

I covered my mouth so my laughter didn't carry.

"That's right, our food is only good enough for shitting," Ramo whispered in my ear, his shoulders shaking too.

Morillon squared his shoulders and took another bite, finishing his slice. He reached for the water quickly, attempting to wash away the pain of a sore throat as the bread burned its way down.

After an hour of watching them talk, my stomach was churning with hunger. "Let's go home," I said to Ramo.

He nodded, and we weaved our way through the crowd to get home. "The Serbs tried to kill Morillon."

"But he's a United Nations General," I said.

"They tried to stop him from coming and after hours of arguing, he finally left. Deep snow covers the road, and it is mined. They were hoping he would crash or the car would hit a mine. When he reached the front line, a truck hit a land mine, and they abandoned it. But he made it. I bet the Serbs are watching us right now and cursing him."

When we got home, we ate half a slice of hazel-bush bread each and a watery stew with one tired-looking carrot in it. I sat on the couch and took out my notebook, drowsily writing.

"Dear Zora, For the first time in so long, I actually feel hopeful. There's a UN General here in Srebrenica, and he's really listening to what life is like for us. When he tells the international community, they'll have to believe him—how the enemy is starving us and how doing nothing is basically letting a genocide happen. Once the UN soldiers come, we'll

finally have peace, and the war will end. Life will go back to normal. Maybe you'll even be able to come home."

Someone urgently knocked on the door.

Mama opened the door. "Fatima, come in," she greeted.

I stood and peered over her shoulder. It was my school-teacher, Mrs Tanović.

"Morillon is attempting to leave. We need to mobilise women and children to stop him. Take all your female-folk to the post office quickly," she said and stalked back up the path.

"Stop him? How?" Mama shouted.

"Peacefully. Naser's orders are to do it peacefully." She ran to the next house and knocked.

If Naser said we had to stop Morillon, it was because we were in a desperate situation.

Mama took her coat off the hook in the hallway. "Paša, Edina, we need to go to the post office," Mama shouted to my aunt and Ramo's mother.

My aunt went to wake up my cousins after my mother told her what was happening.

Nana appeared ambling painfully. "I'm coming too." Her hair was greyer and her face more lined in the year since the war began as her health deteriorated.

"No, Mama, you're not well," my mother said, gently urging my grandmother back to bed.

"If Morillon leaves, we are all dead," Nana said.

The Serbs knew we were weak and hungry. They were shoring up their artillery on the peaks above us, watching and waiting. Morillon was our chance for a reprieve before they made their last push to drive us off our ancestral land.

"I'm coming." My grandmother shrugged on a coat by the door.

My Aunt Paša came down the stairs carrying the baby, my cousins Imran and Minka following slowly, their eyes half shut and creases on their cheeks from sleep.

We put on our coats and ran out the door. A crowd of women and children had already gathered at the post office. One woman was writing with crayons on a cardboard. She handed a placard to a child. "We are hungry! Give us bread!" Mama approached, and the woman gave us directions. "Sit on the ground around the convoy. Don't touch any of the soldiers or shout. We are here for a civilised protest." As she was talking, she continued writing. She handed my cousin Minka a placard that said, "Don't abandon us!" Minka's brown eyes lit up with delight as she marched with the sign. She couldn't read it, but she loved being the centre of action.

Women continued gathering. Belma came, her mother and siblings following her. Belma looked gaunt and tired. Giving birth in a war zone had been brutal, but she'd said that was the easiest part of it. Trying to breastfeed Zikret when she didn't get enough nutrition to produce breastmilk was causing her great distress. She constantly worried about the effect of the malnutrition on his tiny body. I greeted her, and we joined the crowd. Nana and the older women sat around the UN track, forming a circle. The woman wrote on the last piece of cardboard, "If You Leave, They Will Kill us!" As she handed it to me goose pimples raised on my skin.

Kamila and her mother appeared and joined the crowd. Lebiba sat next to my mother, and Kamila edged in between me and Belma.

Morillon was the one person stopping the Serbs from launching a final offensive. He was a high-profile general that they couldn't risk attacking. If they did, the international community would turn on them.

My grandfather and uncle were talking, and they said strategically it was the perfect time to attack because we were starving, weakened, with no fight left. The waves of refugees who were living on the streets were like the walking dead. If Morillon left, the Serbs would attack for the last time, and we would be gone.

Mama and Lebiba exchanged small talk, their breath forming misty clouds in the frosty night air. My ears perked up, the only part of me warm beneath my thick scarf, hat, and coat, when Mama mentioned the missing medicine from the hospital storeroom. "How can we survive when we have such blatant corruption and disrespect for human life?" Mama implored, her words almost tangible in the frosty air.

Lebiba's gaze narrowed with concern, her brow furrowing against the chill. She looked at me, her expression serious. "I need you to come to the Council offices tomorrow afternoon and I'll take a statement. We need to ensure this travesty doesn't happen again."

I nodded, the relief flooding through me like a wave of warmth, momentarily forgetting the biting cold. Losing the medicine had weighed heavily on me, but Lebiba's determination to take action filled me with hope.

Half an hour passed, and Morillon and his soldiers exited the building. He smiled at the women as he opened the truck door. The truck engines exploded as they turned on, the loud noise a physical assault.

I was sitting next to the wheel, nerves making my skin tingle as the vibration of the motor thrummed through my body. If the truck moved, we would be mown down. Women who were behind the trucks, in the path of the exhaust, coughed as fumes spluttered in their faces.

Morillon stepped out. "Dear ladies, it is getting quite late, and I need to return to Sarajevo. I will report on the conditions here and get help."

The women looked to Mrs Tanović. She shook her head and didn't move from her spot behind the APC. Morillon attempted to talk to different women. "I know you are afraid, but once I report what I have seen to my superiors, we will help you."

"If you leave, we will die," Mrs Tanović said in her accented English. "Don't move, ladies. Your children's lives are in question."

No one moved.

Morillon returned to the post office, and his soldiers got out of the trucks and waited in front, smoking and giving us filthy looks.

"I want to get out of this shit hole," one of them said in English.

Morillon came out again with Naser Orić. Naser looked relaxed, his hands on his belt as he walked slowly, while Morillon was agitated, his hand moving up and down as he pointed to the women.

"Please, make them move so we can leave," Morillon asked.

"I can't do anything," Naser said. "These women are scared for their lives and the lives of their children. They won't listen to me."

Naser returned to the post office and Morillon followed. Ramo watched from the back and updated us that Morillon was upstairs with a sleeping bag. Half an hour passed.

I was tired and droopy. Ramo found a piece of cardboard and I lay on it, using his legs as a pillow, while Belma lay her head on my legs. I awoke to a grumbling sound and shouting. Kamila was listlessly leaning against her mother. When I opened my eyes, women were huddling closer to the trucks.

"What's happening?' I rubbed my eyes.

"The driver is trying to leave," Ramo said. "Naser checked, and Morillon is gone. We think the driver is supposed to meet him, so we can't let him leave."

The driver implored the women to move. He said he needed to return to the airfield, or he'd lose his job, but the women resolutely closed ranks and sat.

Mrs Tanović returned with more women and children. Now, we weren't just standing around the vehicles. Instead, we were a force in front of the post office.

"Where is Morillon?" a woman asked.

"He's left," another woman said.

"Should we follow him?"

Mrs Tanović spoke to Naser and returned. "Don't worry, he has no transport and will return."

We waited.

Two hours later, a man bobbed through the darkness. The Bosnian soldiers lifted their torches and lit up Morillon, holding his hand to cover his eyes. He walked past us and smiled sheepishly, acting like he was taking an evening stroll instead of attempting to escape.

The women held arms and swayed as we sang, keeping our morale up. Belma and I were side by side, and I saw her face lit up with purpose and determination. Adrenaline surged through me. If we wavered and Morillon left, we were dead.

A soldier handed out food relief packs. Each woman took a handful and passed it on. The sugar from the M&Ms surged through me. It was months since I'd had any sugar, let alone any chocolate. It stripped my fatigue away and I was buzzing and wide awake.

The hours passed as if in a dream, and dawn lit up the sky.

"Morillon keeps arguing with the President. He said he will report his findings and help us. The President said that by the time he puts in his report nothing will be left of us. That he needs to protect us now," Ramo told us in one of his updates. I handed him an M&M I'd saved in my pocket. He ate it with a look of bliss, his eyes closing as the chocolate hit his tongue. He opened his eyes and smiled, his hand squeezing mine. Then he returned to his post by the window.

The hours passed, and a crowd gathered. Women with small children were now able to leave because we were a bigger crowd, and my Aunt Paša and Belma's mother left.

"Are you coming?" her mother asked Belma.

Belma shook her head. Her chest was damp from leaking milk. "Send Nedjad with Zikret so I can feed him."

Nedjad arrived twenty minutes later, and Belma breastfed her baby, standing up. She quickly burped Zikret and handed him back. Nedjad joined the crowd, holding the baby in his arms.

The crowd was collecting with men appearing too. The sugar wave was receding, and the fatigue returning, but I didn't want to go home. The crowd surged with a palpable sense of agitation. We were waiting for something to happen.

Journalists arrived with their cameras and filmed our faces. I wanted to make sure my face was clean. I looked down at my clothes. They were wrinkled and filthy from sleeping in the street. I finally understood why the refugees with no housing looked as they did. It was impossible to keep yourself clean when you didn't have access to a bathroom or water. My scalp was itchy. I scratched at it, wondering if I got lice from being in close proximity to the refugees around me. That was something to worry about tomorrow, if we prevailed.

"He's going to speak." Ramo ran out, his voice cracking with excitement.

"Who?" I asked, blinking and yawning. Another wave of fatigue was washing over me.

"Morillon, he's going to speak."

My fatigue retreated as a frisson of excitement penetrated the crowd. People were crammed on the street in front of the post office, lined on the edges of the steep embankment surrounding the building.

From my vantage point, I saw Morillon in the window of the second storey, holding a megaphone in one hand and a black notebook that he was reading a statement from in his other hand. The man beside him held a NATO flag that fluttered in the breeze.

"I have decided to stay here in Srebrenica. You are now under the protection of the UN forces," Morillon said in his accented English voice, his voice sounding robotic and stilted over the megaphone.

Thunderous applause rang out.

"What does that mean?" I asked Mrs Tanović, who was standing beside me.

"It means the UN won't let anything happen to us. We are saved, we are saved." She clasped her hands, tears on her cheeks.

Ramo grabbed me, and we jumped up and down, delirious with joy and fatigue. Belma and Nedjad were hugging and kissing, holding their baby between them. As we pulled away, I saw two of Morillon's aides on the street below, they were laughing. Something about the way they laughed seemed off. I walked closer and Ramo followed.

"As if the UN can keep his promise. He's talking nonsense," one of them said.

"Do you believe them?" I asked Ramo after I'd translated what they said.

"That can't be true. Morillon's a General. Of course he can keep his promise," Ramo said.

I smiled and nodded, but something in his voice gave me a pause. I don't think he believed it himself. We'd heard so many empty promises. Was this just another one?

8-Annihilation

12 April 1993

Since Morillon stayed, a feeling of calm settled over Srebrenica. People ventured into the streets and fields, their faces turned towards each other instead of scanning the sky for enemy planes or the trees for enemy snipers. We shook off our fear savouring the beauty of the spring day, coming together for a community event at the school playground.

A cacophony of shrieks and laughter filled the air, rising from the players engaged in basketball and futsal games in the other two play areas. Their joyous sounds mingled with the music of a folk band on the sidelines, where a harmonica and violin played lively tunes. It appeared everyone in Srebrenica had come out to celebrate Morillon's promise that we were in a safe area.

Ramo stood watching as Emir played soccer, his movements fluid and graceful, his skill evident even from a distance. Kamila joined him, her eyes taking on a longing look as she watched Emir, her admiration clear. Despite his thin frame, Emir's shoulders were broad and his physique muscly, a testament to his love for sports.

Ramo and I exchanged an amused look, sharing a moment of understanding. Kamila nodded at me, her gaze fixed on Emir, not lifting her eyes.

"Come and sit with me," Belma called, spreading a blanket on the concrete stands built into the hillside near the road. She sat down, cradling her son Zikret in her arms. At five months old, he was growing more alert, his green eyes darting around with curiosity.

I glanced longingly at Ramo behind me. He was waiting on the sidelines, observing Emir in the scrum of the football game at the playground in front of the elementary school, but making no move to join in.

"We were just going for a walk," I explained to Belma, extending my hand to Ramo. He stepped forward and took it, our fingers intertwining.

"Oh," Belma murmured, looking down to hide her disap- pointment.

"I'll come sit with you later," I promised, feeling a pang of guilt for leaving her looking so lonely. But I knew I needed to seize this moment of privacy with Ramo.

Kamila barely acknowledged my words, her gaze still fol- lowing Emir as he weaved and dodged on the field, lost in the game's excitement.

We strolled past the stands where my parents were sitting with my aunts and uncle, enjoying the sunshine as they gos- siped with others. The school abutted a hill with the forest framing it from behind, the conifer trees spiky and unruly as they covered the hill. We walked through the basketball court in front, through the carpark at the front of the school. As we got close, people streamed out the front doors. The schoolhouse became a shelter for refugees, like most public buildings, and it was full to bursting with people using its empty classrooms to sleep on sponge mattresses.

Behind the school, a stack of rubbish bags loomed, overflowing with refuse from the refugees. As we passed, one bag suddenly moved, emitting a soft ripping sound. I jumped, startled, as a German Shepherd's head emerged from the bag. Its black fur glistened in the sunlight, contrasting with the matted brown fur on its body. Ignoring us, it focused on the bag, trying to extract the last crumbs of food from within.

We walked up the hill, which seemed steeper than I remembered, or perhaps I was weaker than I thought. My stomach churned from the stench of bodily functions as the desperate refugees searched for places to relieve themselves. As we ascended, the smell gradually faded, replaced by the scent of pine and earth. We could see over the school.

Finally, we reached the copse of trees that had once been mine and Zora's hideout. A fallen tree had created a makeshift seat, hidden from view by the surrounding foliage. Here, Zora had once planned a birthday surprise for me, when she'd written us a romantic play and we acted out the parts, laughing uproariously as we read her lines and then ate sweets she'd brought. I couldn't believe that nearly two years had passed. My birthday would be next month, and I wondered if anyone would remember to celebrate it this year. I'd write to her when I got home about revisiting our hideout.

As Ramo and I sat down, our thighs pressed together tightly. It felt like ages since we'd been alone and could be free with each other.

"I wonder when the convoys will begin?" I mused aloud as I turned to Ramo, the sunlight filtering through the canopy, dappling his features with light and shadow. The gossips said that as the convoys delivered food, people could leave on the empty trucks.

"Even when the convoys start, we won't be leaving." He gently nudged me with his shoulder. "Morillon promised us we're a safe area, and my sister and her husband live with her parents. They have no more space for us."

Relief filled me. He pushed my hair behind my ear and bent, gently touching his lips to mine. We kissed, my arms twining around his neck and tugging him closer. My head was spinning, and when I heard the whistle, I thought it was in my mind.

Ramo pushed us both to the ground, and we watched as the shell landed in the middle of the playground. A grey plume of smoke appeared, bits of gravel exploded and then screams rent the air as glowing pieces of metal sliced through flesh. I watched stupefied as another shell hit the stands, smashing through the wooden benches on which people were sitting, shards of wood and body parts flying in the air. I closed my eyes and covered my ears as the next two shells fell. The shelling paused and the only sounds were screams.

My family. My whole family was down there. I looked at Ramo mutely, my body frozen.

"Let's go." Ramo yanked me up by the hand. We ran down the hill, turning the corner of the school. Blood and pieces of flesh covered the white render of the walls, looking like abstract paintings that my art teacher had shown us in class. Dust floated around, affecting visibility. A woman bumped into me, her eyes half-crazed, blood covering her whole torso. She ran past me, stumbling like she was drunk. I tripped on something and fell. I'd slipped on the blood that formed into a puddle from a severed leg. Ramo came back and lifted me off the ground.

A car screeched, and I turned my head. It was a van that used to deliver bread before the war and was driven by a man who we called the 'Bread Man.' When he screeched to a stop, people helped place the wounded into his van. When it was full, he drove off quickly towards the hospital.

We passed by the playground, and I saw bits of brain, the white and pink whorls like little mince balls, and long glistening intestines hanging on the fence. My legs weakened and my knees buckled. Ramo steadied me. The smoke cleared, revealing large craters in the concrete, body parts strewn like a mannequin factory—a torso here, a leg here, an arm. I looked closer at a strange bone, my stomach lurching as I realised it was a spine.

Children stumbled around, looking for their parents. A young boy with a hole where his left arm should have been walked dazedly in circles as if he couldn't remember how to get out of the playground. Women were screaming children's names, rising over the screams of the wounded, their desperation increasing each time they didn't hear a return scream back.

A tiny hand was stuck in the fence's mesh. It was the size of a five-year-old's hand. I remembered holding my cousin Minka's tiny hand and kissing it, loving the way it was plump and dimpled, like a perfect doll's hand.

I stepped forward and my eyes caught on the red cardigan. One more step. A red torso. I looked closer. A red torso wearing a red cardigan. My eyes swam, and I blinked, forcing them open. A red torso with no arms, no legs, no head. All that was left of Minka was a red torso.

The smoke cleared, and my Aunt Paša walked towards us, carrying Imran in her arms. "Minka, Minka," she screamed, blood-curdling cries.

I lifted my hand and pointed. Paša's face cleared in relief as she looked on the ground to her left. When she saw the torso, her knees gave out, and she fell, still holding Imran. "No, no, no!" she screamed.

Imran turned his head to see. Ramo left my side and pushed open the gate, his hands touching the flesh stuck to it, walking to Paša's side and lifting her up.

"Take Imran home." He walked Paša backwards so that Imran couldn't see. Paša walked down the footpath, slowly and dazedly, as if she was re-learning how to walk.

"Mama, Babo," I whispered, turning towards the stands.

The stands were filled with seated people. As we approached, I saw one was a headless body, still sitting in position. Another one, a man with brown hair and blue eyes, half his head caved in.

Two boys passed by, wheeling a wheelbarrow with a third in it. The boy in the wheelbarrow had blood pouring from his eyes.

"Where are my eyes? Give me my eyes!" he screamed.

Spectators searched the stands for survivors, collecting those who were still moving. A woman wearing a blue and yellow dress, with large patches of red now covering it, was bent down "Mama," I shouted, letting go of Ramo's hand and running.

"Seka." Mama stood and quickly hugged me.

"Babo, Emir," I demanded.

"They're fine. Babo found Emir, and they were looking for you."

Someone screamed. I looked back and saw my Aunt Adna lying in the stands. Her leg had been mangled, and her stomach was bleeding. Mama helped Adna up. A Canadian soldier ran towards us, and he and Mama walked Adna to a white UN truck that was on the street in front of the school.

"Go find your father and Emir," Mama said over her shoulder.

I heard my father's voice and turned to see him running towards me. Blood covered his blue shirt. "Are you okay?" Babo demanded as he looked me up and down.

I nodded. "Emir."

"Over here." Babo led me to the side of the oval. A boy lay on the ground, curled up in the foetal position. It was only when I saw the number 10 jersey that I realised I was looking at my brother.

"Is he hurt?" I demanded, running to Emir's side.

"Not physically," Babo said.

"Emir, Emir," I kneeled beside him, shaking him. He didn't respond. I heard a keening sound and realised it was coming from my brother.

Ramo knelt and grabbed Emir's arm, yanking him up to stand. Babo quickly wedged himself under Emir's other arm, and the two of them walked briskly off the field while I followed. Emir's legs barely touched the ground. His head lolled as if he was unconscious, but his eyes were wide open.

When we arrived home, my grandmother was holding the baby and sitting beside Paša. Paša was holding Imran in her lap, smudges of dirt and blood covering her face, her eyes blank. My grandfather came back into the living room carrying a bucket and a cloth as my father and Ramo carried Emir and placed him gently to sit on the armchair.

"Where is Minka? Paša won't tell me where Minka is," my uncle said, his face distraught. He looked from me to Ramo to Babo.

I turned my head away.

"I'm sorry," Ramo stepped forward, placed his hand on Ibrahim's shoulder. "A shell hit Minka."

"No, no." Ibrahim's legs collapsed, and he dropped to his knees. His arms folded across his chest as if he were hugging Minka as his screams cut through the air.

Babo stepped forward, hugged my uncle.

"Adna," my grandmother whispered, her face white.

"Mama took her to the hospital," I said.

My grandmother nodded, tears streaming down her face. My grandfather put his arm around her and stared at the ground.

Memories of Minka, the playground, and the body parts flooded my mind. My stomach lurched, and I ran to the bathroom, bent over the toilet as I vomited bile. Even though my stomach was empty, the painful cramping wouldn't stop. Finally, I stood shakily and wiped my mouth. I saw my reflection in the mirror over the vanity. Bits of gravel and dust coated my hair. Smudges of dirt and blood on my shirt. I looked closer.

Drops of flesh dotted my shirt like asymmetrical polka dots. I ripped off my clothes, stepped in the bath and ladled cold water from the bucket of water beside the tub, scrubbing my skin raw. Afterwards, I wrapped myself in a towel. There was a knock on the door. When I opened the door, Ramo handed me a change of clothes.

I dressed and took my dirty clothes outside, throwing them in the rubbish bin, and returned to the living room. Ibrahim and Paša were still on the couch, sitting side by side and yet completely oblivious to each other.

"Let's go, Paša. You need a wash." Nana attempted to take Imran from her arms, but Paša clutched him tighter. "All right, let's all go together," Nana said, helping Paša to stand and walk to the bathroom.

Babo washed himself and changed, and now he was wiping Emir's face and arms with a bucket and cloth.

I closed my eyes and leaned my head back on the couch. The screaming woke me. My heart sped up, and I panted with fear. It was morning. I'd slept the night through.

Standing in the hallway was my Aunt Paša. "She was by herself all night at the playground," she screamed.

"She would have been collected," Mama soothed. Mama was wearing jeans and a top, her hair wet. She must have just come home from the hospital.

"No, she's not. She's by herself." Paša fell to her knees. "Please, I have to get her."

"We'll go to the hospital. We'll find her and take her to the Mosque," Mama said, kneeling next to Paša and rubbing her back.

"She wasn't transported to the hospital," I said, recalling how the aid workers bypassed her torso to assist those who were alive.

"*Bože Sačuvaj*," Nana gasped, covering her mouth, uttering God Forbid.

Mama jerked upright and looked at me. "Do you know where Minka is?" she demanded.

I nodded.

"You'll have to show me." Mama helped my aunt stand. "See Paša, Seka and I will go get Minka." Nana led Paša up the stairs to what was once my bedroom, and where Ramo and Ibrahim were. Since the weather warmed up, we'd returned to our rooms upstairs.

"You can't take Seka back to see that horror," Babo hissed.

"Which horror is better? Torturing a grieving mother by not burying her child or our daughter, seeing what she's already seen once?" Mama asked.

"I want to go." I stood. "I can't leave Minka. I can't..." I stopped, my voice cutting out. I straightened my back and wiped my face. I could cry later.

"Where did Ramo go?" I asked Mama as we rushed up the street.

"He came to the hospital this morning so I could come home and have a change in shift."

"Things are even worse now. Stretchers are lining the halls with all the injured. He's guarding Adna."

Mama continued racing.

We reached the playground, and I saw five to six dogs. Mama picked up a rock and threw it at the one closest to us, the German Shepherd I'd seen the day before. The dog turned to us, picked up an arm with its mouth, and ran towards the forest. I gagged and bent over.

Mama rubbed my back as I got myself under control. "Can you show me where Minka is?"

I nodded. We walked towards the playground. The bits of flesh and brain stuck to the metal fence looked even darker a day later. A smell rose from the playground. The uncovered flesh was rotting in the sun. I saw a flash of red and pointed. Mama approached and knelt. She opened the bag she'd been carrying and laid down a white sheet she'd brought. Mama gently lifted the torso, and as I blinked, I saw she was holding Minka, her dark hair lying against Mama's shoulder, her tiny feet dangling. then I blinked, and the image was gone.

"The dogs haven't reached her, thankfully."

I cried as Mama gently wrapped Minka and placed the package back in the bag.

"You can go home now, Seka," Mama said as she stood. "I'm going to take Minka to the Mosque for burial." Mama looked around at the playground and further afield at the soccer field. The dogs were wary of us and were edging from the woods onto the soccer field away from us.

"We must collect and bury these body parts."

Mama helped me up, and we walked out of the playground. "I'll come with you to the Mosque." I wanted to go to the hospital and find Ramo.

At the Mosque, Mama handed over Minka to the Imam. Muslim burials took place within 24 hours, however, in war conditions, they now took place under the cover of darkness to ensure that the gravediggers and attendees would be safe from snipers. Mama said that the family would attend Minka's burial at dawn.

When we reached the Council offices, Mama received a form to ask for a work detail to collect and bury the bodies. Lebiba came out to speak to her and nodded sympathetically, promising that the burial would happen the same day.

A man ran in, shouting, "Bread on the convoy! Bread has arrived on the convoy!"

"Let's go." Mama tucked the form in her handbag and took my hand. We followed the crowd and ran to the department store, where a heaving mass of humanity surrounded the trucks, shifting and pulsing.

We hadn't eaten proper bread in months, and as I watched people running with loaves in their hands, my mouth watered, and an urgency filled me. I pushed through people, trying to get to the front. The ripe smell of unwashed bodies bit my nose. I pursed my lips and kept shoving. When I got closer, I breathed in deeply, the smell of bread filling me with strength. I felt transformed from a girl to a beast. A UN worker tossed a loaf into my hands. Safely stowed in my coat, I presented them again. I got another loaf. Securing it under my arm, I swiftly took a third loaf from a woman on my right. I quickly hunched over and hobbled back through the crowd, using my hands to crawl. I recognised Mama's shoes and tugged on her skirt.

"I got one loaf," Mama said, holding it in her arms.

"Good, good." I adjusted the bread under my coat and held my stomach as if there was a baby in it. Mama's eyes sharpened, but I sped up. We needed to get far away from the rabid crowd before I disclosed my secret.

I wanted to tell her how many I got, but too many desperate people would knife me to eat. Even though my treasure was three loaves of bread that would barely satisfy the hunger of eleven people who hadn't eaten properly in a year. No ten people, I corrected as I remembered Minka was gone.

"Mama, open the door," I urged when we reached the house. In the kitchen. I unbuttoned my coat and handed Mama the first loaf.

"We'll be able to eat a proper meal." Mama clapped with happiness.

I reached into my coat and pulled out the two loaves and placed them on the table. Mama looked at the four loaves, her face dropping. "We've taken too many. People will go hungry."

"We are going hungry, and we didn't take too many," I shouted. I'd expected her to be as happy as I was. "This is two days' worth of food."

"What's the ruckus?" Babo asked as he entered the kitchen. His eyes caught on the loaves of bread and his eyebrows lifted.

Mama was playing with the button on her coat, rubbing it as she pondered our ethics. "I think we should take one loaf to the refugees next door."

"You can take your loaf." I snatched a loaf off the table. "This one is mine, and I'm not sharing it with anyone."

"Seka, we're not animals." Mama reached for the bread.

I bared my teeth at her, my fist raised and aimed for her face, anger and hunger ripping me apart. I wanted to hurt her for her stupidity. She would see us all starve over her idiotic principles.

Mama stepped back in fear.

"Seka, calm down." Babo took my fist in his hand and slowly brought it down. He turned to Mama. "This bread is for our family only, Esma. We have to take care of our own before we can take care of anyone else."

Mama nodded. Babo took my bread and returned it to the table.

Paša and Ibrahim were standing in the hallway, and behind them, Nana and Dido.

"A convoy arrived?" Paša asked.

"Yes, we got bread." I pointed at the table.

Paša looked at the bread and away. "Good. We'll take one loaf and be on our way."

Mama and Babo looked at each other in surprise. "On your way?" Babo asked.

"Yes, I'm leaving this hellhole while I still have children to live for." Paša stepped forward and took a loaf of bread. She ripped off a hunk with her hands and handed it to Imran, and ripped off another small piece that she placed in the baby's mouth.

"We can't just decide to leave," Ibrahim said, picking up his son and holding him tight.

"I'm leaving with my children. If we'd left on the last convoy the way I wanted, my child would still be alive." As Paša spoke, Ibrahim stepped back as if she'd punched him.

"She was my child too," Ibrahim cried deep, heaving sobs, hugging his son to him.

Paša watched him as if he was an insect in a jar. She left the kitchen.

"She's mad with grief." Mama hugged her brother.

"Is she? So many children suffocated on the last convoy that I thought it was safer to stay here, at least where we had family and hope that things would get better, but now..."

Paša returned from upstairs with a parcel. She'd used a sheet to collect their few pieces of clothing, tying the corners to create a makeshift bag to carry with her. She picked up the baby who was sitting on the floor, and took Imran from his father, holding his hand as she walked to the front door. My uncle didn't fight her. He crumpled into a heap and sat on the stairs, crying as he watched her leave.

I ran to the kitchen and told my parents my aunt had left.

Mama followed her and reached my aunt on the footpath. "Minka's funeral is tomorrow morning."

Paša's steps slowed. "It doesn't matter. She's gone. These are the ones left." She lifted the baby higher against her and clenched Imran's hand. "You should leave too. Get out and save what family you can." She nodded at me.

My mother stepped back. "I could never break up my family."

Paša shook her head. "You'll lose them all, anyway." She turned and walked down the street.

My mother hesitated before hurrying to catch up to my aunt. Mama took the bundle of clothes from my aunt and walked with her down the street.

"Go tell your grandparents they have to go to the department store to say goodbye to their grandchildren," my father said as he grabbed his coat and followed.

I found my grandparents in the room upstairs. Nana was pale. She'd taken to bed since Minka died, and Dido stayed with her. I quickly told them what had happened.

Nana nodded and slowly got out of bed. She went to the wardrobe and ruffled through the socks until she took one out. "I'm going to give them what we have," she told Dido.

He nodded, and they trudged down the stairs, Dido holding her arm as he helped her down step by step.

Emir appeared in the hallway. His eyes were red, and his face pale. He hadn't moved from the armchair all night, even when my father urged him to bed.

"Do you want to come and say goodbye to Paša and Ibrahim? They're leaving on the convoy."

Emir was shaking his head before I finished. He hadn't left the house since the shelling. His ears rang, and he flinched constantly as he heard the phantom whistle of a shell. "Tell them I wish them luck."

The huge aid trucks attracted crowds in front of the department store, with trays filled with women and children. Paša pushed through to the front, the baby in her arms. Mama was next to her carrying Imran, while my father walked in front, carving a path for them.

The trailer of the truck was getting crammed with women sitting on each other, and that's how they would travel for the two hundred kilometre trip. While they travelled through Serb territory, individuals jeered at the refugees and pelted rocks at them. At each checkpoint, the Serbs made all the refugees disembark to screen them, ensuring that no so-called 'war criminals' passed.

Ibrahim could not leave. If Ibrahim attempted to leave, the Serb checkpoints would detain him, and once the convoy was out of sight and the foreign witness of the Swedish driver was removed, they would shoot him at point-blank range.

We reached the edge of the crowd. "Call them," my grand-mother urged.

"Paša!" I shouted my aunt's name until my throat hurt, but my scream disappeared into the din created by the desperate refugees milling around.

My grandparents were struggling in the melee. Nana was weak and wilting. Dido was propping her up. "Here, take this. Give them a kiss for us." Nana handed me the wad of cash.

"Hide the money and run. We'll wait over here and wave at them." Dido pointed at the hill to the left of us.

I nodded and put the money in my dress so that it rested against my stomach. My size worked in my favour, and I could weave through the crowd and reach my aunt. I put my hand on Mama when I was close.

"Fadil, stop," Mama shouted, and my father stopped and waited.

"This is from Nana and Dido," I panted, handing my auntie the bundle of notes. She took the money and tucked it into her bra. I pointed at the hill where my grandparents stood. Nana was holding a handkerchief to her face and Dido was standing stoically by her side.

Paša told Imran to wave at his grandparents. He waved his tiny hand as he looked at them. My grandparents waved back. Paša lifted her hand and waved quickly, her face expression-less.

"Go back to your grandparents," Mama said. "It's too dan-gerous here."

This time, it was hard pushing against the crowd in the wrong direction, but most people let me pass, I was one less person to compete with. I reached the hill with my grandparents. Nana was bent over, while Dido comforted her.

My aunt was on the truck with my cousins. My parents and uncle walked through the crowd to join us on the hill. As the trays filled, a palpable sense of tension swirled through the seething crowd. This was not an organised evacuation. It was a free-for-all as desperate people clambered one over the other, knowing that this could be their last chance to escape Srebrenica and save their children.

As more and more women and children climbed onto the tray, I clenched my fists in agony. They crowded together with no space to sit, no space to breathe. Finally, the UN soldiers intervened and surrounded the truck, preventing any more from getting on. Those who were still on the ground desperately reached their arms towards the truck, trying to wriggle past the soldiers. The truck turned on, its large engine rumbled, and drove down the main road out of town. I kept watch until it was out of sight behind a curve in the road.

9-Resolution

13 April 1993

The day after my aunt Paša left on the convoy, Ramo and I went to the hospital to bring Mama food while she cared for my Aunt Adna. All the beds were filled, so patients had to lie on the floor. The doctor told Mama that they were organising an evacuation of the high-priority patients.

"Did you hear that?" Mama told her sister. She kissed her hand. "They will evacuate you tomorrow," Mama told her sister.

Aunt Adna nodded weakly. The nurses insisted that we leave, assuring us that now that Adna had a hospital bed, they would take care of her and keep her safe.

The next day, we returned to the hospital to find another woman in my aunt's hospital bed. "Where's my sister?" Mama asked.

The nurse looked at the chart on the bed, which listed my aunt's name. "She's supposed to be in this bed."

We spread out in the hospital, calling for Adna. We found her two rooms over on the floor. "What are you doing here?" She told us that during the night, the stronger patients pushed the sicker patients out of their beds to be evacuated.

"*Bože Sačuvaj*," the nurse said. God Forbid.

She called over a UN soldier whose name tag read Johnson, who was African American, and told him what happened. Johnson's hair was a flat top afro, his dark brown skin like the mellow-brown shine of a walnut. He looked shocked for a moment, but quickly rallied.

When we helped Adna back into her bed, her stitches were jostled, and she started bleeding again. The nurse re-bandaged her while my aunt's face took on a sheen of sweat from the pain.

Officer Johnson entered my aunt's room. He used a pen and cushioned my aunt's hand in his dark brown one and marked the back of it in purple. "Indelible ink. You can't wash off or forge it," he said. "We will evacuate your aunt now."

"I'm not taking any chances," Mama said. "I'm not leaving her side."

Around noon, the soldiers began carrying the wounded on stretchers to the soccer field, which was a helicopter landing zone. They placed Adna on the flatbed truck with other patients. We followed on foot to the soccer pitch and joined other family members gathered along the graffiti-covered walls surrounding the soccer field. A military cordon of trucks and APCs prevented anyone from getting too close. Three white helicopters marked the UN were on the field with their rotors churning as UN and Bosnian soldiers loaded the bandaged patients onto the helicopters. In the middle of the soccer pitch, three soldiers waved their hands. It looked like they were air controllers who were telling the helicopters when to leave.

"Where is she?" I asked.

"There." Mama pointed at the red scarf fluttering in the breeze. She'd tied it around my aunt before she left the hospital. I found it strange at the time, but now understood she ensured that Adna was visible.

The soldiers placed about thirty of the wounded into the helicopters and pulled the doors shut. The helicopters slowly lifted off the ground, the sun glinting off the metal as it hovered in the sky.

"Adna will be next." Mama squeezed my hand.

An explosion rocked the soccer pitch, sending smoke and earth flying up. The soldiers on the soccer pitch crouched down. Some of them were talking into their radios.

I blinked, spat out dirt from my mouth. Some women around us were screaming, others were running for the exit.

"What's happening?" I cried.

"The Serbs are shelling," Ramo said.

Another explosion hit. The air blackened with smoke and debris.

"We have to go." Ramo tugged on my arm.

"Adna? Where is Adna?" Mama peered at the soccer pitch. The smoke was obscuring our view. Finally, we saw her stretcher next to an enormous crater, with fresh brown earth beside her, and bodies strewn like dolls.

"No, Adna," Mama screamed. She ran, and we followed. We reached Adna's stretcher. I thought she was dead, but Mama leaned in close.

"She's breathing. She's breathing," she said.

The UN soldiers attempted to move towards the landing zone with patients, but the Serbs responded with artillery fire, the bullets ripping through the grass and dirt.

Mama covered Adna on the stretcher. We waited another hour as the UN soldiers talked into their radios. Soldiers returned the injured to the flatbed trucks.

"What's happening?" Mama asked.

"They're calling off the evacuation."

"No, no. She's going to die."

The soldier wouldn't meet my mother's eyes.

We ran back to the hospital. When we arrived, a UN helicopter swooped down and hovered overhead. Its rotors whipped the air, and the gale pushed against me, making it hard to stand. Debris hit my face. I covered my eyes with my hand and squinted through my fingers. The helicopter winched up two injured Canadian soldiers and three air controllers, then it glided away and disappeared into the sky.

"Are more helicopters coming?" Mama shouted to the empty sky.

I heard soldiers talking to each other in English.

I translated. "The evacuation is called off until a ceasefire is called."

We ran into the hospital, searching for my aunt. She wasn't in any of the beds. We found her stretcher in the morgue. She'd died on the way back from the soccer field.

That night, I stood next to my grandmother and held her hand in mine. My eyes were red and sore as I stood by the open grave. My grandmother stood beside the grave, hunched over as if the weight of losing her daughter burdened her. My grandfather held her arm, his spine rigid and straight, not making a sound.

My father, brother and Ramo were pallbearers, helping to carry my Aunt Adna on planks, her small body wrapped in muslin, and then carefully placed her into the grave. As the Imam recited the prayers, Emir kept looking at the surrounding hills, his head twitching from side to side like a bird on an electricity wire, waiting for a jolt. My father put his arm around Emir's shoulders, and Emir startled for a moment before taking a deep shuddering breath and settling slightly.

My mother stood on the other side of me, a handkerchief held to her mouth, her body heaving as she sobbed. Edina stood on the edge of the grave, watching Ramo use the shovel to throw in the dirt. I wondered if she was thinking about her husband and three sons who were murdered in a field, their bodies left to rot, lost and unburied. Was she thinking that at least we had the mercy of a body and a burial in order to mourn properly?

The Imam finished his prayers, and my father, Emir and Ramo took turns shovelling dirt to cover my aunt's body. My Uncle Ibrahim stood opposite me, holding his beret in his hand. He stood apart from everyone, leaving a gaping space between him and my mother. It seemed as if he had become accustomed to leaving space for his wife and three children, as if the habit had become ingrained, even though they were all gone. I hoped my aunt reached safety in Tuzla and my cousins survived the convoy.

After moving the last heap of dirt, we covered the grave. We shuffled out of the cemetery. I followed from the back, watching my diminishing family with sorrow.

Ibrahim stopped in front of Minka's grave. He said a prayer for his daughter, while the rest of us slowly shuffled past him.

That night in my dream, I saw my aunt Paša on the convoy, holding Imran by her feet, the baby tightly gripped in her arms.

I floated above the convoy, and I saw her stressed face staring out at the passing landscape, a speck of red at her side. As I descended, I witnessed Minka tightly embracing my aunt's lifeless body while the truck rattled along the rural roads. I woke up, feeling momentary relief. Minka was with my aunt. She was safe. Then I remembered the massacre, her torso on the ground, her tiny hand in the fence. I closed my eyes, rubbed my fists into my eyeballs, and pushed the images away. As I lay back on my mattress, I was on the truck again with my aunt, my cousins holding onto their mother tight, Minka's dark brown eyes serious as she sucked on her thumb and closed her eyes, the motion of the truck sending her to sleep.

I woke up and trudged downstairs, achy from a sleepless night. The radio was on, and my grandfather and Ramo were in the living room, hunched around it as they listened to the news. My brother and father returned to the front for their service, as it was their duty to report every third night. I heard them getting ready earlier, my father urging Emir, who was reluctant and attempting to claim he was sick. I remembered the days when he'd been bounding to go to the front, hoping it would be the day he'd get to hold a gun as soldiers took turns. Being a soldier filled him with pride, and all he'd talked about was killing the Serbs and chasing them away. Now it seemed he realised that no matter how many Serbs were killed, there were always more to take their place.

Even though grief had dulled my appetite, I recognised the importance of eating and proceeded to cut myself a slice of bread with marmalade on it. The bread from yesterday was slightly stale and would not last.

"Where is Mama?" I asked as I sat next to my grandfather.

"She went to the Council to get a work detail to collect the bodies from the playground," he said.

The bread stuck in my throat as I saw Minka's torso again. I blinked rapidly, replacing the image with Minka on the convoy truck. I saw my father hand her up to my Aunt Paša.

"Ibrahim went to the ham radio station to call Tuzla," Ramo said, pre-empting my question. I hoped Ibrahim would return with good news that my aunt and cousins were safe in the Bosnian government-held territory of Tuzla. From Tuzla, they would go to Germany to live with Paša's sisters. In Germany, they wouldn't go hungry anymore.

The radio announcer spoke about the playground massacre. Dido hushed us. I waited with bated breath.

"We have confirmation from the United Nations that the playground massacre that took place yesterday morning was retaliation by the Serbs for an action undertaken by the Bosnian Muslims. A UN official has confirmed that one of Naser Orić two tanks fired its cannon at the Serbs and that the Serbs shot into the schoolyard only in retaliation."

"*Jebem im mater*," fuck their mother, my grandfather swore at the radio without heat, his face defeated.

The bread dried in my throat, and I swallowed it hard. "How could they think we fired tanks and purposely started a fight? We just wanted to have one nice day." I was crying by the time I finished, the unfairness burning through me.

"They have to lie to cover their own arses," Ramo said. "They can't admit that the safe zone is a joke."

He put his hand on my arm, gently caressing it. My grandfather saw, but said nothing.

After I finished eating, I took my plate into the kitchen to wash. Ramo followed a few moments later. He hugged me hard. I breathed in his scent and relaxed for the first time in days, crying silently against his chest. He looked down and gently kissed my cheek, making his way to my lips, brushing them against mine, before lifting his head and hugging me again.

My Aunt Adna had been only twenty-three years old. She'd always dreamed of having a husband and family. When I was small, she'd told me that Seka was her favourite name, and she would give it to her oldest daughter. *You'll be Big Seka, and my daughter will be the Little Seka.* And now all her dreams were gone. She would never get married. Never have children. I shivered in Ramo's arms, and he held me tighter.

I stepped on tiptoes and kissed Ramo tightly, a hunger overtaking me. A hunger to feel his flesh on mine, to touch his skin. I put my hands under his top. He shivered as my palms smoothed his torso, revelling in the feel of his soft skin and hairy chest.

"Ramo," Edina gasped.

I opened my eyes and saw Ramo's mother standing in the hallway, anger and fear on her face.

I looked down at myself and flushed with embarrassment at my dishevelled clothing. Ramo hid me from sight as I put myself back in order. My legs felt weak and trembly, and my body hungered for more.

"Come here," Edina lifted her finger and gestured to Ramo, leading him away.

I ran upstairs, hesitating on the top step to eavesdrop.

"Stop this. If they suspect you are ruining Seka's reputation, they'll ask us to leave," Edina said, her voice low with tension.

"But Mama, we love each other," Ramo said.

"Then you need to do the right thing. You need to be friends only. Do you understand?" Edina demanded.

Ramo nodded.

I tiptoed off the stairs and stood in the corridor, staring out the window above the stairs. It was a sunny day, the kind of day that made you want to walk around outside and enjoy the sun and fresh air. But I couldn't. I couldn't do anything but be in this house. The only thing that made this nightmare bearable was being with Ramo, and now I had to be careful about that too.

I went to my former bedroom where my grandparents slept. Nana was lying in bed. I pushed the door open and was about to leave, not wanting to disturb her. I peered deeper into the gloom and saw her eyes were open.

"Nana," I said.

Nana lifted her hand and gestured for me to come in. I lay down on the bed, my head on the pillow next to hers as she put her arm around me.

"Adna was a child of nature. She loved nothing more than to be with animals," she said, gently caressing my hair. "She named all our cows, and she was the one who delivered our calves safely, after an incompetent veterinarian killed a calf." I felt my grandmother's tears on my neck. "She would have been a wonderful veterinarian, but girls like her couldn't go away from home to study." Nana stopped speaking as she sobbed. "She was so proud that you wanted to be a veterinarian and that you shared that dream."

I sobbed with my grandmother, taking comfort from her embrace. Crying made me tired, and I blinked sleepily, drifting into unconsciousness.

I dreamed that I was walking on a mountain, and a thunderstorm clapped, the loud sound thrumming through me.

"Seka, Seka, wake up."

I opened my eyes to find Mama above me, shaking me awake.

"We have to go down to the basement." She urged me to stand up and helped my grandmother.

I tried to stand, but it was like my arms and legs had forgotten how. My muscles ached and my head was fuzzy. *Boom.* A grenade exploded, making the house shake.

"What's happening?" I asked.

"Mladić's artillery has opened fire again. This is his last offensive to try to claim Srebrenica before they sign off on the peace plan," my mother said. "We need to take cover."

Ratko Mladić was the Commander in charge of the Serb troops.

Mama ushered us to the basement. I huddled in the corner with my mother on one side and my grandmother on the other. Ramo and Edina were in the other corner. It sounded like the world was ending above us. The shelling was unrelenting, and the bang of artillery fire was getting closer and closer.

My grandfather brought down the radio, and we hunched around it, listening to the news. The UN was debating a resolution to declare Srebrenica a Safe Zone.

"Once the United Nations passes the resolution declaring Srebrenica a Safe Zone, the Serbs will not attack." The UN

Army will bomb them into the ground," my grandfather said. "We'll be safe."

I remembered seeing the images on television of the UN Council in their raised chairs, serious-faced diplomats staring into space before them, wearing headphones, as translators frantically paraphrased what other diplomats were arguing into their headpieces. These men and women in the safety of their chambers had all the time in the world.

"Why are the Serbs doing this now?" Morillon's promise was supposed to protect us.

"Once the resolution is introduced, these incursions would become illegal. This is their last chance to take Srebrenica with all its bounty and add it to their territory," my grandfather explained. "The city is too valuable with its minerals and manufacturing, while we are expendable."

"Turn it off," Mama shouted, her face flushed.

My grandfather turned off the radio. Now the bombs seemed even louder in the quiet.

I closed my eyes, attempting to block out the sound, the thrumming through the concrete below me. I tried to imagine a good day, but nothing could help me escape my reality. Hours passed. My mouth became dry and the more I tried not to think about the thirst, the dryer my mouth got.

My grandmother wilted against me. She was perspiring and pale. Mama attempted to shake her awake, but she was unconscious. Mama gently lay her down, using a blanket as a pillow for my grandmother's head.

"I need to get us water and something for her to eat," I told Mama.

"No, I'll go. You stay here." Mama went to stand, but I beat her, running for the stairs.

"Seka," Ramo and Mama shouted behind me, but I didn't turn around. I'd reached the corridor when I felt arms grab me.

"It's okay. I'll come with you," Ramo said.

I nodded. We held hands as we walked to the kitchen. I searched through the cupboard and found all the empty bottles we'd collected. We filled the bottles.

"I need to know what's happening," I said, looking up at the stairs.

He hesitated and then nodded.

We climbed the stairs to the second floor and entered my parent's bedroom to the balcony. We crawled on the cold, rough concrete to the window. My top lifted. I winced as I scraped my stomach.

We peered over the edge of the balcony fence and saw soldiers running between buildings from the forest, bullets whizzing between them. The front line was on our doorstep, the soldiers fighting with frantic desperation. We had nowhere to run.

The fog burned off, and the sky was clear. Ramo and I looked at the sky and at each other. We knew what the clear sky heralded. As if we had conjured it up, a shadow appeared. I looked up, my mouth dropping as I saw a jet plane flying over the town at high speed, so quickly my eyes barely followed its path, white fog enveloping it so that it was like a flying cloud. The jet plane was getting ready to rain down deadly bombs and sharp pieces of shrapnel that would slice flesh like paper.

As it passed, a boom filled the sky. The jet broke the sound barrier and vanished again.

Ramo grabbed my arm, and we ran to the basement. I heard the whistle of the bomb dropping. We'd reached the basement stairs. Our mothers stood and reached the bottom of the stairs, sweeping us up into their arms. I saw Ramo's face over his mother's shoulder and knew I had the same expression, a feeling of relief that we could be children again and let our mothers take care of us. We told them what we saw. That the fighting was on the street in front of our house.

"They have entered the town. We should surrender," I said.

"Even if we surrender, Mladić will show no mercy. He'll do what he did in Vukovar."

I remembered the images on television after the surrender of the Croatian town of Vukovar. The city reduced to piles of rubble. The journalist reported the Serbs separated the menfolk, took them away in buses and executed them in the cornfields, while they dumped the women and children near battle fronts and forced them to walk across no-man's land.

Mama held the bottle to my grandmother's mouth. She barely moved as the water touched her lips. Mama wet the bread and made it soft and placed it in my grandmother's mouth. She slowly chewed and swallowed. A few minutes later, my grandmother opened her eyes.

"How are you feeling?" Mama asked.

"Better," my grandmother said.

My grandfather turned the radio on. The reporter announced that Srebrenica's hospital reported five deaths per day due to lack of treatment. As night fell, we heard the gnarl of chainsaws.

"What are they doing?" I asked.

"Probably clearing firing positions for machine guns and tanks on the hilltops around the town."

I imagined the Serbs on the hilltops, cutting down swathes of trees so they could better shell us. My grandmother's face was sallow, a sheen of sweat coating her. My mother hugged me to her. She was bereft of hope. My grandfather turned off the radio, and we waited.

I took out my notebook.

"Dear Zora, this might be the last time I write to you. The enemy is coming. I love you. Being your friend has meant everything to me, and I'm so grateful you chose me. I hope we'll see each other again someday—if not in this world, then in the next."

I saw my Aunt Adna standing on the stairs, her smile wide and happy. She was here to welcome us into heaven with her. My aunt walked towards me, her hand reaching for mine, when my grandfather spoke.

"Do you hear that?" he demanded.

I blinked, and my aunt was gone. An eerie silence enveloped us. What was happening?

My grandfather turned on the radio. "The UN has signed the resolution declaring Srebrenica a Safe Zone."

"We are saved," exclaimed my grandfather as he hugged my grandmother.

Nana smiled weakly.

Ramo and I jumped up and danced with joy. The Serbs wouldn't kill us today. We made our way slowly upstairs. The house was a mess. Crockery and glass had shattered as the shelling disturbed gravity. Shards of glass were everywhere.

Ramo and I went outside. Holes from mortar shells pock-marked the asphalt. Concrete and debris covered every surface. We stepped away from the front of our house and I looked at it. The mortar shells damaged the tiles on our roof. A giant hole gaped on the wall beside my parent's bedroom window. People were coming out of their houses, looking bewildered and dirty from hiding in basements for days. We'd survived the end of the world.

UNSAFE HAVEN

10-Termination

November 1993

The next day, Ramo was at the back of the house, chopping wood to prepare for winter. I followed him and sat on the back stairs, watching as he swung the axe high above the ground. Soon he was perspiring, and he took off his shirt. My mouth went dry.

"Seka, can you bring me some water?" He wiped his forehead with his arm.

"Of course." I went to the kitchen, my legs weak as I walked and poured water from the jug. I returned and handed him the glass, my hand trembling slightly.

"Are you okay?" His eyes narrowed in concern, and he took my hand in his.

"Mmm," I nodded. I swayed towards him. His eyes widened, and he put the glass on the chopping block, took my hand and led me down the side of the house. He kissed me, pushing my back against the wall.

The desire within my thighs was like a gnawing hunger. I dug my fingernails into his bare back, feeling the smooth skin and rigid muscle underneath, my hips writhing against his hardness. I wanted... I wanted... everything.

"Seka," someone shouted my name.

Ramo lifted his head, and it took a moment for the desire to clear from my head. Mama was staring at us from the back door, her face horrified. "In here," she shouted.

Ramo stepped away, and I walked towards her. When I was close enough, she yanked my arm hard and tugged me upstairs. When we were in her bedroom, she closed the door.

"How long has this been going on?" she asked, pacing up and down the room.

"Not long."

"How long?" Mama stepped towards me and grabbed my arm, gripping tightly as her nails dug into my skin.

"Just a few months."

"Have you had sex?" Mama demanded.

"No, no, we haven't had sex. We've just kissed."

"That did not look like just kissing."

Ashamed, my eyes watering, I looked down at the ground. "We're not doing anything wrong. Ramo wants us to get married. We love each other."

"Married!" Mama gasped, covering her mouth. "You're only sixteen. He's eighteen. How in the world do you think you can get married?"

"People get married young. Belma did it."

"Do you want her life? She's seventeen years old and mother to a one-year-old and is pregnant again," Mama demanded. "She'll be an old woman by the time she is 20."

I said nothing. I did not want Belma's life, and we both knew it.

"This can't go on. I have to do something about it."

"Please don't tell Babo. Please, please, don't tell Babo," I begged. "He'll send him away. He and Edina will be homeless."

Mama said nothing. If Babo suspected Ramo was a genuine threat to my virtue, he would show him out of the house, regardless of the war.

"How can I make sure that this doesn't happen again? That the two of you don't lose your senses and start rutting like animals?"

"We weren't rutting. We love each other. It's natural. You and Babo do it even during the war."

Mama blushed and looked away. "Your father and I are different. We are an old married couple." She went to the window and looked outside, crossing her arms.

"Please, promise you won't tell."

Mama sighed, her shoulders slumping like the fight had gone out of her. "There are consequences to what you're doing, Seka. If you get pregnant, you will ruin your future. You'd have to marry Ramo, and even though you think that's what you want now, you'll never have the opportunity to find a different path. This war will not last forever, Seka." Mama put her arm around my shoulders, and we looked out together.

I looked out over the ruined rooftops we could see. The pockmarked mortar. The plastic sheets fluttering in the breeze from blown out windows.

"One day, our city will be back to normal. Our lives will be what they once were. Hold on to hope and don't give up," Mama said.

She was talking about fairy tales.

Before the war, I dreamed I would go to university, have a career. That girl was someone else, her future dashed and broken by artillery and shells.

"Promise me you won't be with Ramo like that again," she said, gesturing towards my genitals. "Make sure you don't get pregnant."

"I promise I won't." I forced myself to hold my mother's gaze. Memories of the overwhelming heat and desire flooded my mind. I had to control myself.

"You had better keep your promise," Mama said. "If you end up pregnant, your father might take things into his own hands, and you might be a widow longer than you're a bride."

A chill went down my back. Mama was exaggerating. Babo wouldn't kill Ramo. Then I remembered my father's fearsome rage when a drunken guest at a wedding had groped Mama. Babo had beaten him to within an inch of his life. It had taken four men to pull him off and a whole day of chopping wood to calm down the rage. I had to protect Ramo.

"I'll keep my promise," I told Mama, gripping her hand tight.

Mama kept an eagle eye on us and I couldn't talk to Ramo for a few days. Only when Mama went to the market, and Edina was making a phone call on the ham radio were we able to sneak down to the basement.

"What happened with your mother?" He reached for me.

I pulled away. "She said we can't do this anymore."

"You mean we can't get caught doing this anymore?" He put his hands on my waist and bent, nuzzling my neck.

I had to fight my urge to put my arms around him, let myself sink into his embrace. "No, no." I pushed his hands down.

Ramo stepped back. "You don't want to be with me anymore?" His face showed pain.

"I do, but if we get caught, my father will kick you and your mother out, or worse."

"I don't care. I want to be with you."

"What about your mother? Would you be okay with her living on the street or in lice infested public building like the school, just because we were so selfish we couldn't control ourselves?"

Ramo turned away. He lifted his hand to his face and wiped his face.

"I'm sorry. I love you, but I don't want to lose you," I said, gently placing my hand on his shoulder.

"What about marriage?" Ramo turned back. "If we were married...."

He stopped as I shook my head again. "No, Mama was very clear about that. Marrying now is out of the question, and if I got pregnant and we had to get married, well, Babo wouldn't handle that well.

"Then we won't get pregnant."

"How do we do that?" I demanded. "Every time we get more and more..." I stopped, caught by his blue eyes. His eyes dropped to my lips. "See, you're doing it right now. We can't do this anymore." I ran up the stairs, uncaring of how loud my stomping was. I hid in my room and cried. Even though I was doing this for Ramo, it felt like a little death. How was I going to be around him and not touch him?

A few weeks later, Mama took me to the bathroom. "You're not bleeding." She looked at me suspiciously.

"So?" I'd been relieved to not be bleeding and dealing with all the mess associated with it.

"It's been six weeks." Mama opened the cupboard and the cloths we used for our menses were untouched.

"You told me you didn't have sex and now you're pregnant." Mama sat on the edge of the bathtub, covering her face.

"I didn't have sex and I'm not pregnant," I told her.

"Then you should bleed," Mama said.

I started thinking. Usually, Mama and I had our menses at the same time and the cloths would be used by both of us. "Are you bleeding?"

Mama hesitated and shook her head.

"Maybe you're pregnant?" I said and laughed.

Mama looked at me with a cross face. "We'll go to the doctor and sort this out."

We dressed in our best clothes and walked down to the health spa where Kamila's father, Dr Harun Hodžić, was seeing regular patients. There were women filling the waiting room. Among them Belma, who was three months pregnant, with her mother-in-law, Dželila who was holding her baby Zikret. We greeted each other. Belma was there for a checkup for her and the baby. There were dark circles under her eyes and she looked listless, as if her spine would not hold her and she would slide out of the chair.

"I lost my period," Mama said, holding my hand tight to stop me from saying anything. She had warned me not to tell anyone that I had also lost my period because, "Rumours spread like wildfire. Your father will know before we even get home from the doctor."

Belma was called into the doctor's office. As we waited, we heard two women talking behind us. They had both also lost their period. I looked at Mama in confusion. She shrugged.

Belma came out. She had anaemia, and the doctor had given her iron tablets that he had received from aid agencies. Zikret was undernourished and small for his age. Belma looked defeated and broken.

"It will be okay," I said as I hugged her. She sighed and didn't reply.

We waited for a few hours after Belma left and were finally called in. After Mama explained her concerns, the doctor asked us to do a pregnancy test.

It was the first time I'd had to pee into a cup, and I couldn't accurately predict my flow to hold the cup under. I lifted the cup to see only a tiny amount at the bottom. I hoped it was enough.

When we returned, the doctor put on gloves and took my cup from me and placed a strip in the urine. "Not pregnant," he said after a few minutes.

I looked at my mother with a smug smile. As the doctor took Mama's cup, I saw her tense. The doctor held the strip in again. "Congratulations Esma. You're pregnant."

Mama nodded, tears forming in her eyes. "I'm told that you can provide a solution to this predicament."

"Perhaps we should ask your daughter to wait outside."

Mama shook her head. "She thinks she's old enough to get married, then she's old enough to hear this. I need an abortion."

Harun nodded without expression. "Yes, we can perform that procedure. The payment is 100 Deutschmarks."

I gasped. Where would we find that kind of money?

"However, since your family did us such a kindness by providing wood during winter, I'll do it for half the price."

"Thank you," Mama said, white-knuckled as she held her handbag handle.

"See the nurse, and she'll make an appointment."

We stood, and I followed my mother. She made an appointment two days from now in a whispered conversation.

I opened my mouth to speak when we walked out, but she covered it with her hand. "Not here." She looked around and smiled at a woman she recognised. "Walk first."

We walked down the street, and when we were away from the town centre with no one around, I demanded, "How can you have an abortion? You're killing a baby?"

"I'm not killing a baby." Mama walked briskly. "I'm taking out a foetus. It only becomes a baby at 20 weeks."

"But it could be my little brother or sister."

"This is only another mouth to feed when we are already starving. Do you think Belma is enjoying having a baby and trying to keep him from starving in these conditions?" Mama turned towards me and shouted, her face flushed. "This needs to be done." Mama turned and began walking again. "Besides,

I never wanted more than two children. When I fell pregnant last time when you were eight years old, I had an abortion."

"You did?" I gasped.

"Yes. It was necessary. I wasn't going to be like the women from my village who became trapped at home cooking and cleaning. I'd gotten a job at the factory in the office. I loved being out of the house and having a purpose, and I didn't want to lose that."

"Did Babo agree?"

Mum harrumphed. "He's a man. While he liked the idea of having another child, he wasn't the one who would take care of everything. He came around." Mama had reached the park, sat on a bench, and patted the seat beside her. "After that, I went on the pill and was careful about taking it at the same time every day."

"What is the pill?" I asked.

"A contraceptive pill that you take every day that prevents you from falling pregnant."

I remembered seeing a round packet in her dresser once when I was ten years old. Mama had told me they were special vitamins that only older women take and that if I took one, it would make me sick.

"Yes, that was my pill packet," Mama said, when I reminded her about that incident.

"If you were taking the tablets, how did you get pregnant?"

"Because the war started and there was no longer any contraception available. Your father and I tried other methods...." Mama paused. "He didn't spill his seed inside of me, but we got careless. And now here I am, six weeks later." She took my hand in hers and gripped it. "That's why you can't take the chance. There is no safe way once you have sex."

She turned away, looked down at the ground, and sighed.

"Are you going to talk to Babo about the abortion?" I asked.

"I will tell him I'm having an abortion. He won't argue. We are too old to be dealing with a baby, and these war conditions are not any place or time to try to have a baby." Mama stood decisively and took my hand as we walked home together. "I'll need your help. It's better your father finds out after the fact."

I nodded. Mama squeezed my hand. I saw her quickly brush a tear from her eye.

Two days later, Mama woke me before dawn. We tiptoed down the stairs, and Mama handed me a hunk of bread that she carefully cut from the loaf.

"Aren't you going to eat?" I asked as we sipped hot water Mama had made into tea from the rose hip tree she had picked and dried in the basement. Usually she made it only with half a teaspoon, being frugal to stretch it out longer. This time, she used a whole teaspoon, making the tea dark red and adding half a teaspoon of sugar.

"My stomach has to be empty for the procedure."

"Are they going to use anaesthetic?" I asked, remembering when Mama had tooth surgery before the war and hadn't eaten before the appointment because the anaesthetic would make her nauseous.

Mama shook her head, biting her thumbnail. "No, they're going to do it live."

I blinked, my throat becoming thick as I found it hard to swallow my food. "But, but..." I remembered the screams of patients who were operated on live without anaesthetic. The guttural screams of agony that sounded like they would tear out the vocal cords of the sufferer.

"I know." Mama quickly rubbed my arm. "The cure is still better than the disease." She looked at the clock and got her coat. "We have to go."

After the doctor called my Mama, time passed slowly in the waiting room. I had remembered to bring a book, but every time I attempted to focus on the words on the page, my mind wondered. Mama would be in so much pain. I had asked little about the procedure. Did they perform the same procedure to remove the baby as the one used to conceive it? Nausea rolled inside of me as I imagined a surgeon cutting into my Mama's private bits.

Another hour passed, and the door opened. Mama's face was pale and sweat-covered. "Let's go," Mama said, panting shallowly as she slowly walked. I went to her side, and she leaned against me.

"You're in too much pain."

"I want to go home."

We laboriously made our way home, Mama walking slowly. There was a boulder beside the road, and Mama nodded. "Let me sit." I slowly helped her down, and she moaned slightly as she sat down. We had only walked five hundred metres from the clinic and had another kilometre to go.

"I'll get Emir and Babo to help," I said.

Mama nodded, biting her lip. I ran home, adrenaline and fear moving my feet. My father was in the living room playing chess with my brother. I called both their names loudly, and they followed me to the boulder where Mama was.

As they helped lift her, there was a small stain of blood on the boulder and her dress. I took off my coat and draped it around Mama's shoulders. Babo and Emir held it in place.

When we got home, Babo carried Mama up the stairs and into their bedroom. Mama insisted I bring a towel before she would lie down, and after my brother and father left, I had to help her change her underwear and rags.

I opened Mama's dresser and found the flannel pieces we had cut up from a sheet and used during our menses. Even though we had boiled them in an iron pot and scrubbed them after use, they were still slightly stiff and stained. I took out a clean pair of underwear and walked over, carefully pulling down Mama's underwear from under the dress. I gasped as I saw the blood-soaked pad with bits of shiny red clots. While feeling weak and shivery, I focused on placing the pad in Mama's new underwear and pulled it up her legs.

Mama lifted herself up and pulled it on. "Give me my night-gown and put this dress to soak."

The next three days, Mama stayed in bed, getting weaker and pale. When I helped change her pad, the blood clots were getting thicker.

"Mama needs antibiotics," I told my father later that night in the kitchen.

He nodded. "We used the last of our money for the pro-cedure." Babo looked down at his hand and I noticed his wedding ring was gone. I flashed back to Mama attempting to use the spoon and realised her hands were bare of her wedding and engagement ring.

I was in the kitchen crying as I washed dishes when Ramo appeared in the doorway. Since Mama discovered us and I told him we had to stay away from each other, Ramo spent the day outside of the house, walking and wandering with friends. When he was home, he remained in the attic with his mother.

"I know how we can help your mother," he said, holding up his father's watch. "We can sell this and buy her antibiotics from the black market."

The watch was an old-fashioned pocket watch made from silver that was engraved on the cover. Ramo's mother had hidden it in her brassiere, and when the Serbs had searched everyone on the bus, somehow it had remained undiscovered as they pilfered money and belongings from the Muslim refugees. It was Ramo's most treasured possession, the only thing he had from his father, and he was too fearful of carrying it anywhere. Instead, he held it in his hand before bed every night, rubbing its engraved surface, remembering the faces of his father and brothers. It was all he had of them. There were no other moments, or photos, just this watch.

"You can't sell it," I cried. "That's the only thing you have from your father."

"What's the point of having a watch if you lose your mother?" Ramo said.

"She won't die," I said, my voice unconvincing. It was war. People died from regular illnesses just as easily as they died from artillery fire. With all the depravation and hunger, immunity was weak, and death was a constant visitor.

I looked away to hide my tears, then straightened my shoulders, drying my hands. "I'm going to go to the hospital and see if I can get the doctor there to help."

"I'll walk with you." Ramo got our coats from the hallway closet.

As Ramo and I ventured into the bitter cold of winter, the town lay shrouded in a blanket of snow, each step echoing with a muted crunch. The icy air bit at our faces, leaving our cheeks flushed and numb, while the distant rumble of artillery reverberated through the stillness, a constant reminder of the war raging around us. Ramo remained outside the hospital, the security guard not allowing him to come inside.

Inside, the corridors were dimly lit, the flickering fluorescent lights casting eerie shadows that danced along the walls. The cries of pain echoed through the halls, a haunting melody that underscored the desperation of our situation.

I approached the supply room and stopped in shock, a wave of despair washed over me. There was now a padlock on the door, preventing anyone from entering. I realised Labiba had taken my statement seriously and taken steps to prevent supplies from being stolen.

I looked around, searching for someone I know, and spotted Vahida briskly walking down the corridor, her hands full of bandages.

I ran up and walked with her. "I need to get some antibiotics for Dr Tonal from the supply closet," I lied. "Do you have a key?"

She shook her head briskly. "Only the administrators have access to that. They have to sign out supplies for patients. Send him to speak to one of them."

I nodded and let her walk off. I paced the corridor, trying to think how I could get into the supply room short of breaking the lock and running away. The thought hit me, and I stalked to the front door and Ramo.

After I told him about my predicament, I told him to go home while I went to see Kamila alone. He protested, but soon realised that it was the only way.

As I dashed through the icy streets to Kamila's house, the biting wind whipped against my skin, stinging my cheeks and blurring my vision with tears frozen against my lashes. Each footfall echoed in the silent streets, a frantic rhythm propelling me forward through the desolate landscape of war-torn buildings.

My fists beat at her door until Kamila opened it, looking harried and annoyed, a crease on her cheek showing she'd been napping.

"Seka, are you all right?" she asked, grabbing my shoulders and peering at me with concern.

That's when I realised my face was damp with tears. She put her arm around my shoulders and ushered me into the house and to her living room. I gasped for air, my chest heaving with exertion. Kamila left and returned with a glass of water that I drank greedily, the cool liquid washing away the salty tang of tears that lingered on my lips.

"It's my mother," I confessed, the words tumbling from my lips in a torrent of desperation, telling her about the termination and infection while Kamila rubbed my back. "We can't afford to buy antibiotics, and I wanted to see if there were some at the hospital, but someone padlocked the supply room."

"Can you help me open it?" I gripped her hands, staring into her eyes pleadingly. The gravity of my request hung heavy in the air, the silence broken only by the ragged rhythm of my breath.

"Are you asking me to use my father's keys?" she asked, her voice sombre.

"Please, please. She's going to die."

"But that's unethical, to steal supplies." She looked away, the lines of her face drawn tight.

"I know," I sobbed, gasping. "But she'll die, and I can't live with that."

"If I do this, no one can know," Kamila said. "My father would get in a lot of trouble for leaving the key at home where I could access it."

"I promise. I won't tell anyone," I gasped gratefully.

"All right. I'm going to get it."

She left the room and returned wearing her coat. After she put on her boots, we hurried to the hospital, the bitter cold biting at our exposed skin.

"Be the look out," she told me. "Make sure no one comes in while I'm there."

I nodded, remaining in the corridor as she unlocked the padlock with a flick of the wrist and slipped in quickly. She was in there for two minutes, and slipped out again, locking the padlock. We left the hospital, and she took a bottle of pills, the tablets clinking against the plastic.

"No one can know that I did this."

I nodded, not telling her I'd already told Ramo about my plan, as I took the bottle with trembling hands.

"We can never speak about this again," she whispered.

"Thank you," I murmured, my voice barely above a whisper as I struggled to contain the tumult of emotions that threatened to overwhelm me.

"That's what friends do," Kamila said softly, her words a balm to my troubled soul as she turned and walked away.

I raced back to the house and handed the pills to my stunned father. The air crackled with tension as I recounted my fabricated tale, each word tasting bitter on my tongue as I wove a web of deceit.

"How?" he asked, stupefied.

"Ramo sold his watch," I lied.

Ramo's gaze bored into mine in consternation before quickly nodding.

"Hide your watch," I whispered to Ramo. His nod of understanding was a silent reassurance.

"I'll place it in our special spot in the basement," he murmured, his voice barely above a whisper as he carefully concealed the precious timepiece among the bricks where we had hidden our cigarettes. And as he disappeared into the darkness of the basement, a sense of gratitude washed over me.

I spent the night next to my mother, my ears straining, listening to the ragged sound of her breathing. We gave her a second dose of pills before dawn, and an hour later, her trembling ceased, and she fell into a restful slumber. Babo and I exchanged a look of relief over her still body. The antibiotics were working.

I spent the next few days at my mother's side, and it was a relief that three days later I snuck out of the house in the morning, waiting for Ramo to cut wood. "Psst," I called his attention when he came out.

He put down the axe and walked over. I pulled him to me and kissed him, hard. He returned my kiss for a moment.

"We can't." He stepped away. "I never want you to go through what your mother went through. She could have died. We need to stay away from each other."

"No, no. I don't want that." I desperately tugged him towards me. I couldn't face the thought of not feeling his touch again.

"You know that we're getting too heated. We need to take a break."

He walked away, picking up the axe and heaving into the wood with a frenzy. I watched him, hoping he would change his mind and return. After five minutes, I quietly slipped back into the house, wiping the tears on my lashes. I knew why he was doing this, but it didn't make it any easier to bear.

11-Corruption

I heard the door knock, a sharp sound that cut through the quiet of my room. The murmur of my mother's voice drifted to me, mingling with the distant sounds of the outside world. With a sense of urgency, I tossed aside *Pride and Prejudice*, the familiar weight of the book leaving my hands reluctantly. It was my fifth time reading it, but every encounter with Mr. Darcy and Elizabeth felt fresh and comforting.

Eager for any chance at human contact, I hurried out of my room. As I approached the door, I caught sight of a figure, a dark-haired woman, standing in the doorway. It took me a moment to recognise her—Alyssa Jones, the reporter who had visited two years before. She wore her usual attire, which consisted of cargo pants, a brown t-shirt, and a leather satchel slung across her torso.

"Alyssa Jones," I gasped, the name slipping out like a long-forgotten memory surfacing.

"Seka, how are you?" Alyssa greeted me with a warm smile, her eyes alight with recognition.

I returned her smile, a rush of joy flooding through me. She served as a link to the outside world, reminding me that we weren't forgotten. Hope blossomed within me, fuelled by the possibility that the designation of a Safe Zone might bring salvation.

"Come in, come in," Mama urged, her voice filled with excitement as she ushered Alyssa inside.

Leading Alyssa to the living room, I watched as Mama's hands flew to her mouth in surprise when Alyssa presented her with a kilo of coffee and a bag of sugar cubes.

"For you, Mrs. Torlak," Alyssa said.

Mama's legs trembled slightly as she made her way to the kitchen, her movements unsteady with emotion.

"How have things been?" Alyssa asked, settling down on the sofa and placing her backpack beside her.

"Okay," I replied, unsure of how to encapsulate our reality in a single word.

"Are you getting enough food?" Alyssa inquired, her concern clear in her eyes.

I shook my head, a faint smile tugging at my lips. "Supermodels have to work for this figure," I joked, raising my arms in a mock display of thinness.

Alyssa chuckled at my attempt at humour, her smile genuine.

"What are you doing here?" I asked, curiosity getting the better of me.

"I'm doing a follow-up story about life in Srebrenica now that it's a Safe Zone," Alyssa explained.

"Do you want me to translate?" I interjected, eager for a chance to be of help.

Alyssa nodded gratefully. "That's why I'm here." She reached into her satchel and withdrew an envelope, handing it to me.

I glanced at the envelope, my heart skipping a beat as I recognised the familiar cursive handwriting. "Zora."

Alyssa confirmed my suspicions with a nod. "She and her family are in Melbourne, living as refugees. She knew I was coming and brought this letter to the office."

Tears welled up in my eyes. I longed to read the letter immediately, but I knew I needed to compose myself first. I retreated to my room, hiding the letter under my pillow for safekeeping, before returning to the living room to continue our conversation.

Mama returned to the living room with a tray of coffee, the rich aroma enveloping the room as she moved gracefully. Following her were my grandparents and uncle, their presence filling the space with a sense of familial warmth. My father was out working with the Swedish organisation, overseeing the reconstruction of the secondary school, while Mama took on work details assigned by the Council offices. My own responsibilities included attending what passed for school and undertaking translating jobs at the hospital, although the latter was becoming increasingly difficult. Each visit to the hospital exposed me to the sights and sounds of live amputations and surgeries, a grim reminder of the harsh realities of our existence.

Mama served the coffee on a tray, using her largest džezva and lining up dozens of fildžani. She saved Ramo and me for last, as we were the youngest. I had never been fond of coffee before the war, but today, I savoured each sip, the hot, bitter tang awakening my senses. The sweetness of the sugar cubes added a layer of comfort, and I relished the textured, flavourful experience of the drink.

Alyssa asked questions, and jotted notes in her notebook, while I translated the conversation with my parents and grandparents. When we finished our coffee, we posed for photos that she took with her large camera, recreating our daily life. Mama posed in the kitchen, preparing watery stew. Ramo chopped wood that we were stockpiling for winter, while my grandparents prayed in their rooms, while Alyssa respectfully took photos of them.

Afterwards, she wanted me to introduce her to other families and people I knew, so she could get a sense of what life was like for ordinary citizens living under a siege. I took her to meet Belma and her family, Bilal and his, and Kamila's family.

Kamila vanished after opening the door, and returned with her hair brushed out and glossy, her cheeks rosy and lips shining. Before Alyssa took photos, I cursed myself for not taking a moment to prioritise my vanity, considering that these would be published internationally and anyone could see them. Alyssa had wanted us to look the way we did every day, and I'd taken her words to heart.

Alyssa thoughtfully asked questions of Lebiba and Harun, about the Council, the running of the hospital, the lack of resources and struggles to care for people, and that they carefully avoided any mention of the corruption with the black market in operation.

"Should you talk about the corruption?" I asked Lebiba while Alyssa was jotting down notes.

She shook her head energetically. "No, no," she gasped. "We can't have the international world looking down on us and not wanting to help."

I furrowed my brow but didn't pursue it any further. Alyssa took snaps of the family posing, Harun in his home office, peering at a medical chart, Lebiba reading a file, and Kamila posing on the staircase, looking like a cast member from the Sweet Sixteen movie rather than a war survivor.

Alyssa thanked them warmly, and we left.

"I know about the corruption," Alyssa said, snapping photos of the pockmarked buildings, showing the shelling and devastation.

"You do?" I exclaimed. "Are you going to write about it?"

She shook her head. "I can't. There are too many important players involved, and they'll prevent me from returning." Alyssa returned her camera back to her bag. "And it's not a great look to get help for the town, showing how there's no unity."

"But nothing will change unless it's made public," I exclaimed in frustration. "My mother nearly died because she couldn't get medication, and there are those dying every day from simple procedures because only those with any money can get treatment and food."

"Mmmm, you know, if someone who was a citizen wrote about it, how it affects everyday life, and the issues, did an expose from the inside, that could get published." She glanced at me from the corner of her eye.

"Me," I said, in disbelief. "I'm not a reporter."

"I'd be able to help with editing and smoothing it out, but it's probably not a good idea. If you did write it and I had it published under your name, it would put a target on your back. I guess we could publish it anonymously."

"How would I even get the article to you?" I asked, my imagination caught up in the idea of being a writer, having a purpose, something to make every day worthwhile rather than merely surviving.

"I have a friend at the base, one of the Dutch UN soldiers, who could pass it to me. His name is Bart Muis, he's so blonde he's almost albino. Can't miss him."

The Dutch, known as DutchBat, replaced the Canadian peacekeepers. They set up camp in what was the former Canadian base of an embroidery factory in Srebrenica and further afield in the former industrial zone of Potočari, which was nearly five kilometres away from town. My father was derogatory about the might of the peacekeepers. The Canadians struck him as naive schoolboys who thought they were out to a disco, getting drunk during the day and flailing around in public, while he said that the Dutch looked like models with their buzz haircuts, perfumed skin, and stylish glasses. He complained they walked down the streets as if they were on a holiday and not on a peacekeeping mission where the lives of 60,000 people rested on their muscular shoulders.

When the Dutch peacekeepers first arrived, I struck up a friendship with one peacekeeper to practice my English. The peacekeepers were my window to the world. Unlike us, they were not trapped in Srebrenica. For those of us who were trapped, it felt like a magical trick when they could go on leave and return. My Uncle Ibrahim hadn't been able to get in touch with my aunt since she left. The letters that were sent out and came in from the Red Cross were on forms, with the length determined by the dotted lines on one side of the paper, while the other had the space for both the sender's and recipient's addresses. Before sending out or receiving, the Red Cross Office censored them by covering big chunks of black text. There was a whole glossary of forbidden words: army, killed, perished, Chetniks, executed, slaughtered, captured, hunger, black market, crimes, prostitution, despair. And yet, these were the words that made up our lived experience as we shared news of those who were alive and those who were not. With all the blacked-out texts, they became almost incomprehensible and meaningless.

My uncle begged me to help him ask a peacekeeper to send a letter out. We heard some soldiers sent letters when they went on leave, and one family in the street said that a soldier returned with prescription glasses for their child that he'd picked up from an aunt in Germany.

I took my uncle's letter and looked for Bram, who the children called Mr Moustache because of the thick, black handlebar moustache on his face. He was the one who was kind. As the children begged at the front gates, clamouring for attention, a few soldiers swore at them or banged on the fence to chase them away. Finally, I saw Bram. He agreed to post the letter for me.

Returning every day to see if there was a reply was a way to fill the time. When it was quiet, and there were only a few children, the peacekeepers gave the children whatever they could. But when there were too many, they couldn't do anything. Bram once gave me a toothbrush and toothpaste, slipping it into my hand under the pretext of a handshake so it wouldn't draw attention.

Three weeks later, Bram came out with a smile on his face and handed me a letter from Germany. I ran home, handing it to my uncle, who skimmed it. As soon as he finished, Ibrahim cried with happiness. "They're safe. They're well." For a week afterwards, he read and re-read the letter to us—we heard about how my aunt and cousins were eating, had toys to play with and clean clothes to wear. They'd applied for a refugee visa, and hopefully, my uncle would join them. That was a year ago, and Ibrahim was still here, and his children were growing up without him.

Five months later, Bram completed his tour and returned to the Netherlands; I never heard from him again. After this, I stopped visiting the peacekeepers. I didn't want to get attached to any other soldiers who would then leave and forget I ever existed.

Alyssa gripped my elbow. "But you need to think about this carefully. This would require you investigating the corruption, finding evidence of who is involved, and it would be very dangerous. You wouldn't be able to trust anyone. No one can know."

I nodded, picturing my Ramo. I could trust him with my life.

I walked Alyssa back to the city centre, where her escort was waiting. She opened her satchel and took out her notebook, jotting down a note. She tore it out and handed it to me. "If you want to write to me, this is my address and the name of my contact." She handed the paper into my palm, holding it tight. "But don't put yourself in danger." She looked around the town warily. "There are enemies within, too."

I shivered as she spoke. "Do you remember when we met two years ago, and I asked you why do you do this? Come to dangerous places and write about them. You said someone has to so that people know and help."

Alyssa nodded. "Yes, but I can leave, Seka. You can't." She patted my shoulder.

I deflated, looking around the hills that imprisoned me. Zora's letter beckoned me, and I rushed home. I found it under my pillows and went to the basement, hiding under the stairs in the shelter we'd created to escape the shelling. I peeled open the envelope reverently, my heart skipping a beat as I read the first line. *"My dearest Seka, how I have missed you."* Tears began, and I had to wipe them and clear my vision before continuing to read. Zora and her family were living in Melbourne. They were renting a house. She was going to high school after spending a year learning the language in a different school. Her life was good, full of normal high school rituals of homework and excursions. Her father was working as a taxi driver, her mother in a factory, and her older brothers in hospitality.

I cried after I finished reading, holding a fist to my mouth to muffle my moans of pain. I was so happy that she was well and happy, living a normal life in Australia, and yet there was also a biting bitterness tearing me apart. Why didn't we leave when we could? Why didn't we run and claim refugee status and get out of this hellhole? I felt a flash of anger towards my parents for their stupidity and my father's refusal to leave our house and belongings.

I gasped, realising I'd been scrunching Zora's letter as rage coursed through me. I carefully smoothed it out, gently returning it to its envelope, before inserting it into the back of Zora's notebook. I knew I wouldn't read it again while I was living in Srebrenica. It would just tear me apart. I leaned my hot cheek against the cool brick wall as I hugged my knees, imagining myself in Zora's life in Melbourne.

A few days later, my mother sent me to collect the first aid packet. It was a warm day, and I was wearing my parachute dress, the nylon fluttering the breeze. As I lined up with everyone else at the warehouse, I noticed a woman in tight-fitting jeans and knee-high leather boots, her face carefully coiffed and makeup slathered on, cut the line and get her packet. It was too warm for jeans and boots. A few of the women before me shouted, their *dimije* and headscarf-covered hair identifying them as refugees from the nearby villagers. The woman in boots looked at them and spat out "refugees," her face screwed up in contempt and making her previously lovely visage now resemble a nasty troll. The women in *dimije* swore at her as she sashayed down the street, purposely swaying her hips.

"That's the girlfriend of a councillor," a man before me said to his friend. "She's showing off the brand new boots her sugar daddy bought her from dealing with humanitarian aid and I'm wearing this." The man kicked his foot, and I looked down. He was wearing runners that were covered in black creases from wear. The sole had detached at some point and was duct taped back together, and there were holes on the sides where the leather had worn out.

"At least you're lucky. You've got summer sandals," his companion said.

Frayed Runners let out a bark of laughter. "Sandals indeed," he said bitterly, wiggling his toe, which poked out from under the duct tape. "We need to do something."

Ramo was in the line behind me with my brother Emir and their new crony Bilal. In the six months since our breakup, we avoided spending time together. Ramo was getting his aid rations for him and his mother, and even though we lived in the same house, he had left earlier and gone to meet his friends first. Ramo and my brother had drawn together and become best friends and had met Bilal at the Cultural Centre, where there were youth programs established to keep us entertained. The three of them had started a band, and Ramo had been using Emir's old guitar and teaching himself chords while Emir played bass. They practised every day in the great hall of the culture centre and were going to perform at the concert.

There had even been a chess tournament organised, which involved the best players. Even I had attended the tournament. Life in Srebrenica was boring and anything that passed for entertainment was acceptable. I had expected to watch the chess game sleepily and leave when I couldn't stand it. Instead, the tournament had been the talk of the town when a 15-year-old ended up in the finals and played against an old man who was a miner.

The miner had been arrogant and boastful, saying that he could beat him with his back turned. He teased the young man about his youth, his pretty-boy face, and that he had reached the finals on luck and guile. When the boy claimed to have studied tactics from books, the miner laughed and laughed. The last tournament had lasted hours, and everyone had been on a knife edge. The young people all urged the young boy to win and groaned when he made a wrong move, while the adults all cheered the miner.

When the 15-year-old won with a quietly spoken "Check Mate," the miner had been incredulous, his face a perfect picture of disbelief that made so many of us laugh. The miner had picked up the chess set and thrown it against the wall, swearing and shouting, until his friend urged him out of the hall. Finally, everyone hailed the young man as a winner and enjoyed the surprise victory.

Conversations sprung up around me as people started muttering about all the injustices. Ramo approached Frayed Runners and began interviewing him. He and his cronies had started a newspaper that they typed on a typewriter that had belonged to the previous occupants of Bilal's apartment.

I approached and eavesdropped on their conversation. The man was Kerim Viskovic, and he had organised a protest at the Council offices the next day. This was my opportunity. I needed to attend, take notes, interview Kerim and get the story on corruption. Ramo finished his interview and glanced at me, my body flushing with heat as we gazed at each other. A woman to my right shuffled in place and nudged me, breaking my concentration. I looked away quickly. Ramo and I were on a break, a necessary evil. Ramo left with his friends while I remained in the line.

When I came home with the aid packets, Ramo was sitting at the kitchen table, his tongue protruding from his mouth as he concentrated on drawing. I approached. He was drawing a girl in knee-high boots who looked like a cartoon character with her boobs and hips exaggerated, her boots decorated with a yellow dollar sign buckle.

He was recreating the councillor's girlfriend who cut in line, wearing tight-fitting jeans and knee-high leather boots the councillor had obtained from the black market.

"What are you doing?" I asked.

"The cover for our next newspaper." Next to him were already three copies of the drawing, each one slightly more polished.

In the year since the Safe Zone resolution was passed, Ramo started a newspaper with Emir and Bilal that they called the Srebrenica Proclamation and produced it on used paper that they got from the municipal authorities. They laboriously re-typed twenty copies, each copy an original with its unique typos, with Ramo and his friends taking turns typing. The front page was coloured, drawn by Ramo to represent the theme of the issue. I'd contributed in the early days, enduring Bilal's ridiculous editorial notes that were riddled with spelling mistakes, until the day my anger spilled over, and I threw a log at his head, barely missing him. Bilal claims he fired me for disrespect towards hierarchy. My story was I'd quit before he provoked me into becoming a murderer.

"Are you sure it's a wise idea to write an article about the President of the Municipality? After all, they're the ones who are your paper supplier."

"Why not? We uncover facts and report the truth," Ramo said.

He sounded like Bilal, who was their unofficial leader.

"I hope you enjoy publishing your last issue," I muttered under my breath.

"I heard that," Ramo said. "You forget we have a man on the inside. Bilal's friend."

"It's not like anyone will know that the paper is still from the Council."

"We're careful," Ramo said, and bent his head over his drawing again. "Here, you can read the first copy."

I took a copy upstairs and found the article about the corruption in the Council. It contained Bilal's trademark blow-hard commentary with words like "malfeasance", "purloining" and "perfidiousness." I got my dictionary and looked up the words which I'd never read before. All three were misspelled. Ramo told me that Bilal found a thesaurus at the flat he was living in and always selected the longest word he could find when editing his first draft to make himself sound smarter. My nervousness about Ramo getting in trouble about the article faded. No one in the enclave could understand the article, not without the help of a good dictionary.

I finished reading the typed newspaper pages and flicked through poems and a fictional story. The newspaper was not for real news; we used a radio for that. Instead, we founded it as a cultural activity, and the first few issues provided fun reading with stories, poems, and interesting articles. Since then, each writer attempted to outdo themselves by using as many big words as possible, even if it meant that their writing was hard to understand. I finished reading the typed newspaper pages and flicked through poems and a fictional story. My head hurt by the time I finished reading. I flipped the newspaper over and read the pages from the Council, finding drafts of letters to aid organisations begging for aid, or orders for materials to unclog the sewer lines by flushing them out, and letters to the UN demanding that the Dutch military contingent do the work to clear the sewers.

I took out my notebook from my side table. I'd stopped carrying it with me since I received her letter and hadn't been writing to Zora as much. It was getting harder to keep the hope alive that we would see each other and to keep writing in the notebook for her. I attempted to write in it as a diary for myself, but there weren't many moments I wanted to re-live.

"Dear Zora, life has settled into a plodding routine of forgettable days and constant deja vu. Time in the enclave seems to stretch out forever, taking on a different meaning. It has been two years since the war began and you left and yet it feels like so much longer.

I can barely remember what life was like before all this, or the fun times we used to have. Thinking about it just makes everything now feel worse, so I try not to. I push it all aside and just focus on getting through the day.

Writing in this notebook was supposed to be a way to keep you close, now it has just become a way of torturing myself. If we ever see each other again, I'll just tell you the things that really matter."

I closed the notebook and returned to the newspaper, turning the page to read a letter from the President that stated epidemics, including hundreds of cases of yellow fever, intestinal disease, scabies, and eighty cases of tuberculosis, had hit Srebrenica. When I showed my father, he dismissed it. "He's exaggerating in order to try to get the UN to come in and help."

Mama glanced at the page and harrumphed. "Didn't they send a UN Field office to investigate the claims?"

"Yes, and he found no evidence to support them and now our name is mud. They keep constantly making false public appeals on the ham radio and now they think that everything we say is a lie." Babo got another cigarette.

I heard a whistle of a shell and then an explosion outside. I looked at the clock. It was midday. The Serbs were testing their aim again. Since the resolution passed, they sporadically shelled and shot at us to keep reminding us to fear their might. We all ran to the cellar and took our spots, waiting to see how long it would take to stop. The house thundered above us. Hours later, the shelling ceased. We remained in the cellar for another half an hour, our usual procedure. The Serbs loved to lull us into a false sense of security and then restart the bombings when we thought we were safe.

As the family descended to shelter in the basement, I mulled over whether I should tell Ramo about Alyssa's offer to write an article, especially since he was just as invested in exposing the corruption as I was. As if he knew I was thinking about him, he glanced at me, his blue eyes full of longing. I quickly broke eye contact. No, we needed to stay away from each other. Besides, he was already behaving recklessly with his newspaper writing. I didn't want to encourage him further.

The next day, I followed Ramo and Emir to a protest at the Council offices. When we arrived, there were hundreds of people gathered in front of the large imposing two-storey built during the Austro-Hungarian Empire for old aristocratic families and visiting diplomats, the elegant striped limestone of white and grey, the arched windows with delicate floral flourishes moulding, harking of a time gone by.

Kerim Viskovic was standing in front of the crowd, stalking back and forth in his worn-out tracksuit and threadbare sneakers. "Look at this building behind me. It houses corrupt officials who believe that they are the aristocrats of our impoverished town and deserve the fat of the land. They wear new boots while the rest of us walk in shoes that are splitting apart, and warm winter coats while we shiver." He shouted to the crowd, waving his hand at the building behind him. In the windows were the councillors he was complaining about, but even though they listened, none of them came down.

"Look at the cowards listening. Look at them. They are few and we are many. We need to tear them down from their lofty perches. They are no better than us and should be in the muck like we are. We need to get rid of the corruption that steals food from our mouths and those of our children. We need new leadership."

As he spoke, the crowd cheered, getting more and more excited and voluminous while he walked up and down, castigating the officials, listing all their crimes and all the ways they had failed the people.

Afterwards, the crowd surrounded him, clapped him. Kerim shook hands and kept urging the crowd to take action, and they all nodded.

I'd been plotting all night about how to approach him and talk about an interview. I was wary of doing it in front of witnesses; this article and the support I had from an international journalist had to remain a secret. I had prepared some props in my bag and was wearing my longest dress. Slowly, protestors dispersed, and Kerim left the offices, surrounded by an entourage. I tracked them through town. They went to a park and hung outside, talking and laughing, sharing a bottle of what was probably homemade *rakija*. While they were occupied, I ducked behind some trees and donned my disguise, tucking my dress into the *dimije* I was wearing beneath them, tugging on a loose and billowy shirt, and putting my hair into a *šamija* I'd taken from my mother's drawers. I was going to use a fake name when I spoke to Kerim and didn't want him to identify me too easily.

An hour later, Kerim's cronies departed, leaving me to shadow him to an apartment block. Silently, I trailed him up the stairs, my steps careful. After he reached the third floor and entered an apartment to my left, I paused, peering through the staircase banister to ensure he was settled before proceeding.

After a few moments, I ascended the remaining stairs and knocked on the door. Kerim opened it, looking puzzled. "Sorry, I don't have any food," he began, moving to close the door.

"I'm not here for that," I interrupted, pushing back against the door to prevent its closure. "I'm here to interview you. I'm writing an article with the help of a journalist on the outside about the corruption and need to gather some facts."

His gaze narrowed as he scrutinised me, clearly thrown off by my appearance. I bit my lip, realising that my disguise, intended to blend in with the local women, was now a hindrance. Most of the villages discouraged schooling for women, expecting them to be domestic drudges and remain illiterate.

"It's a disguise. Here," I hissed, handing him the paper on which Alyssa had written her contact details.

Understanding dawned in Kerim's eyes. "Come in," he invited, leading me down the hallway and into the living room. "Would you like something to drink? I've only got water."

"Yes, please." I'd spent the afternoon following him around and had long finished the bottle of water that I'd carried with me, and was parched from the warm day.

He returned with a glass, while I admired the view from the apartment out onto the town, the surrounding hills.

"What do you want to know?" he asked.

I took out my notebook and pen. "Everything you know about the corruption. I'm going to write an article and smuggle it out of the enclave to Alyssa. She has a contact in DutchBat who'll get it to her."

"Great. Let's begin." Kerim sat, a smile lighting up his face.

There was a harsh banging on the door, and we both jumped. The banging continued until the door splintered. "They're coming for me. Hide." Kerim hissed, opening the balcony.

I slipped outside, crouching to the left out of view from the window. Three men burst into the living room, wearing balaclavas. One of them had a gun, another a plank of wood, and the third a knife. They took turns beating him, until the large man with the gun lurched forward and cut his throat. Kerim's gaze caught mine through the window, and I covered my mouth to hold back my scream. His eyes rolled back and turned lifeless as blood spurted from his neck. The men ran out of the apartment while I rocked myself.

I don't know how long I remained there, frozen and horrified. Finally, adrenaline kicked in. I needed to get away. I crawled from the balcony back in the house, struggling to stand up, my gaze averted from where Kerim's body sprawled on the floor.

I walked down the stairs, holding onto the banister, fighting not to fall down. Neighbours were coming out of the apartment, and I heard shouts and screams as they discovered Kerim's body.

I stumbled out of the building, my legs trembling beneath me. The night air was cool against my skin, sending a shiver down my spine. As I walked, the shadows seemed to grow deeper, the darkness closing in around me.

Suddenly, a figure lurched from the darkness, heading straight for me. My heart leaped into my throat, and I screamed in terror, my voice echoing through the empty streets.

"Seka, Seka, it's me," Ramo's voice called out, breaking through my fear.

I blinked, my vision clearing to reveal Ramo's worried face above me. Relief flooded through me as I realised it was him. "What happened? Where were you?" he asked, concern etched in his features.

"I was with Kerim. They killed him," I replied, my voice hollow with shock.

Ramo's body tensed. "He's dead. Oh, God. You were there," he murmured, his arm coming around me, urging me to hasten.

"Why are you here?" I asked, confusion clouding my mind.

Ramo flushed, his embarrassment clear. "I saw you leaving the protest and wanted to know where you were going. Then you were hiding out at the park and changed into this." he gestured to my attire. "So I followed you."

His voice carried a hint of jealousy, but I was too shaken to dwell on it. I recounted the events of the evening, telling him about Alyssa and the article.

"You could have been killed," Ramo burst out as he stopped and shook me by the arms.

"I know," I whispered, feeling drained and overwhelmed. I leaned into him, seeking comfort and support.

He held me tightly, and I felt the warmth of his tears mingling with mine. "I can't live without you. Please tell me you'll stop this madness," he pleaded.

I nodded, not wanting to argue, but a flicker of anger burned within me. Could I really ignore the injustice and violence I had witnessed?

We plodded home, holding hands.

I thought about Kerim, about the hundreds of people gathered to protest today. He had inspired so many people to stand up and was becoming a force of justice and truth. That's how you kill a movement. You kill the man with the idea.

12-Recreation

It was night when we arrived at the Cultural Centre. Ramo and Emir joined Bilal, Belma's brother-in-law, who insisted everyone call him Billy. Bilal was holding an electric guitar that he'd found in the flat he and his family were living in, left by the Serb family the flat once belonged to.

"You brought it," Ramo said enthusiastically as he touched the guitar.

"Yep. Here you go Iggy." Bilal passed the guitar to Ramo. He was attempting to get all of them to use English names, but Ramo was not keen on Iggy. "Come on pip-squeak." Bilal gestured to his younger cousin, Ismail. We had no electricity, and the only way to generate it was to pedal on the bike set up in the corner that was connected to a generator.

"I'm not doing it." Ismail crossed his arms over his chest, his bottom lip protruding as his brown-haired fringe covered his eyes.

"Now." Bilal pushed him towards the bike.

"You always say I can be a part of the band and then use me to pedal." Ismail was nearly in tears.

"I know what we'll do." Ramo picked up the guitar and the instruments and carried them over to the bike. "You can be our backup singer while you're peddling." Ismail smiled and got on the bike.

"Are you ready Emmett," Bilal said to Emir.

Emir stood in place without responding. He'd learned the only way to stop Bilal's Americanisation attempts was not to respond to his re-naming.

"Alright, alright," Bilal said with exasperation. "Are you ready, Emir?" He pronounced Emir's name with an edge.

"Yes, I am." Emir plugged in his guitar.

Bilal pressed record on the cassette recorder he'd found in his flat and then gestured that they were to start. They were playing *Twist and Shout* from The Beatles with Bilal singing in English, his pronunciation flawless. Bilal grew his white-blonde hair, and it hung to his shoulders and as he twisted and gyrated it flew into his face and mouth.

Ramo played the electric guitar, wincing every time he got the wrong chord. He'd attempted growing his hair but didn't have the patience for it and I'd cut it short for him. I was getting good at giving homemade haircuts to the men in my family.

He and Ismail sang the chorus together, Ismail forgetting to pedal as he sang, and as the electricity waned, the guitar twanged unpleasantly. Emir played the guitar tolerably well, his blue eyes squinting in concentration, while Bilal did his best John Lennon impression, his howling reaching high-pitched tones that made my ears ring.

A trio of girls, led by Kamila, had established a dancing troupe and were practising as they eyed the band. The boys were handsome, tall and lanky, wearing t-shirts and tracksuit pants. Ramo was nearly Emir's height, and while Bilal was the shortest at 180 centimetres, he was still relatively tall.

I heard someone call my name and turned to see Belma arrive with her son Zikret in her arms. He was now two and a half years old, and she put him on the ground. He toddled, his green eyes lighting up when he saw his uncle Bilal. Belma followed him slowly behind. She'd ditched the village outfit of dimije and headscarf and was wearing a long skirt and t-shirt, her shoulder-length hair framing her face and making her green eyes pop.

When she reached me, we hugged, while Zikret hugged Bilal's legs. Bilal stopped the song and bent to pick him up, giving him a quick cuddle and kiss. He handed him back to Belma, who placed Zikret back on the ground.

"How are you doing?" I asked.

She looked tired and wan, with dark circles under her eyes. She'd given birth to her second child, a daughter, who was now one. "Good, good," she smiled wanly. "My mother-in-law is taking care of the little one while I take this ragamuffin for a walk."

"Great."

"What about you? Still at school?" she asked, her voice envious.

I nodded. I used to love school but wasn't sure about this new revamped post-Communist model. The high school had reopened after being renovated by a Swedish humanitarian organisation. The school resembled barracks, with bags of sand in front of the entrance and sandbags in the classroom windows. I had no stationery and used old pencils that I could barely write with on the back page of Emir's notebooks, and I was one of the lucky ones. Other students brought old receipts or pieces of packaging from food aid.

University students or specialists, like my father, who was a former engineer, were teachers instead of certified teachers, and they were paid with a bag of cigarettes. Most classes were theoretical due to the lack of required equipment. Moreover, they added a new subject, religion. Our education system had been firmly secular, and any talk of religion was only in a Mosque, which I never went to. I already disliked the Imam when he called me by my given name, Dževahira, and refused to use my nickname Seka because it wasn't Muslim.

On the first day of school, the Imam asked the class who knew how to pray. I'd looked around the class. Most of the students were refugees from the villages around Srebrenica and, like Ramo, they spent their childhood attending *mejtef,* religious classes at the Mosque once a week. There were only three of us who I knew from Srebrenica, me, Kamila and a boy who I'd never talked to before the war.

The Imam approached me. He was wearing a black robe that reached his ankles. His white shirt collar was slightly visible against his neck and matched the white turban he wore on his head. "Who are your parents? Why haven't they taught you anything?" he demanded, staring at me with his white eyebrows furrowed.

"Because I was taught to recite the Pioneer Pledge, and my father is Fadil Torlak. You met him in the staff room."

The Imam's face turned red. "Get out of my classroom," he shouted, pointing to the door.

I heard students snicker as my cheeks turned pink and I walked into the hallway. I'd never gotten into trouble before and I didn't understand why I was in trouble now. I'd answered the Imam's question honestly.

Later, I spoke to Kamila, watching her suspiciously as I demanded to know how she'd learned to be a Muslim when I knew both her parents had been Communist Party members. She told me her parents had been indoctrinating her into the faith since the war began. "Haven't your parents been praying and teaching you?" she asked, her blue eyes guileless.

"Of course," I lied through a tight smile. Mama had started praying with my grandparents and attempted to get me to join them, but I steadfastly refused. My father still clung to his atheist principles and refused to let Mama force me.

"School's good," I lied to Belma.

"I wish I could go." She looked down and lunged at Zikret, moving him away from the speaker he was about to rip wires from.

I was taken aback. Belma had been relieved to give up schooling and get married, but I guess the war had given her a life she hadn't signed up for. Instead of living comfortably with her in-laws in their large house with indoor plumbing, she was struggling to feed her two children.

"How is everything with you?" I asked, concerned about her welfare.

"Difficult. Nedjad is attempting to practice the withdrawal method so we don't get pregnant again. I can't enjoy myself at all because I'm so worried he'll spill his seed inside of me, and he's frustrated that I keep avoiding relations." She teared up as she spoke and quickly wiped her eyes. "I wanted a big family. I want so many children, but not like this. Not like this." She looked at Zikret, who looked so thin and frail, her face wreathed with despair. Zikret glanced at his mother, and seeing her melancholy, toddled to her. He gently patted her cheek, and she smiled and gave him a kiss, making him giggle.

"Oh, oh," Belma said, looking at something behind me.

I glanced back and saw that the trio of girls were now standing in front of the band in formation, dancing their choreography with Kamila front and centre; she and Emir eye-fucking each other. Kamila was still thin but had obviously been getting more nutrition than the rest of us and had hips and boobs that were bouncing every time she swayed. She was also the one who was the best dressed in tight-fitting jeans and a tight top. The other two girls wore frayed tracksuit pants and tops, a sure sign they were refugees. Kamila had probably picked them for their lack of wardrobe options so she could shine.

The band finished the song, and the girls swarmed them. Belma waggled her eyebrows, sweeping Zikret into her arms as we stalked over. One girl stood with each of the boys. A blonde was with Ramo, her head tilted with interest as he showed her the chords of the guitar. Kamila and Emir were talking intently about them joining forces for the concert, with the girls being their back up dancers. The girl with dark hair that reached her waist was laughing with Bilal. When Belma and I approached Bilal introduced us, the blonde was Enisa.

"Maybe Torlak can join you," Bilal said,

Enisa followed his gaze to look at me. "You don't look like a dancer," she sneered.

"I'm not," I said.

I approached Ramo, placing my hand in the crook of his arm. He smiled at me, and Enisa retreated.

"Now that we've got that settled, let's review our performance." Bilal rewound their cassette recorder, and they listened to their recording, and they mocked each other good-naturedly, wincing as they missed the notes and giving each other feedback about how to improve.

"Let's play again," Bilal said.

"We have to get going," Ramo said, glancing at the clock.

"What's your rush?" Bilal demanded. "There's nowhere to go."

"It's Seka's birthday," he nodded at me.

As all eyes turned to me, I blushed.

"Happy Birthday," Belma said and hugged me.

"Thank you." It was my eighteenth birthday, and I was excited about our night out to see a movie.

"Where are you going?" Belma asked.

When I told her, she looked despondent. "I wish I could have a night out." Zikret toddled to her, and she picked him up. "But this little cutie pie keeps me busy."

"You should come to our hangout at least for a few hours," I tugged on her hand. "Your mother-in-law can watch the kids."

She looked torn.

"Bilal, tell her," I urged him.

"Yeah, come tonight," he said, sounding anything but enthusiastic.

I glared at him, and he shrugged. "What? She's a young mother with children. She's not interested in our adolescent shenanigans."

Belma's smile faded. "Of course. He's right." She cleared her throat and picked up Zikret, heading for the door.

"You're a jackass," I muttered at Bilal. "I'm going to go after her. I'll meet you at our spot," I quickly said to Ramo. Seeing Enisa's calculating stare, I leaned in and kissed him on the cheek, marking my territory.

"Wait up, Belma," I called, as I ran after her.

She was holding Zikret to her chest, tears streaming down her eyes as she walked. "Is it so wrong to want one night to be doing what other young people my age are doing?"

"No, it's not. You need to come tonight. We're going to have a little hang-out session before the movie for an hour. You can take an hour out of your duty being a mother and wife and have some fun."

Zikret looked at his mother with concern and gently nuzzled his face into her neck. She sighed and held him tighter. "I know, but you also don't have this." She squeezed Zikret. "It's hard being a mother, but it's also the best thing that happened to me."

"I know, but you can still come and spend an hour celebrating the birthday of your oldest friend," I pleaded, leaning my head against hers.

She laughed. "I'll try."

We hugged, and she continued on home. I realised I'd walked halfway to town and was close to the hospital. This was a good opportunity to work on my secret project. I arrived at the hospital, and the security waved me in, used to me popping in and out for translating. Most staff had gone home for the day and only a skeleton staff remained to care for the injured patients. When I reached the floor where the supply room was, I waited a beat, ensuring no one was in the corridor. I glided towards the padlocked door, taking out the wire I had wrapped around a scrunchie on my wrist. During one of my book scavenges a few months ago, I'd discovered a find, a torn and beaten book titled *The Sleuth's Toolkit*, supposedly written by Sherlock Holmes as a guide to help amateur sleuths undertake investigations. I'd read the chapter about picking a padlock with a hearty laugh and attempted it on a beaten and forgotten padlock in my father's workstation, if for no other reason than complete and utter boredom. When the padlock had snapped open after I used a wire in the motion the book described, I'd gasped with shock. The next day I snuck into the hospital and attempted it on the supply room padlock, and was stunned to find it worked.

The padlock gave a satisfying click, and I entered the supply room, checking supplies and noting down quantities in my notebook. There was a ledger that doctors were supposed to record medication that they were dispensing to patients. I opened it and moved my finger down, jotting down patient names and the doctors who had prescribed them. When I finished, I made my way to a corner shelf and moved around the plastic bedpans until I reached the indelible ink marker that I'd found in an old cupboard a few months ago. It was the marker that Officer Johnson had used nearly two years ago during the evacuation. I took out bottles of antibiotics and drew a dot on the label, quickly returning them back to the box. After I hid the marker back, I exited from the storeroom, locking the padlock with a flick of my wrist.

Vahida stood at the nurse's station, and I chatted with her, checking in on patients who had been admitted over the past few days and learning about updates at the hospital. When she was called by a patient, I seized the notebook that the patient rooms were in and recorded them. I wandered down the corridor, entered the patient rooms, brought water, and asked if they had received the antibiotics they had been prescribed. The answer was no, always no. I left, feeling disheartened and broken. I walked out of the door, looking back at the hospital in despair. A picture was emerging, a heartbreaking picture of corruption and the doctors who were involved.

I tried to shake off my melancholic mood. Tonight was my birthday celebration, and everyone expected me to be happy. This article and the dark undertow of corruption would have to wait, but I knew the time was coming soon when I would have to make the final decision—to draft and send it to Seka through her DutchBat contact.

I returned home and got ready for my night out, leaving again an hour later. Ramo and Emir had already gone ahead. It was still daylight when I passed by the playground where grenades and shells wreaked their havoc and massacred hundreds two years before. My cousin Minka would be seven years old now. Sometimes I pretended she wasn't buried in Srebrenica in pieces, and instead imagined she was with my aunt and her siblings in Germany, living a normal life.

I entered the smaller street leading around the school and reached the rubble of a house that was hit by a shell. I walked up the stairs and through what had been the living room, half torn walls around me, and to the back, where one bedroom had debris and slats had fallen down to create a roof. The sky was visible and when it rained it was wet, but on warm nights like tonight it was a cosy nook.

Refugees claimed it for a few nights but abandoned it because they heard screams of terror from those who'd perished on the playground next to us. When my friends and I used it for the first time on one of our nightly sojourns, I was jumpy and fearful, but we had heard nothing, perhaps because we didn't stay the whole night.

I lifted my t-shirt and unwrapped my mother's red silk wrap-around dress that I'd hidden around my waist, together with her dainty black handbag. My parents thought I was visiting Belma, so I'd snuck out my dress. I put it on and shivered as the cool silk slid on my skin in the balmy night. The bodice enveloped my waist, and the pleated skirt draped down to my mid-calf. I folded my tracksuit pants and t-shirt and placed them in the corner. I'd have to change back into them before I returned home tonight. I opened the handbag, took out my mother's compact mirror and placed it in a hole in the wall. I rubbed the lipstick on my lips. Using my finger, I dabbed blue eyeshadow on my eyelids. I looked at myself and felt a flutter of excitement. I looked sophisticated, like a real woman.

Ramo arrived, a big smile lighting up his face when he saw me. I ran into his arms, and we kissed, revelling in being able to touch each other. At home, we hid our relationship from my parents, and only in these stolen moments could we just be a boy and a girl in love. His hands caressed my back, pushing me tighter into him, and I shivered with delight.

"Are you here, Torlak?" Bilal called out, and we quickly pulled apart.

I wiped my mouth as Bilal came in, followed by my brother. Bilal always announced his presence, so we had time to be presentable for others. *Thanks*, I mouthed.

Bilal took out a bottle. "The first sip for the birthday girl?" He smiled devilishly as he handed me the bottle.

I placed the top of the bottle against my lip and took a big gulp. The acrid homemade *rakija* that Bilal made in the bathtub of the flat he lived in burned my stomach, and warmth spread to me. The first time I'd taken a sip months ago, I'd coughed and spluttered for ages. While the taste was still revolting, I loved the carefree feeling it left me with. For a few hours I could forget that I was in a war zone with no escape, and pretend I was a regular teenager, with regular problems. I passed the bottle to Ramo, noticing that my lipstick rubbed off on him. I wiped his chin with my finger. When the bottle completed a circle again, I snatched it back and took another gulp. I also loved that the alcohol filled the gnawing physical hunger that invaded my body nearly every minute of every day.

"How are you feeling?" Emir's right cheek became swollen after a tooth broke, which was a side effect of our wartime diet. Babo used pliers to take out the broken pieces, leaving Emir's gum red and swollen. I'd found him in front of the bathroom mirror, practising his smile so he didn't reveal the gap.

"Better." He took another swig of *rakija* and sloshed it around in his mouth before swallowing. The only other benefit to the plum brandy was as a pain reliever. Emir was lucky. When my tooth broke, I suffered through days of agonising pain without the benefit of any pain relief.

I reached for the bottle, but Bilal snatched it off me. "We have to save the rest for the others."

I sullenly nodded. As if I had conjured them, Kamila and Enisa appeared in the demolished doorway. They had both changed, and Kamila was now wearing a dress, the top tight with her boobs spilling out, while Enisa was wearing jeans that hugged her butt, with her trademark red bow in her ponytail. She must be wearing a child's size for it to be so tight-fitting on her thin frame. There was only one reason a refugee girl like her was wearing jeans like that — she was benefiting from the corruption in town and receiving smuggled counterfeit goods.

Kamila approached me and handed me a rectangular box wrapped in a tea towel and ribbon, kissing me on the cheek. "Happy birthday, Seka."

I didn't expect a present and knew no one else had one to give.

"Don't worry, it doesn't cost anything," she added, seeing my shocked face.

I opened the ribbon and found a book, a copy of *Wuthering Heights*, my favourite novel that I'd borrowed from her on many occasions in the past year.

"I can't—" I went to hand it back.

"It's fine. One read was enough for me, and no one else in my house will ever read it. At least I know that you'll treasure it."

I nodded, my cheeks flushing as I flashed back to the investigation of her father and the suspicion I was forming about him.

Kamila went to stand beside Emir, and he glanced approvingly at her cleavage, having a perfect vantage point because of his height. Enisa walked towards Bilal, her blonde wavy hair swaying, her cheeks flushed on her pale face. Bilal's glazed eyes remained fixed on her hips, causing his cheeks to flush.

"Wow, you look amazing." Bilal hugged her, and they kissed before us, their mouths making a slurping noise.

"I like your dress," Kamila complimented me.

"Thank you." I appreciated her making the effort, considering I was wearing my mother's hand-me-down while she wore her own dress that she'd bought pre-war and was now tight. I'd grown too tall for my pre-war clothes and my mother had donated them to refugees.

"Yeah, it's great your mother lent you her dress. You almost fill it out." Enisa glanced at my chest, where the dress was hanging loosely, exposing more of my boob than it should have.

I quickly lifted the dress up over my shoulders and glared at her. She was always making small put-downs. Ramo told me I shouldn't get worked up. She was jealous that I lived in my home with my own things, but it still grated on my nerves. "Are we leaving?" I demanded.

"Relax," Bilal said. "It's too early in the night."

"Yes, there's no point getting there before nine at least," Enisa said, flicking her blonde hair over her shoulder.

I glared at her. The superior way she spoke grated on my nerves.

We all settled into a loose circle, each taking our seats. Ramo and I sat on a stack of bricks he'd formed as a makeshift chair, while Bilal and Enisa sat on a log that we'd brought in, and Emir and Kamila sat on the demolished wall that used to divide the house.

Ramo took a jar from Bilal that contained petrol and lit the wick, the glow from it casting light into the dark room.

"How does it feel to be eighteen, Torlak?" Bilal asked.

I was the baby of the group. Emir was the oldest at twenty one, Bilal and Ramo were twenty, and the girls were already eighteen. As the days were unfurling to this day, I was full of anticipation. It was a milestone, the moment when I officially went from youth to adulthood.

I was holding the bottle and took a sip. "Not the way I thought," I finally said. If it wasn't for the war, I would be in my final year of high school, planning to leave home to go to university, probably to live in Belgrade to study to be a veterinarian. Instead, my whole life was on hold.

"Who would have thought we'd still be in this shithole three years later?" Emir said, his voice bitter. He should have been in his second year of university. Instead, his days of boredom were punctuated by getting odd jobs on the work brigade through the Council, doing menial jobs like cleaning public areas or repairing pipes.

Ramo's hand tightened on mine, and I knew he was thinking about his life before the war. Living in the village with his father and brothers, working the land. He probably would have been married by now, maybe even expecting his first child. His father promised each of his sons a plot of land and Ramo would be building his house on his plot, his brothers helping him.

A pall descended as we each wrestled with our thoughts, thinking about the life we should be living.

"I didn't think the war would last this long," Emir said. "I thought the international community would intervene, end it, and our lives would return to normal." He laughed bitterly. "Instead here we are, the disenchanted youth of Srebrenica with our rotten teeth and our dying dreams." He lifted the bottle and gulped a sip of *rakija*.

We cheered as he passed the bottle. I took a drink and wiped the tears seeping from my eyes.

I opened my handbag and took out three cigarettes. I handed one to Emir, one to Bilal, and one for me and Ramo to share.

"Make sure you don't smoke them all," Bilal said, holding his cigarette over the wick. "You need two each for entry."

"Is that makeup?" Enisa gasped, peering into my handbag. She squinted as she looked me over. "Are you wearing eyeshadow? Give me some." She reached for my handbag.

I held it away from her. "It belongs to my mother."

"Since you stole it from Mama, it's only fair you share it with the girls," Emir said, his voice carrying an edge. He stared me down, daring me to defy him.

"Fine." I took out makeup and sullenly handed it over.

Kamila and Enisa looked at it like eager magpies confronted with a bright object. They took turns holding the compact and rubbing makeup on. Enisa pressed her finger so hard into the eye shadow she crushed it.

"How do we look?" Enisa demanded when she finished preening for the boys.

"Gorgeous," Bilal said.

"Beautiful," Emir said.

As I looked at the two of them, I was angry. This was my opportunity to distinguish myself, instead we now looked identical. I licked my finger and surreptitiously wiped the eyeshadow from my eyelids.

Enisa caught me in the act. "What is it Torlak? You don't want to look like a refugee."

"No, I just don't want to look like you," I said.

"You think you're better than us?"

I glared at her. "What did a nice girl like you do to earn jeans like that?"

Enisa looked at me and scowled. "I borrowed them from my sister."

Ramo's hand tightened on my shoulder, urging me to stand down.

"Calm down ladies," Bilal said, the bottle in his hand sloshing as he held up his hands in a sign of peace. "Let's go for a walk." He stood and held out his hand to his girlfriend. He walked out, taking the bottle with him.

"That was really low of you," Emir snapped when they were out of earshot. "You know about her sister."

I flushed with embarrassment. Her sister sold herself to the UN soldiers under the cover of night. Their mother was widowed with six children to raise, and as the eldest, she took on the responsibility of earning cigarettes that she traded for food with the only thing she had to sell.

Emir and Kamila went to sit on the stairs in front of the house.

Ramo and I were left by ourselves. "You really didn't want to share the makeup," he said.

I laughed hysterically, his dry tone setting me off. We sat in silence for a minute.

"When did I become such a mean girl? All she wanted was to feel special." I clutched the handbag tighter against me. All these small luxuries meant so much when I sneaked them out of my mother's bedroom, dreaming of my big night out, and now I had tainted them with my own hand.

"This is what happens in a war. Survival turns us into savages," Ramo said wryly.

There was truth in what he was saying. We were all becoming harder and embittered under the toll of deprivation.

"I'm going to try to be kinder to everyone. I don't want to be this mean person."

Ramo smiled gently. "Okay."

He'd felt the sharp edge of my temper too many times to be fooled by my false promises.

"I am," I said, leaning towards him.

He kissed my nose. "I like you exactly the way you are."

We heard cheering outside. Everyone returned, followed by Nedjad.

"Look who's joining the party," Emir said, clapping Nedjad on the back.

"Where is Belma?" I asked.

"The baby is sick," Nedjad said, taking a sip of *rakija*.

"So you left her at home by herself with the baby," I snapped.

Nedjad looked down at the floor.

"Stop picking on my brother." Bilal hugged him. "He deserves a night out."

"Belma deserves a night out more. He should stay home and let her come," I snapped. "It's my birthday."

"So much for being kinder," Ramo muttered into my ear.

I glared at him, and he put his hands up in surrender.

"No, she's right." Nedjad stepped back to the door. "I'm not supposed to stay. Belma wanted me to tell Seka that she couldn't come and then go back home."

"Tell her I'll come and see her tomorrow," I told Nedjad.

He took one last sip of *rakija* and left.

"You're quite a ray of sunshine," Bilal said.

"I'm loyal to my friends, first, last and always." I glared at him.

"I'm not going to argue with you tonight, Torlak. Only because it's your birthday." Bilal stepped away.

"Good." I straightened my shoulders. "Enisa, I'm sorry," I said to Bilal's girlfriend. "Your eyes look beautiful. Would you help me put on eyeshadow?" I handed her the compact.

Enisa looked at me with surprise. "Yes, I will." She smiled and approached, dabbing her finger in the blue eyeshadow and then smoothing it onto my eyelid.

I looked in the mirror afterwards, and the blue sparkled, making my brown eyes stand out. "Thank you."

We headed out, all of us holding hands as we walked to the cinema and lined up.

Ramo and I each held our two cigarettes to pay the entry fee for the cinema. Ahead of us, people were paying for entrance with flour or other food. We finally moved to the front of the line and Ramo handed over the cigarettes. We walked into the cinema. Rows of mismatched chairs faced the wall cabinet that contained the television and video recorder.

Amid the chairs was a couch and armchair, re-arranged into rows too, extra plush seating for the patrons. They squashed the chairs in to fit maximum capacity, leaving a small path next to the wall for patrons to walk to the chairs. They didn't have to worry about any of the patrons being too large to make their way down the narrow path. With the war diet we were all skin and bones and had no trouble slithering to our seats.

To our right was a wooden wheel about three feet in diameter that was connected by a belt to a pulley and a generator. Members of the family took turns spinning the wheel by hand to power the VCR and the television set until someone wandered in with no cigarettes to pay for entry and instead bartered their entrance fee to spin the wheel.

Even though the 'cinema' was a former living room in a residential house, it still felt special. After the Safe Zone resolution was passed, Srebrenicians started thinking past day-to-day survival and used their ingenuity to provide some normality. The residents of Srebrenica built many power plants, typically using small motors to operate mill wheels, and placed them in the Red River to generate electricity.

Ramo and I nodded to a few acquaintances, but I didn't want to talk to anyone and spoil this moment. This was our special night out to celebrate.

"Have you seen this movie before?" We were watching *Three Days of Condor*. All I knew about it was that Robert Redford was in it.

Ramo shook his head. "I love Robert Redford."

"Me too." I squinted as I looked at his face. "You know, you look a little like Robert Redford. Your eyes are so blue, and your hair is the same shade of blonde."

Ramo blushed and turned his head away. I cupped his face and leaned in to kiss his reddened cheek. He turned at the last minute, and my lips landed on his. I closed my eyes and lost myself in the moment. I was like a regular girl in a pretty dress on a date with a handsome boy.

We broke our kiss, and the cinema filled up. The lights turned off, and one of the sons from the family pressed play on the VCR. The VRC whirred on, and the screen lit up. Everyone clapped as the screen filled up with colour. I felt a grin split my face as the action on the screen washed over me.

During the movie, we heard a commotion. One of the cinema owner's sons ran out of the house, swearing. I looked through the plastic of the window and saw a hole. A few minutes later, the son returned. Someone attempted to drill a hole through the plastic so they could see the movie without paying.

Afterwards, we walked out hand in hand. I was on a high. For a few hours, I forgot about where I was or who I was. We walked through the park and found a spot in a darkened corner where we could hear others in the darkness.

"I have something for your birthday," Ramo said, shyly. He reached into his pocket and took out a rose-coloured ring with an infinity swirl at the top made from copper wire. "I made it myself. Infinity, because our love will last an infinity," Ramo said as he slipped the ring on my finger.

Now I knew what he'd been doing for the past few weeks in the basement by himself.

"Seka, I know we said we would wait to get married," Ramo said, his cheeks flushing. "But we don't know how long this wretched war will end, and I want us to begin our lives together. Now that you're eighteen, your parents can't interfere in our relationship. Will you marry me?"

Tears seeped from my eyes as I nodded jerkily. "Yes, yes," I said.

He handed me a larger ring that was from silver wire. I cried as I placed his ring on his finger. We held hands, and I watched the two rings side by side, a symbol of our love and commitment.

"The war will end, and we'll have a proper life." I placed my arms on his shoulders.

"We'll go to Australia and start again away from this madness." He placed his hands on my waist, and we swayed together.

"I'll go to university and become a veterinarian," I said dreamily, imagining our life together.

"And I'll be a carpenter. I'll build you a beautiful house."

"And give me babies," I said and laughed.

"We'll have a little Dževahir," Ramo said, referring to the masculine version of my first name.

"Please no. I hate it. His name won't be Dževahir. Although if it's a girl, we should call her Rama," I said.

Ramo scrunched up his nose. "We can do better than that. Anyway, we should think of an international name. Something that would make it easier for our child in Australia."

"Yes, an international name. Aida is international, or Azra."

"Adnan and Amir," I added.

"So we're stuck on names beginning with A?" Ramo asked, holding my hand in his.

"No, we're just going to begin with A and work our way down."

"Good idea. Tomorrow we have to propose B names."

"You've got it."

This was how we spent our days, dreaming of a better life away from Srebrenica and all the death we saw.

"Nothing can tear us apart."

"Yes, nothing," I said, but in my head, the sentence kept finishing itself. Nothing but death, and death was too close in a war. Ramo must have been thinking the same thing because his arms tightened around me.

"Not even that. Not even death will come between us," he whispered in my ear.

My skin broke out in goose pimples, and I shivered.

"Are you cold? We should get home," Ramo said, misunderstanding the source of my goose pimples.

13-Deprivation

May 1995

"Are you sure this is a good idea?" I whispered to Kamila as she unlocked her front door.

"Yes, absolutely." She opened her door and yanked me in. "No one is going to be home this afternoon, and we can finally have the house to ourselves." She briskly walked to the backdoor and opened it. Ramo and Emir were waiting, looking around nervously.

Kamila had suggested that we use her house for some much needed privacy as couples while her parents and brother were working, and had sent the boys to the backdoor so that neighbours wouldn't see them entering.

She took Emir's hand and walked towards the stairs. "We're going to my room," she said, jauntily over her shoulder. "You can have the downstairs."

Ramo gingerly walked through the hallway and into the living room, admiring the antique-looking furniture, the lushly wallpapered walls and marble tables. "Wow, they really do live like royalty," he said.

I nodded, not as awed by the surroundings due to my numerous forays over the years. "I don't really care." I pushed him so he sat on the couch and sat on his lap, my legs on either side of him.

This was the first time we were ever in such comfortable surroundings, without the need to constantly be alert to interruptions. I bent my head and kissed him, his hands holding me tight. Soon, passion overcame us, and he was grinding against me, and ecstasy filled my head. He undid my jeans and yanked them off, and I gasped. This was the first time we'd engaged in nudity. Usually, we had to sneak off and engage in furtive moments in my parent's house, putting our hands down each other's pants, always with one ear listening out. He yanked off his own jeans and lay between my legs. I gasped at the pleasure of the friction.

"We can't," I stammered, coming to my senses briefly. "I don't want to get pregnant."

He nodded, shifting so I was sitting on his lap. His hand went beneath my underwear in a practised motion, and after I climaxed, I returned the favour.

We sat on the sofa, half undressed, holding each other. This was the first time I was able to enjoy just lying together, and I didn't want it to end. I was drowsy and replete, almost dozing.

"We could be doing more of this if we told your father we were getting married," Ramo said, running his hands through my hair.

My drowsiness receded, and I tensed. Ever since Ramo had asked me to marry him, and I'd agreed, we'd been having this conversation. "I don't think the time is right." I stood, dragging on my pants.

"Why? We're both adults. We can do what we want."

I sighed. "Yes, but if we get married, then we'll want to have sex, and then…" I zipped up my jeans. "I am not having a baby in a war zone."

"We'll do other things so that you don't get pregnant."

I quirked an eyebrow and glanced at him. He knew as well as I did that it was hard to not cross the line now. If we were married and didn't have to worry about the consequences of pregnancy, it would be nigh impossible to restrain ourselves.

Ramo sighed, sitting up. "Would it be the worst thing in the world if you got pregnant?"

I whirled to face him. "You're not the one who would be pregnant and having all your nutrients leeched. Belma lost three teeth in her last pregnancy. Then there's the birth. Women still die giving birth. We had a woman whose placenta detached, and she bled out in the hospital and no one could do anything. And then the difficulty trying to feed her son and daughter and the toll of breastfeeding. So when you can carry the baby, give birth, and breastfeed, then it wouldn't be the worst thing in the world." I was shouting in the end, trembling with rage.

"I'm sorry. I'm sorry," Ramo stood, reaching for me.

But I whirled and stomped away. I didn't want him to touch me now. We'd been bickering for a month now, and each time my anger had built. I wanted to marry him just as much as he wanted to. I wanted to begin our life together and be able to share affection and be seen in public. But I was also aware of all the difficulties that we would face. Babo would ask us to leave my home, forge out onto our own in a shared household with other refugees. His pride would not allow his grown daughter to remain under his roof after I defied his decree not to marry. And then there was the lack of contraception and the risks with pregnancy and birth. And yet, I also dreamed about having a baby that was a replica of Ramo, a tangible reminder of our love.

After washing myself in the downstairs bathroom, I wandered through the other rooms, avoiding returning to Ramo before I calmed down. There was a closed door next to the basement, and I realised I'd never seen it open. I turned the doorknob and peered in. It was an office, a large walnut desk facing me, a matching built in shelf with cupboards on the bottom covering the wall next to it. I tiptoed inside and saw medical files on the table. This must be the doctor's office.

Before I'd realised what I was doing, my hands opened the drawers under the table, and I scanned its contents. Files, stationery. I opened the cupboard drawers and gasped as I saw boxes in there. I took out the box with eager hands, peering in, and saw the antibiotic pill bottles. I took one out, looking at the table. Sure enough, there was the dot I had placed next to the logo.

I sank back to my haunches, processing. While I'd suspected that Kamila's father was involved in the corruption, having it confirmed one hundred percent was still a shock. I thought that I would be full of glee at being right and cracking the case; instead, I was filled with devastation to know that the people I'd thought were good were secretly corrupt.

If the antibiotics were in his house, then that meant that his wife knew. All those fake statements about caring for the community, the locked padlock and ledger recording medications, were not an attempt to stamp out corruption. Instead, they were done to keep it even more disguised so that no one could discover them. Did Kamila know? I flashed back to two years ago, when my mother had her abortion and needed antibiotics. Kamila had said she was getting a coat before we left, and yet I'd seen her go into this very office. I bit my lip as I realised she hadn't been getting the antibiotics from the hospital supply room. Instead, she'd pocketed them from home and then pretended that they were in the storeroom. And ever since she'd been pretending to be my friend when she was well aware of the evil that her parents were wreaking and all the ways she was benefiting.

I quickly returned the boxes back to the cupboard and closed the doors. I hadn't truly known what I would do in this moment when I discovered the true perpetrators of the corruption. Whether I would have the courage to write the article and try and get it published, knowing how dangerous it was after Kerim's death. The rage burning through me made it easy though. Harun and Lebiba had to pay for their duplicity. They were worse than the Serbs who circled us and were attempting to wipe us off the map. At least the Serbs were upfront about their deadly agenda. Harun and Lebiba were playing the perfect Bosnian patriots, reverting back to Islam and proclaiming their faith to all and sundry, while they were exploiting and cheating their own people of lifesaving aid.

I left the office, adrenaline surging through my blood-stream.

"Seka," Ramo called from the living room.

I hesitated, wanting to go to him and tell him everything. Scream to him about Kamila's parents and everything I had discovered. I remembered Karim's death and stopped. No, I had to keep Ramo safe. I headed for the backdoor and left for home, walking briskly, drafting the article in my mind. I was going to stop them once and for all. No one knew about my investigations and my findings. Alyssa would publish my article anonymously, and the Dutch UN soldier who was our go-between wouldn't be sharing that he was smuggling letters out of the enclave, so my secret would be safe. The only thing I had to worry about was how to secretly get the article to him.

I avoided Ramo for the next few days as I drafted and re-drafted the article. He assumed I was still angry about our fight, but couldn't approach me directly with my parents around. I finished the article and placed it in an envelope, writing down Alyssa's name and address details. I walked the seven kilometres to the Potočari base where DutchBat was stationed. There were still crowds of children and some adults dotted around the gates, but not as many as I'd seen last year when I'd gotten Bram to send a letter to Aunt Paša.

Children were gathered in rows in front of the fence, and as the peacekeepers drove through, they begged for bonbons from the peacekeepers. The children were waiting for the garbage truck to leave the compound so they could jump onto the moving trucks and rifle through the bags to find something to eat, until the peacekeepers stopped and yanked them off. Once the rubbish was dumped in the field, it was a free-for-all as starving children fought each other for food.

I stalked the gate, attempting to get a soldier to approach me, but they all avidly avoided the fence. Some went as far as to yell profanities at those of us who were here. When DutchBat first arrived, boys brought chess sets they placed under the fence and they played with the peacekeepers, kept apart by the chain link fence, while the rest of the children watched with hushed wonder. One of the girls next to me explained that things changed after an incident when peacekeepers accidentally ran over a child when they were collecting bread from the town bakery and the Commander forbade interactions between children and the peacekeepers.

I spent the whole day being ignored by the peacekeepers and realised that this wasn't going to get me any closer to sending the article. I needed to find another way.

My opportunity came a few weeks later when Bilal came to hang out at the Cultural Centre, bragging about getting a job as a bouncer at the local disco. There was only one disco in town, and it was reopened soon after demilitarisation. It was near the market and operated only on Wednesdays and Saturdays. The owner was a member of one of the families that ruled the town. He used a generator unit that was run by a tractor connected to an alternator inside until late at night. Bilal bragged that anybody who was anybody went to the disco: local thugs, officers, UN soldiers on their nights off. This was it. This was my in.

"So, do you get a friend's discount?" I put my hands on Bilal's shoulder. "Friend." I waggled my eyebrows, jokingly. "Wouldn't you love the opportunity to hobnob with Srebrenica royalty?" I urged Enisa, his girlfriend.

"Please, Bilal." She approached him and leaned on her tiptoes, kissing him on the lips, suggestively.

I knew our invitation was as good as issued. Enisa wouldn't give up until she attended the disco, and Bilal wouldn't be able to resist Enisa's charms. Sure enough, a week later, Bilal arranged for us to go on his night off.

Ramo and I walked to the centre of town, holding hands as we'd made up again. We passed by other young people walking the streets. In the days before the war, it would have been scandalous for a girl to be out after dark. But with the war raging and houses packed to the rafters with people, everyone walked at night to take advantage of the clear nights and no shelling. Bilal and Enisa walked ahead. She was once again in her tight jeans and boots, wearing an even smaller t-shirt that hugged her torso. Kamila too was in a new top and jeans, while I was wearing my parachute dress again, the only new piece of clothing I owned.

When we arrived, we lined up in pairs. The bouncer at the door was tall, wide and fierce. He eyed those seeking entry and took a cruel delight in being able to turn some of the boys away, and some of the girls who were wearing tracksuit pants and threadbare clothes.

We moved up the line.

"How are you, brother?" Bilal said, clapping hands with the bouncer. "Good night?"

"Good enough," the bouncer said, looking me up and down. "Go in," the bouncer nodded to Bilal.

We handed our cigarettes for entry and stepped into the disco. I blinked as my eyes adjusted. My ears were assaulted by the loud music, and I winced. The disco was full. There were Dutch soldiers hanging around the bar, a few local officials I recognised. I watched the girls as they gyrated looking like catwalk models in their high heels and shiny dresses, shimmering lipstick and gleaming eyeshadow flashing in the neon lights. I hadn't seen women who looked like this in three years and my eyes danced back and forth.

Enisa pulled Bilal onto the dance floor. He attempted protesting, but she didn't stop. I saw Emir stand by the back wall, Kamila next to him. He drummed his fingers on his thigh, but didn't get onto the dance floor.

Ramo and I danced. At first I felt stiff, uncoordinated. It had been so long since I danced, I'd almost forgotten how. Slowly the rhythm took over and Ramo and I found our groove. I'd never seen him dance. He was beautiful in his euphoria, his golden hair streaking in the bright lights, his blue eyes lit up as the disco ball mirror shone in his face. I lost my breath watching him.

I don't know how long passed when Bilal gestured towards the bar. He leaned in closer and shouted, "Let's get a drink." He put his arm around Enisa's shoulders and led her off the dance floor and to what passed as the bar.

"A plum brandy." He placed a five-mark note on the bar.

My eyes widened at the exorbitant price.

"Do you want something?" he asked. "There's juice, which is just humanitarian aid juice diluted from powder or plum brandy?"

My mouth watered at the thought of tasting fruit juice for the first time in years. I opened my handbag and rifled through for the notes that I'd brought. "Two fruit juices, please."

The drinks came in a small glass. I handed Ramo a glass, took a sip, closed my eyes, and moaned. It was delicious. I looked at Ramo and he was smiling as he slowly sipped it.

I looked around, remembering my mission. I needed to find Alyssa's contact. I had only a name and a vague description. He had white-blonde hair and a beard. I checked all the soldiers in my vicinity. There were a few blondes, but no one that was white-blonde. I sighed, hoping this wouldn't be a wasted errand.

The mirrored ball rotated above the dance floor, lighting the dancers who heaved beneath its twinkling. Video monitors were in two corners, showing film clips that went along with the music blaring from the speakers around us.

"I love this song." I clapped my hands as *Rhythm Is A Dancer* by Snap played.

I turned to Bilal and saw he was unimpressed. "Don't you like it?" I demanded.

"I did, the first 100 times. Those are videotaped film clips and they are now permanently playing on a loop. The next song after this will be Dr Alban's *It's My Life* and then…"

I covered his mouth with my hand. "Stop. You're ruining it for me."

I took Ramo's hand, and we returned to the dance floor. I lost myself in the music, the anonymity of the darkness around us, the heaving bodies, and closed my eyes as I moved.

I gestured to Ramo that I had to go to the toilet, and we left the dance floor. Ramo followed me. When we came out, I glanced at the Dutch soldiers and my blood hummed. There was a tall man with white-blonde hair and a moustache in the middle of a scrum, all of them laughing jocularly and smiling. I glanced behind at Ramo. Now I just needed to find a way to approach him and give him the envelope unobtrusively. We returned to the dance floor, but this time, I couldn't lose myself. Instead, I constantly surveyed the soldiers, searching for my opportunity.

I saw Emir stumble towards the soldiers, Kamila attempting to tug on his arm. Ramo must have noticed my face because he turned.

Emir had reached the three Dutch soldiers and was gesticulating towards them. Ramo grabbed my hand and we walked quickly off the dance floor and towards Emir. As we passed Bilal, I pointed. He followed my gaze and quickly followed us.

"You're all cowards." Emir pointed his finger at the Dutch soldiers. "You're letting the Serbs take all the checkpoints." When the Dutch soldiers first arrived in the enclave, they demilitarised the Bosnian army and took over the checkpoints on the pointy peaks above town. In the past few days, they'd surrendered them one by one as Serb soldiers advanced and took them prisoners, outraging the Bosnian military who said we were being left defenceless to attack.

"I'm sorry. My brother is drunk," I said in English to the Dutch soldiers, forcing a smile.

"Tell him we're only here to save his thankless arse. Why isn't he fighting?" a Dutch soldier with a black beard said.

"Emir, you need to calm down." I stood in front of Emir, holding him back and not translating the Dutch soldier's words. "We are leaving," I said, instead in English. I tugged on Emir's arm, but he wouldn't budge.

"Three hundred Dutch are worth 30,000 Muslims." Emir shouted. The presence of the Dutch contingent was tiny, and the Serbs took soldiers hostages whenever they wanted the UN to stop military attacks. And it worked.

Ramo and Bilal tugged him towards the entrance while I stepped in front, preventing the Dutch soldiers from launching at him.

We got him outside. "He's not coming back here again," the bouncer told Bilal as we walked past him.

"Okay, I got it," Bilal said. He slapped Emir on the arm as we walked down the street. "You really fucked that one up."

Emir shook him off. "I don't care. At least those cowards know what I thought of them." He stalked ahead, Kamila running to catch up with him. "Where were you?" he demanded as she reached his side. "You vanished when I confronted those cowards."

"I didn't want to be seen with you. You were embarrassing me." Kamila tugged her handbag higher on her shoulder and continued ahead of him.

"I embarrassed you!" Emir shouted, stopping in his tracks.

Kamila didn't respond and instead stalked ahead of him, her high heels clacking on the concrete road.

I was dejected. I was so close to achieving my objective, and now my brother had ruined my chances.

"Are you all right?" Ramo asked as he put his arm around my shoulders.

"Yeah, just disappointed," I told him, being honest for once.

"Me too." He kissed the top of my head. "It was nice to be like normal teenagers for once."

I wiped the tears that were seeping from my eyes.

"Hey, we can still go back, maybe. This time without your brother," Ramo said. "We'll just have to wait a while for the dust to settle."

I nodded, forcing a smile, letting him think that I was dejected because of the disco, and not the missed opportunity.

Two days later I was at the hospital, doing my latest shift translating during a live amputation, and had retreated to the back of the hospital for some much needed fresh air. I heard Kamila's voice as she approached, and ducked behind some bushes. Since I found out about her father's dark deeds it was difficult being around her, as my anger bubbled under the surface, and so I did my best to avoid her. I was thankful she and my brother had broken up, and this made it all easier.

"I can't believe you scored such a sweet gig working in the Dutch command cafeteria," Vahida said.

I saw plumes of smoke drifting over the hedge and realised they were having a smoke. I'd have to wait until they finished and returned to the hospital before leaving. I settled in more comfortably.

"It's because of Mum. She knew how desperate I was to get the chance to practice my English. This way I could be more helpful by translating more at the hospital." Kamila's voice was full of pride.

I dug my nails into my palms, fighting back my anger. Of course, Kamila got the plum assignment of working in the Dutch complex. I couldn't believe I was so naive in believing her family weren't involved in the corruption.

"I wish I could get that job. Working in the hospital is spirit-breaking, but I'm a nurse, so it's my lot in life."

They changed the topic of conversation, with Kamila now complaining about how much she missed Emir, and she hoped he would realise his error and apologise.

"If he just says sorry, I'll forgive him immediately. I miss him so much," she sighed.

They butted out their cigarettes, and their footsteps retreated, but I remained in my hiding spot, formulating another plan.

I returned to the hospital and saw Kamila at the nurse's station. She would be leaving soon, so I briskly headed down the corridor, the fading summer light from the window behind casting long shadows that danced along the walls. I ducked into a doorway, the coolness of the metal door against my palm a sharp contrast to the warmth of the hallway.

My plan was dependent on me crying and conveying despair; the only issue was that after so many years of deprivation and loss, I didn't have any more tears left. Kamila was approaching, and my eyes were dry as a bone. In desperation, I threw my body into the protruding door jam, the metal slamming into my back with a thud, making me gasp with pain. Tears began immediately and quickly became earnest as the pain spread. By the time Kamila reached me five minutes later, I was a snot-covered mess.

"Are you okay?" Kamila asked, stopping at my side.

"I can't take it anymore," I gasped out between sobs, struggling to breathe from the very real pain radiating through my back. "I've been here for two years, and it's killing me seeing all this pain and suffering."

Kamila's face wreathed with concern, and she reached out an arm, putting it around my shoulders. I turned away, pretending it was because I didn't want her to see me cry, when I actually had to hide my revulsion and anger. I wanted to punch her in the face, instead I continued my pitiful act. "I was hoping that with you and Emir getting serious and you becoming my sister-in-law, I could ask for a favour."

"Sister-in-law?" Kamila asked, with surprise.

"I wasn't supposed to say," I wailed, covering my mouth.

"Emir was going to propose!" she exclaimed, her eyes wide.

"It's a surprise. He's going to kill me if he finds out I ruined it. Please, you can't tell him." I gripped her arm, begging.

"Of course, of course. I won't say anything."

"Anyway, I was hoping I could ask you for a favour to do another job and get away from all this blood and bile before I have a breakdown." I paused, gauging the effectiveness of my performance. Kamila's lips were tilted in a smile. This was not the reaction I wanted.

"And now you and Emir had a fight, and his pride is stopping him from apologising and making up, and the two of you moving on with your lives." I embellished. The truth was that Emir didn't seem to be cut up at all about his break up with Kamila and hadn't mentioned her once, but that wasn't going to do me any favours.

"He won't apologise," Kamila's voice was full of consternation.

"I mean, he will, and I wanted to nudge him that way. I'd love for us to be real sisters," I gushed, wiping my face. "But it takes him so long to come off his high horse, and I just can't talk to him the way I'm feeling now."

I stared at the floor, continuing to sob, hoping that I'd given her enough clues to connect the dots.

"I can speak to my mother, see if you can join me on the detail to work in the UN Headquarters kitchen," Kamila said, thoughtfully.

"Really," I exclaimed, my joy real this time.

"Of course."

"And I'll talk to my brother. Try and get him to overcome his stupid male pride so that the two of you can be together, as you belong." I hugged her, forcing myself to hold on. "I'm going to go right now." I hurried away, before I gave away my true feelings.

Two days later I sat on the back of the lorry as it drove past the steel fence and the concrete cinder block outside the base proclaiming it HQ DutchBat, stopping in front of the former battery factory that now housed the UN soldiers. The factory was made of white walls which were a mosaic of windows and white panelling, the backdrop of the hills behind it making the headquarters look like a faded postcard. Houses dotted the hill behind the factory with cultivated fields harvested by those who still had the luxury of their own houses with the protection of the UN at the foot of the hills.

I entered the Potočari factory, looking around me with wide eyes. For the past three years since the war began, I was on the outside, looking in. One of the spectators hanging around at the fence when the UN troops first arrived. Now I was entering this forbidden territory, and even though I was here to work in the kitchen, it was as if I was going on a magical blind date.

I lifted my hand to push my hair behind my ear, only to ruffle my now short hair self-consciously. I only became aware of this nervous gesture since cutting off my long hair. I was told this was a requirement to ensure hygiene. An obvious precaution considering the proliferation of head lice and skin conditions in the enclave because of the lack of water. When I'd looked at myself in the mirror to see my face transformed into suddenly more masculine lines, I'd wondered whether this was an effort to make the women less attractive. Fraternisation between women and the UN soldiers was strictly forbidden. The last group of women were supposed to do the usual stint of six months, but they all lost their jobs because they took photos with the soldiers.

Kamila sat across from me, looking dejected. Her long, lustrous blonde hair was now shorn off, accentuating her prominent, sticky-out ears and making her nose appear more pointed. I was grateful I'd mediated a makeup between her and Emir before her haircut. I'd never realised my powers of persuasion and manipulation until I'd tried them on my brother and Kamila. He'd crumpled like a tissue when I told him she was in despair about their breakup and that the only reason she'd reacted the way she did to the fight was because she'd been afraid that her parents would hear of them dating and break them up.

Zaim, the interpreter, led us to the toilet block. "Have a shower here before you enter the compound and dress in the clothes you have been provided with." He pointed to the shirt and pants hanging on the hooks in the bathroom. "When you finish your shift, you will return here, have another shower and change back into your clothes."

Zaim left, and the women began taking off their clothes. There were three cubicles for ten of us, so I waited my turn, averting my eyes.

"God, an actual shower," a woman with dark hair said, haphazardly throwing her underwear onto the seat beside me. "I haven't had a shower in three years. Not since the Chetniks chased us out of our houses and to Srebrenica."

"I've had to use a bucket of water for the past six months," another woman said.

Since the water plant was destroyed, access to water was uncertain. The Dutch and UN had repaired it, but because the water went through the main pipes, and some of those pipes were destroyed, some houses had access to water, while others didn't.

After our shower women in groups of five were allocated duties: the laundry group, the cleaning group, and the kitchen group. I was among the last to leave, and Zaim took me and five others to the kitchen.

"Do you know any English?" Zaim asked. All of the women shook their heads.

"A little," I said in English, earning a look of respect from Zaim. "I hope I can practice with you."

He smiled.

"Me too," Kamila said, stepping in beside us.

I pressed my lips together, reminding myself that my plan depended on me keeping Kamila on side, at least until I saw Alyssa's contact and gave him the envelope with the article.

We entered the kitchen and Zaim pointed out the hairnets which we put on. I washed dishes while Kamila dried.

A Captain in an apron gave Zaim instructions about our duties. Zaim introduced him as Captain Luuk Van Dijk. Luuk mixed batter, and as I washed the dinner dishes, I snuck looks at the captain's wizardry with a frying pan as he made the most beautiful fluffy pancakes. My stomach cramped with hunger, and my mouth filled with saliva as he instructed one of the women to assist him by putting toppings on the pancakes, spreading thick slathers of strawberry, apricot and plum jam, the jam glistening and tantalising with its sweet aroma.

The woman helping was biting her lip, probably fighting the urge to stuff one of the jam-filled pancakes into her mouth. Another woman kept carrying the plates of pancakes out, and we heard the soldiers in the dining area laughing and talking as they ate.

The dining room became quieter and emptied as soldiers finished eating. I peered through the door and saw smears of jam and pieces of pancake left on the plates. I couldn't wait to collect the plates and roll my fingers in the tiny bits of jam.

Luuk made one more large plate of pancakes. "You eat." He pointed to all of the women and mimed eating by putting his hand to his mouth. He called Zaim and asked him to take a plate to the women in the laundry and those cleaning.

I hesitated, eyeing the pancakes. The woman opposite me slowly picked up a pancake and lifted it to her mouth, as if she were waiting for Luuk to shout at her to stop. Luuk nodded encouragingly. "Eat, eat," he said, miming even more.

The woman bit into the pancake and closed her eyes, letting out a moan.

"Good, good?" Luuk asked, smiling.

"Da." She nodded as she stuffed it in her mouth.

The rest of us quickly took a pancake. I moaned as I ate, the tartness of jam making my taste buds dance with pleasure.

Kamila ate daintily, as if this was her everyday fare, and I had to turn away so I couldn't see her.

"I want to take some home to my children," a dark-haired woman said.

I was determined to do the same. Leave at least half a pancake to take home to Ramo.

Zaim shook his head. "You can't take any food home. You will be searched, and if they find food, you will lose your job."

The woman's face fell. My cheeriness dissipated. The pancakes that went down so sweetly now seemed so much heavier in my stomach, sloshing around with my guilt.

"At least we can give them our rations to eat," I said, thinking aloud. I'd had my meal for the day and wouldn't eat again at home so my portion could be shared by everyone else.

The woman nodded. "Yes, that's something." She wiped a tear.

As we collected the dishes in the mess hall and brought them to the kitchen, we ate as many leftover morsels as we could, scooping up every tiny bit of jam. Soon, my stomach was hurting, and I couldn't eat anymore.

Our shift finished at three pm, and we showered before leaving on the lorry.

"I saw the soldier throwing the leftover food behind the factory for the birds," one of the women to my left said, her voice shrill. "They scattered it onto the ground, and the birds came to get it. They'd rather feed the animals than let us take food home."

I sunk hunched deeper into the seat, hugging my bag to my chest as the lorry engine turned on and we trundled slowly down the driveway.

At the gate, the soldiers brusquely demanded all of our bags and searched them thoroughly. A soldier found a banana in a woman's bag.

"Please, it is for my children," she begged. The soldier threw it on the ground and squashed it under his foot.

Zaim translated as the soldier spoke. "You have contravened the UN rules, and your services will no longer be required."

"Please, please, I need to work. I need to work for my children," the woman cried, gaping sobs as she begged.

Zaim shook his head. The soldier finished searching all the bags and gave the driver the signal to continue. We drove the seven kilometres back to the town in silence. It was a ten-minute drive, and yet the woman's sobs and entreaties made the drive so much longer and barely tolerable.

Ramo was waiting for me at the bus station, and I jumped off the lorry with relief, barely saying goodbye to my workmates. The woman who was fired was the last to disembark and slowly trudged back home, her shoulders bowed from defeat.

"See you tomorrow," Kamila jauntily said, unaffected by the woman's tribulations.

I waved, biting back my words.

"How did it go?" Ramo asked as we walked towards home.

I burst into tears when we were away from the women. Ramo hugged me, holding me tight against his chest as I sobbed. I told him what happened between shuddering sobs.

"Why are they so heartless?" I demanded, leaning back to look at Ramo.

"Maybe they're trying to ensure fairness. So many people don't have food and if the workers brought food home to their families, well, there would be riots."

I knew there was truth to what Ramo was saying. I'd spent the day fearing telling him and my family the food I ate while they were going hungry. I'd thought about sneaking food out but resisted because I had time on my side. For the woman, it would have been unbearable having small children clamouring for food, stomachs distended and aching with hunger. When my cousins were with us, they'd plaintively begged, and it had broken my heart.

"So what were the pancakes like?" Ramo asked.

"Stop, you don't want to hear." I pulled away from his embrace.

"Considering it's the closest I'll come to something like that, I want details."

"Are you sure?"

Ramo nodded.

I used all my descriptive words to try and bring to life the smell and taste of the jam, the softness of the pancakes, the fullness I felt.

"I'm so happy for you," Ramo said. "At least you're getting food and pay and a shower." He bent and smelled my hair. "Delicious."

Working at the UN gave me the chance to develop my English-speaking skills, a skill that was a step towards a better future. As soon as the war was over, Ramo and I were emigrating to Australia and leaving this blood-soaked land behind, but first, I needed to bring the corrupt bastards to justice.

14-Cleaving

11 July 1995

Ramo walked with me to the bus stop in the morning. The past few weeks, the shelling had intensified, and we struggled to be away from each other. It was July, mid-summer, and it was already hot.

Someone called Ramo's name behind us. I turned and saw it was Bilal. He waved us over.

"Have you heard," Bilal demanded when we were within hearing distance as he puffed on a cigarette.

"Heard what?" Ramo asked.

"Naser is gone."

"What? He's dead?" I said. Naser Orić was like a God. He couldn't be dead.

"No, he left town," Bilal said.

Ramo and I looked at each other in confusion. Left town. It was Naser's guerrilla tactics that kept the Serb forces at bay.

"Why?" Ramo asked.

"He's a rat leaving a sinking ship." Bilal looked at the hills around us.

Kamila arrived, and Bilal asked her if she knew anything more. She frowned and shook her head.

"Come on, your parents would know more," Bilal pushed.

"If they do, they're not telling me," she snapped.

The UN jeep wound down the road towards us.

"Should I return home?" I asked Ramo. Was it really a good idea to be separated at this time? I'd been trying to speak to the Dutch soldier for the past month, but he had been stationed at a checkpoint and hadn't returned to base.

"No, go. We have to behave like normal," Ramo forced a smile. I could see how much it was costing him to remain calm. "Maybe you can find out more information at the compound?"

I wanted to argue with Ramo, but he was right. My secret knowledge of English gave me the opportunity to understand a lot more of what was going on.

I got in the jeep and waved at Ramo as we drove off quickly. When I saw Zaim at the compound, I asked him if he knew anything about Naser leaving.

Zaim jerked back with surprise. "Naser is gone?"

He found me later that morning to tell me that orders were issued by the Bosnian Army for Naser to go to Sarajevo.

The UN soldiers avoided looking or talking to us. A few days ago, a Dutch soldier was killed when the Dutch were abandoning another lookout post, and some Bosnian farmers set up a roadblock. As the armoured personnel carrier bypassed their roadblock to continue, the farmer threw a hand grenade, and the shrapnel killed Van Renssen, who died in his friend's arms. Ever since, the Dutch soldiers were saying they wouldn't risk their life for any Muslim pigs.

In the past few months, the Dutch soldiers had withered as the Serbs stopped provisions from entering the enclave. Their husky physiques shrivelled, and their full-blooded cheeks turned pale and soon the only thing distinguishing them from the Bosnian residents was their green fatigues that now hung on their lanky frames.

Food became scarce in the kitchen, with no fresh produce and only dry provisions available. The workers suffered, not getting as much food, but we were used to surviving on meagre rations. The Dutch soldiers had never suffered such deprivation, and they were short-tempered and outraged.

Rumours swirled as fear built. Some claimed that Sarajevo headquarters wanted to swap Srebrenica for Sarajevo suburbs. Everyone was on edge and fearful. Without Naser here, it was like we were sitting ducks. He was our great hope. The one who kept the Serbs in check because of the fear he engendered.

I left the kitchen to go to the toilet, peering out at the courtyard. I saw a blonde-haired UN soldier, and waited with bated breath. Yes, it was him, Bart Muis. I ran heedlessly into the courtyard, approaching him.

"Excuse me. Can I speak to you?" I asked him.

He turned to look at me, his blue eyes narrowed.

"I'm a friend of Alyssa's." His suspicion faded as he recognised her name. "Can we speak privately?"

He nodded and ushered me to the side.

"Can you get this letter to her?" I took the envelope that I'd been carrying on me for months and handed it to him.

"We're not doing favours for any Muslim pigs," a large soldier with a handlebar moustache said, slapping my hand, and the envelope fluttered to the ground.

I gasped in shock, my hand smarting.

"Stay out of it." Bart shifted in front of me protectively, pushing the other soldier away.

I bent and picked up the letter.

"Seka, are you okay?" Kamila asked to my left.

I gasped, flinching away from her, hiding the letter behind my back as I realised she could see the address.

"Yes, yes."

"Back to duty soldiers," Captain Luuk Van Dijk barked out. Bart and Handlebar Moustache instantly returned to attention.

"We'd better return to the kitchen," Kamila tugged on my arm, pulling me away.

I quickly tucked the envelope back into the pouch around my waist, hiding it from her prying eyes.

"What was that about?" she asked when we were in the kitchen and out of earshot from the soldiers.

"I was asking him to send a letter to my aunt," I lied.

"Probably not a good idea to ask favours now," Kamila said dryly.

I murmured my agreement, frustration building at my missed chance. I attempted another toilet break and searched for Officer Muis, but no luck.

Our shift finished, and we huddled on the side of the building, waiting for the shelling to ease before the Dutch drove us home. We used to joke about our Unsafe Haven as we waited, but the time for levity was long past. I kept glancing around, searching for Muis, but no luck.

As we drove from Potočari, the streets were filling with residents from nearby villages walking towards Srebrenica, carrying bundles of food and clothes. The Dutch driver slowed down to drive around them.

"Why are you leaving your homes?" I asked one of the women as we passed.

"The southern frontline has fallen."

I covered my mouth with my hand. The Serbs were invading. Not even the Dutch contingent was keeping them at bay. The jeep accelerated, and the woman fell behind us.

I passed the post office. It was teeming with chaos and activity. I peered inside and saw the Dutch Commander talking to the Bosnian Commander. The Dutch Commander wanted the Bosnians to take back the rocket launchers and the tanks at the Vezionica factory that were surrendered in 1993.

When I returned home, I told my father and asked him why they would do that.

"So that they can announce that we're not a Safe Zone under their protection anymore. They want to leave us to fight a caged fight with the Serbs."

Either the UN didn't want to protect us, or they couldn't.

As I walked home, the dusty streets echoed with the distant sounds of explosions to the south. A boy of about eight years old, clad in frayed tracksuit pants and a top, approached me. "Are you Seka Torlak?" he asked.

I nodded, and he handed me a note before vanishing into the bustling crowd. I opened the note and gasped with relief. *"Meet me at the Cultural Centre, Bart Muis."*

We couldn't be seen together, as UN soldiers and citizens were not supposed to be fraternising. Today, the Cultural Centre would be abandoned due to the shelling.

I changed direction and walked towards the town centre. Bilal saw me and nodded. "Where are you going?"

"To meet a friend at the Cultural Centre," I told him.

"This is not the time for socialising, Torlak," he said, nervously glancing at the hills above us.

"It's an emergency," I rushed away before he could inquire further. The centre door was open when I arrived, and I entered. "Officer Muis," I called out, my voice echoing back at me.

A man appeared from the backroom. Expecting to see the UN soldier's blonde hair, I was struck dumb by the tall, brown-haired man. It took me a moment to recognise Kamila's brother, Kinan.

"What are you doing here?" I asked him, confused.

"He's here to help me," Kamila's voice came from behind me. I whirled to see her glaring at me. "You see, I overheard some UN soldiers today talking about one of the drudges from the cafeteria trying to send a letter to an Australian journalist."

My stomach dropped, and I tensed. I looked behind me in terror and saw Kinan approaching me slowly.

"And it didn't take long for me to figure out who that was," Kamila said, walking towards me slowly. My chest constricted, and it was getting hard to breathe.

"So what are you writing about?" Kamila demanded, looking at me coldly.

Kinan reached me, and grabbed my shoulders in his large hands.

"You know what I'm writing about, you viper. About you and your parasite family ripping off the town and sending innocent people to their deaths out of greed," I struggled in

Kinan's arms, but he was too strong, and I stopped, wincing in pain.

"I'll have you know my parasitic family has done a lot of good for this town. My father has saved countless lives, and my mother has been working herself to the bone trying to keep everyone in this town from descending into chaos and anarchy."

"And all the while, you've been benefiting from it," I chided back.

"And who helped you when your mother needed antibiotics? You weren't on your high horse then, were you?" Kamila hissed, her breath on my face.

"If you weren't stealing the antibiotics, then she would have been fine. They would have been available at the hospital for those who needed them," I shouted, my voice hoarse with rage.

"You're so naive," Kamila's lips quirked into a smile that didn't reach her eyes. "You think anyone here wouldn't have done the same. At least my parents ensured some fairness."

She reached for my top and lifted it up, revealing my home-made pouch that I carried belongings in. Her hands reached, and I struggled even more, angry that she was going to win.

"I can just write another article," I hissed.

"I know." Kamila looked at me with pity. She stopped opening my pouch and took out a syringe and bottle from her pocket.

"What are you going to do?" I asked, my voice widening, my struggle even more desperate.

"What needs to be done." Kamila inserted the syringe into the bottle and pulled out the plunger, filling it with clear liquid.

I saw the label and realised it was insulin. If she injected me as a non-diabetic with that dose of insulin, it would be fatal.

The front door to the Cultural Centre slammed open, and Ramo appeared, his gaze taking in the scene quickly. His gaze narrowed with rage as he saw Kinan with his hands holding me. He headed towards me. Kinan pushed me away and headed for Ramo, his hands fisted.

I punched Kamila in the stomach and snatched the syringe from her. She dropped to her knees, and I yanked her hair, pulling her head back as I held the syringe against her neck. "Kinan," I called his name.

He glanced at me and stopped in his place.

"You touch him, and I'll plunge this into her."

I yanked Kamila to her feet and dragged her backward, making her stand in front of me. "Let's go," I told Ramo when I'd reached his side. We paced backward towards the door, Kamila panting shallowly as she matched my stride, Kinan's panicked gaze staring at the syringe.

When we reached the door, I pushed Kamila forward, and she fell. Ramo closed the door, and we ran. I dropped the syringe in the street as we ran away from them, not stopping until we'd reached home.

"What was that?" Ramo demanded when we were sure they weren't following us.

I quickly gave him an overview as I bent over, trying to catch my breath.

"How could you risk your life like that?" he demanded.

"Because it matters. Because I'm sick of them getting away with it." I waved my hands in frustration.

Ramo's jaw clenched as he gritted his teeth and glared at me. A shell exploded nearby, making the ground tremble. Ramo and I glanced at where the plume of smoke was blowing and realised the Serbs had changed direction and were aiming closer to town. "And you picked today for your last stand?" he asked in disbelief.

The whole situation struck me as absurd, and I burst into laughter. Ramo stared at me in shock, and my laughter became even more uncontrolled, descending into hysteria quickly.

Ramo hugged me, holding me tightly. "What are we doing to do?"

Another shell exploded, making the ground tremble. The street was filled with people flowing north like a rushing river. Some were carrying duffel bags, suitcases, and rucksacks. There were cattle and sheep interspersed between the people. Those from neighbouring villages who'd managed to keep their farms during the war were now fleeing.

"Where are you running?" Ramo shouted at the crowd.

"Potočari," one of the men shouted back.

"Why are they going to Potočari?" I asked.

"They must think that the UN soldiers will protect them." Ramo hugged my shoulders.

"Well they're wrong. They can barely save themselves," I said. "But don't tell anyone. We don't want to cause a panic when no one can leave."

A shell detonated into the crowd, and dirt flew in the air. Ramo hugged me as he pulled me to the ground. Screams filled the air. After a few minutes, we got up. There were a few people helping to carry the wounded, but the stream of humanity was uninterrupted and now even more frenzied.

We ran into the house and told my family about everyone running towards the UN base.

"We should go too," Mama said.

"Why? The Dutch are toothless tigers. They're not going to do anything against Ratko Mladić and his troops." My father lit another cigarette, his hands shaking. He handed a cigarette to Emir, who took a puff.

"At least the UN soldiers are witnesses. That might stop the Serbs from shelling near them," Mama argued.

My father didn't respond.

"It's settled then. Let's go," Mama said.

We headed upstairs. "Should we take something with us?" I asked.

"Yes, get water and some flour. We might have to stay there overnight until the UN negotiates for a ceasefire, and then we'll come back home," Mama said.

I got a rucksack, filled a bottle of water, and threw in the little bit of flour we had left. I hurried towards the front door and then stopped, hearing Zora's voice in my head. *Promise you won't ever leave it behind.* I groaned with frustration and ran upstairs. "I'll be just a moment."

I opened my bedside drawer and took Zora's notebook, using the belt she'd made to tie it around my waist. It had been mostly neglected for the past year, but I'd made a promise.

Mama went to lock the door behind us. "Don't do that," Babo said. "We don't have money to fix it if someone breaks in."

Mama nodded and left the door unlocked. We joined the crowd in the street. I held Ramo's hand tightly as the crowd jostled us, almost tearing us apart.

We'd reached the edge of the city when suddenly the crowd stopped. I peered over the shoulders ahead of me and saw that Muslim soldiers brandishing guns blocked the asphalt road towards Potočari. "Go on back. Go on back," one of them wearing a baseball cap cried out to the crowd. "This is just propaganda. Our guys won't let them enter the town."

The crowd jostled, and people shouted. "Move, let us go. The UN soldiers will protect us."

Another soldier who was wearing sunglasses tugged Baseball Cap off the road. "Let them go."

"Fuck you and your Dutch supermodels," Baseball Cap said as he moved.

My father approached Sunglasses and gestured for us to follow. "What should we do?"

Sunglasses looked us over. Noting my grandmother hunched and shaking, my grandfather sweaty and pale from attempting to carry her.

"Go to the woods where our guys are," Sunglasses said and left.

We conferred by the side of the road.

"I think we should go to the woods and stick with our soldiers. They're the ones who can save us," my father said.

Mama looked at my grandparents. Even though they were only in their sixties, the war had aged them beyond their years, and they were frail. "They can't make it to the woods. In Potočari, the UN medics will evacuate them."

"We'll go together," my father said.

"No, you take the children and go to the woods," she said, gesturing towards me and Emir. "What about you Edina?"

Ramo's mother looked between my parents, her blue eyes wide with worry and confusion.

"I'm taking my mother to the compound," Ramo said, answering for them. "She can't go to the woods."

"I'll go to the UN base with Mama," I said as my father gestured for me to go. I wasn't going to be separated from Ramo.

Babo wanted to argue, but the crowd surged around us again. He kissed my mother hurriedly on the cheek and hugged me quickly.

Another shell exploded. The crowd screamed and parted.

"Move, move," my father urged and grabbed my brother, tugging him into the woods on our left.

Mama led us to Potočari. As we trudged down the road, the whistles of mortars exploded on the crowd. The clouds of dust and debris filled my vision, the screams of pain rending the air.

I saw blonde hair in the crowd, Kamila, and gasped as I recognised Kinan's hulking shoulders over the crowd. I yanked Ramo's hand urgently, and he glanced back too. If Kamila had another syringe, this would be the perfect opportunity to deploy it. In the chaos, no one would notice another unresponsive body.

I nearly fell, Ramo yanking me upright. A beam of sunlight cut through, and I looked down. A dead man lay on the ground, his chest burst open and his intestines bursting out, I'd stepped on his hand splayed out as he lay.

Ramo looked down and saw him. "Don't look," he urged. He hugged me and attempted to shield my face.

I closed my eyes for a few steps and let Ramo lead me. I opened my eyes and saw a woman crawling on the ground beside me. I quickly looked away. We walked a few more hundred metres. A little boy of about four years old was standing on the side of the road crying, "Mama, Mama," at the top of his lungs, his face red and tear-stained.

I tugged Ramo's sleeve, attempting to show him the child, when another mortar shell hit, and we were toppled over from the force. Afterwards, my ears rang, and I stumbled back to my feet with Ramo's urging. I looked over to where the child had been, and there was nothing but a crater left.

A Dutch people-carrier drove through, and we moved out of the way. The old woman who had been crawling was now on the tray.

Mama ran up to the passenger side and banged on the window. "Please, please, help them." She pointed at my grandparents. The Dutch nodded and we quickly helped my grandparents and Ramo's mother onto the tray. Women were gathering around the tray, begging for their children to be put on.

"No, we need space for the wounded," the Dutch soldier said, attempting to pull them off.

People clambered on, and Ramo and I helped the soldiers yank them off. I was relieved when the truck continued on its way. I hoped my grandparents would make it without being crushed.

We continued walking, glancing back. Kamila's blonde hair had fallen further behind. It was easier walking now that we didn't have to carry my grandparents, and we continued creating a distance between us and our pursuers. We reached a hairpin curve that opened over the town. Among the trees on the main road, we saw the glint of metal, and a long muzzle flashed for a moment between the break in the trees. It was a tank advancing down the main road.

"Look over there." Ramo pointed south, where we could see smoke rising from the roofs of houses. "Serbs must have set fire to houses."

Mama let out a cry. "We should have taken things with us."

"We couldn't," I comforted her. "We have to focus on survival."

She nodded and wiped her eyes.

Suddenly, there was the crescendo of an approaching jet from the north. We peered up at the sky and saw the glint of a wing. The roar of the plane rolled through the valley like far-off thunder. An explosion rocked the hillside, smoke and a cloud of smoke rising from where the tank used to be.

The people around us who saw it cheered. "It's the UN. They're going to bomb the Serbs back to hell where they belong!"

We reached the base, shocked to see so many people already gathered on the grounds. After a frantic hour of searching the crowds, we found my grandparents and Ramo's mother near the headquarters. Belma and her family were nearby. She was holding her baby daughter, while Nedjad was next to her, holding their son in his arms as we looked at the madness surrounding us. The only one missing was Bilal. He was travelling to the villages to forage for food when the town fell. The soldiers said there was no more space inside the actual headquarters and had set up a cordon.

"Does this mean that only those on the other side of the fence are protected?" Edina asked.

"They'll take care of us." Mama herded us towards the battery factory, which was emptier.

Kamila and Kinan found us three hours later.

"Where are your parents, children?" Mama asked, looking behind them.

"We were supposed to go through the woods, but we got separated," Kamila glared at me viciously. "Somehow, we ended up on the street and couldn't turn back because of the crowd."

What she meant was that she and her brother chose to chase us, and then couldn't turn back and were now stuck with us in the compound.

"What do we do?" I asked Ramo in a whisper, while there was a lull in the conversation.

"We have to be on the lookout and take turns sleeping, just in case they got another needle." He held my hand in the fold of my skirt.

"Would they really risk it now?" I looked at the crowd gathered outside, the Serbs shot more shells into them, setting up dust storms and screams with each detonation.

"We can't take that chance," Ramo insisted, locking eyes with Kinan, whose gaze brimmed with seething hatred.

Throughout the day, more and more people arrived, and the din and smell grew as people took turns relieving themselves around the factory.

Night fell, and mortar shells eased, a calm filling the compound.

Kamila stood, waving madly. "Mama, Mama," she called.

I stirred from where I'd been nearly asleep, my head leaning on my bent knees. Lebiba and Harun were carrying satchels, looking weary and worried. Lebiba's face cleared when she saw her children, and they all hugged. They were too far to hear what they were saying, but from Lebiba's wild gesticulating, she was angry with Kamila. Kamila spoke and they all looked over at me. She must have told her parents what had happened. Lebiba looked unfazed. She urged them towards the gate, and they were swallowed up by the crowd.

"They're leaving," I gasped, full of relief.

"Probably going to try and join a column in the woods to get out," Ramo said bitterly.

We slept on the hard concrete floor snuggled together like puppies, hoping that by the morning the UN would have negotiated a ceasefire, and we would be safe. The night was filled with the boom of mortar shells in the distance. I wondered if our house was standing or whether it was reduced to rubble.

In the morning, there was speculation that the UN would start bombing the Serbs. The energy in the compound was lethargic and tension-filled. We were all waiting, but we didn't know for what. The silence was broken by screams of terror. The crowd parted, and Chetnik soldiers appeared and surrounded the perimeter of the fence, herding us together in the middle and away from the possibility of escape.

The Dutch General approached the Serb contingent and spoke to one of the generals. I recognised Luuk, the Dutch Captain that I'd worked with in the compound kitchen and approached him. "What's happening?" I asked.

"The Serbs want to do a search to check if there are any Bosnian soldiers in the ranks." Luuk kept his eyes on the Serbs as he talked.

"Are you going to let them?" Ramo was of an age where he could have been a soldier even though he never fought.

"The Serbs are just following the protocols of surrender. There's nothing to worry about, Seka." Luuk smiled, and I was shocked there was so much happiness and relief in his smile.

"Surrender," I repeated stupidly, thinking I had misheard him.

He turned away from me and nodded along to the Serb General's instructions about interrogating the men.

I turned around and saw Officer Muis a few metres behind me. My hands automatically reached for the pouch at my waist and the letter I'd been desperately trying to smuggle out. I touched the paper, when sanity descended. What did it matter? My hometown had fallen to the enemy. I had a home no more. The Chetnik soldiers walked menacingly into the crowd, circling a tall man while his wife and children cowered.

I turned away in horror, running back to my family to tell them what was happening. Ramo relayed the story to Nedjad. Belma clutched her son tighter to her chest as she looked around fearfully. Other people overheard, and a woman ushered her teenage sons away. The boys returned later dressed in women's clothing. I regretted I hadn't brought any clothes for Ramo to put on, although he would probably refuse me.

Hearing music, Ramo and I approached the compound. The Dutch marching band played a festive song while the Dutch soldiers, wearing olive green t-shirts, and their pants cut and rolled up into shorts, danced in a circle. The soldiers placed one hand on the shoulder of the man in front of them, another holding a beer in their hand, the blue baseball caps that symbolised the UN that we'd relied on to save us a joke. Serb soldiers watched on with smiles.

"We're going home," one of the Dutch soldiers shouted.

For the Dutch, the fall of Srebrenica was a celebration. They were now free of the responsibility to try and save us.

As we returned to my family, we walked past a graffiti-covered wall:

"No teeth.

Has moustache.

Smells like shit.

A Bosnian Girl."

After I translated to Ramo, his jaw was working as he fought his rage. "Those bastards."

"This is what the Dutch wrote," I said. "They hate us."

Later on, I saw Serb soldiers telling the Dutch soldiers to swap clothes with them. One of the Dutch soldiers argued about giving up his bulletproof vest, but the Serb soldier pushed him. The Dutch soldier took off his clothes. Now there was no way to tell who was a Serb and who was a UN soldier.

Night fell. Mama used the wood we collected and made a small fire, making two little flatbreads that we shared among the five of us. Mama kept looking out at the crowds around us, seeking my brother and father. She'd asked all the new arrivals about them, but so far there was no news about what happened with those who went into the woods.

While we were eating my stomach cramped, and I felt a familiar warmth between my legs. "Oh, no," I moaned in horror.

"What is it?" Mama asked.

"I got my period," I muttered under my breath.

Mama came with me outside. She took off her blouse and removed her singlet. "Fold this up."

I folded the singlet and inserted it into my underwear. As we walked back, I was uncomfortable, my thighs pushed apart. I prayed we could go home tomorrow so I could use my rags.

We lay down to sleep.

The Serbs walked in packs, hunting for prey. The torchlight landed on me.

"What's that?" a gruff voice demanded, and hands reached out and yanked me to my feet. Rough hands grabbed the necklace at my throat, the chain cutting into the tender skin at the back of my neck.

His face was so close to mine that I smelled *rakija* as he breathed on me, a gold tooth winking on his incisor. A large silver cross dangled among the dark hair of his chest. "You're a real patriot," Silver Cross said, as his finger rubbed against the surface of the coin that I'd converted into a necklace, caressing President Tito's profile.

I looked into his brown eyes, my back aching at the awkward way I arched towards him from the pressure of the necklace pinching my skin. I knew better than to reply. You don't provoke a beast.

"Anything good there?" another Serb asked from behind him.

"No," Silver Cross said, and dropped the coin. "Keep your coin as a reminder of your silver town."

I quickly stepped away from him, and Ramo swept me against his side.

"I think you're wrong." A torch danced over my body, moving down from my breasts to my stomach, hips and my legs.

"Oh, she's damaged goods," the second voice said, and the torch moved on, and they left me standing there, blood dripping down my legs.

Their torchlight shone next to us, and they took a young girl, who pleaded and screamed as they tore her away from the arms of her mother. Ramo hugged me as they left, and I held tightly onto him, never more relieved to have my period.

Throughout the night we heard screams of pain and terror rending the air. A few hours later, one of the girls that was taken returned, limping as she walked, her clothing torn and blood trickling down her legs.

In the morning, we woke up to anguished screams. I opened my eyes and looked above at the sawtooth factory ceiling, crisscrossed with beams. A doll hung from the walkway above us. My eyes cleared, and I realised it was the young girl who'd returned bloody. She had found a belt and hanged herself.

A Bosnian man climbed up and cut her down, her brother and father receiving her as she fell. They sat with her on the floor, her mother cradled her in her arms and cried.

Two UN soldiers with red crosses on their arms came and placed her body on a stretcher, covering her with a sheet and carried her away to be buried behind the compound.

The next day, the heat built, and the smells and sounds in the compound became unbearable. Fear became a tangible presence, lulling all of us into a catatonic state.

A man returned from the Serbs saying he was tortured all night. There were bruises and cuts all over his body. They'd used their guns to beat him. Butted out cigarettes on his skin. He couldn't sit down.

"They said they would come back tonight," the man said, his voice teary. He stared at the ground. "They made me..." He didn't finish his sentence.

As a beautiful summer day broke over the fallen town of Srebrenica, despair filled the compound. Heat rose from the bare earth, and it was like being basted alive. Mama fretted about my brother and father while attempting to care for my grandparents, who were wilting from dehydration.

The smells got stronger throughout the day. The smell of fear, of human waste, blood and sweat, merging together into an odour that burned the nostrils. The Serbs were more blatant in their attacks, while the Dutch turned away and pretended that they couldn't see anything.

Their dancing and celebrations were over. Some of them looked scared of the Serbs, and when they attempted to intervene in torture, they were pushed away. Soon the Dutch soldiers melted away into their headquarters, leaving us at the mercy of the Serbs. They were pretending if they didn't see any evil, hear any evil, then they weren't responsible for that evil.

"I would have thought that the NATO bombers would be here by now," I said to Ramo.

He didn't say anything, but his face was full of despair.

"They're not coming, are they?" I said out loud.

The next morning, we woke to another anguished scream. This time I realised it wasn't a doll, recognising the man who was tortured by his red shirt and black pants, even though his face was unrecognisable as the summer heat transformed it into a purple blob.

I didn't scream, just watched as the UN soldiers again came with a stretcher.

"He told us he couldn't take another night of torture," Mama murmured. "I thought he was going to try and run away. I didn't realise he had given up hope."

Everything took on a dreamlike state, and I floated above the compound and saw people huddled in their family groups, hunched with fear. I flew further out over the fences of the compound and saw dead men lying on the ground, their bodies seeping blood into the red earth. I floated up further and saw Srebrenica and we were a dot on the map and abandoned.

On the third day, all hope leeched out. We were limp and listless. There was hardly enough water. My grandmother was lying on the ground, panting shallowly. Her skin was grey, and she looked like she was dying. My grandfather held her hand and looked like he was already grieving her.

There was a rustle in the crowd. "It's Mladić," we heard whispered over our heads. "Ratko Mladić, the Serb Commander, is here."

I followed Ramo, and we stepped out of the factory, but the crowd was too large. Those who were closer were listening intently, and a calm settled over everyone. The message was passed on that buses would arrive soon to evacuate us to the free territory in Tuzla.

"Perhaps they have already evacuated your brother and father," Mama said.

I nodded, hoping.

Ramo and I headed to the bus together, holding hands.

"I need one hundred of you for an exchange," one of the Serb soldiers said.

A woman ahead of us was separated from her twelve-year-old son and screamed. "No, not him. Give him back!" shattering the calm.

Why did they have to take a child if they were exchanging prisoners? I looked at Ramo with fear.

"Don't worry," he whispered, gently touching my hair.

Ahead of us, a man was separated from his daughters. "Take care of your mother for me," he said as he was led away.

I looked back at Ramo. He still looked calm.

I saw a blonde-haired girl, screaming, as she held onto a tall man with brown hair. I was so exhausted that it took me a full minute to recognise Kamila, holding onto her brother as he was being dragged away.

"I'm sure we can come to an arrangement fellows," Harun said, reaching for the soldier's arm.

The soldier struck him in the stomach. "Come on, old man. You too." He yanked Harun to his feet and pushed him.

Lebiba stood on the sidelines, her face horror-struck, her hand covering her mouth as she cried.

"Mama, do something?" Kamila entreated, still holding onto her brother and being dragged on the ground.

One of the soldiers turned to strike her, then stopped, his hand mid-air. "You're a sweet treat," he said, caressing her face.

Lebiba finally emerged from her stupor, stumbling forward and yanking Kamila back behind her. Kamila continued screaming, desperate shrieks in a frenzy of fear and pain. Lebiba yanked her onto the bus.

I turned away, holding Ramo's hand tighter as we reached the doors of the bus. The Serb soldier pushed him away from the door.

"Don't worry, I'll be exchanged for another prisoner. I'll see you soon," Ramo said.

I stepped onto the stair, hesitated and looked over my shoulder. Ramo was being led away, his calm face now crumpled and crying.

Edina shouted. "No, not him. Give him back!" She fought to get through the Serb soldiers. "No, no, no!"

The soldiers yanked her away roughly and pushed her onto the bus. I helped her up and into a chair. By the time I looked back, Ramo was gone; I could only see his golden hair among the men being led away.

My grandfather was pulled away from my grandmother, and my mother helped her onto the bus.

Belma and Nedjad were separated at the bus doors. Nedjad kissed Belma and caressed the head of his son before being led away. Belma's mother walked stoically on the bus as her husband was taken away, herding her four younger children with her, while her mother-in-law collapsed onto the aisle, calling her husband and son's names. Other women helped her to a seat.

The Dutch Captain Luuk jumped on and leaned onto the rail next to the driver.

"What's going to happen?" I asked him.

"Don't worry. Our general wants to make sure that there is a UN soldier on each bus so that you safely get to the safe territory," he said in English, and I translated to the women on the bus.

The bus pulled away. Potočari fell away in the distance. We drove for hours. When we passed through Serb villages, there were crowds throwing projectiles and hurling abuse.

The bus stopped, and the bus driver opened the door. "Get out."

No one moved.

"Where are we?" Luuk asked in English.

"You have to walk to the free territory." The bus driver nodded to the hill in front of us.

I translated to Luuk. Luuk got out first, and we followed. As we walked down the road, my muscles tensed as I wondered whether this was an ambush and they would shoot us as we walked.

A soldier appeared on the hill above us, and women shrieked in fear.

"It's all right, it's all right. You're in the free territory," the soldier said.

15-Vanished

Death March-Day 1

He stood in the woods, impatiently stepping from foot to foot as the column waited for the commando unit to clear a path through a minefield at the edge of the enclave. A destroyed bus lay on the hill below him. He used it as a marker to prove to himself that they were inching along, moving a few steps, then being told to sit and wait in a meadow. The column of men and young boys stretched before him as far as he could see.

He was in the rear. A column had already left ahead of them, with Srebrenica's military and political leaders, hospital staff carrying the wounded on stretchers. As always, the pecking order in Srebrenica had to be maintained, and the important ones, those with clout, were the ones who had the full military might and horses, travelled on horseback.

Tension was building within the column; the men were impatient and beginning to mutter threats under their breath about the slow pace. They knew the Serbs were on their heels. They reached a trench and there was a bottleneck. He carefully followed in the steps of the men ahead of him—the only way to ensure he wouldn't become a victim of the minefields the Serbs had planted.

Darkness descended, and they had only moved into the hills above the enclave, looking down at the town that was now ceded to the Serbs.

He slouched against a tree, his stomach rumbling with hunger. Some men had food with them, and he watched with envy as the Director of the aid warehouse at the department store lounged on the ground nearby. The Director delicately took out a cookie and spread orange marmalade from a packet and put it in his mouth. He felt his mouth fill with saliva as he imagined the sweetness of the marmalade and the crispness of the cookie.

The Director asked someone for water, to help him swallow the cookie. An older man, wearing a blue chequered shirt, poured some water for the Director. The Director said thank you, sipped it and turned away from the older man, eating the rest of his cookies.

"Good for you," he said to the Director. "You collected enough supplies from the aid you stole at the warehouse."

The Director looked at him with unease and held his satchel tighter to him. He stared at the Director, filling his eyes with as much malevolence as he could manage. The Director stood and moved to sit closer to the Bosnian soldiers.

He and a few soldiers went into a house nearby and found some pickled goods he inhaled, his stomach sloshing with vinegar as he walked.

He returned to the column and fell asleep under a tree.

Free Territory

"I'm going Mama."

Mama didn't reply. She lay on the sponge mattress we were given, facing the tent wall. If it wasn't for her chest moving, I would have thought she was dead.

I met Belma at her tent, and we trudged through the mud between the white tents that the UN had set up at Tuzla airport. Before we arrived, the army used the airport as a base. When we arrived from Potočari a week ago, we had received hand-me-down clothes and shoes. I was wearing green nylon tracksuit pants and boots that were two sizes too big. I'd had to insert bits of fabric in the toes to keep them from being sucked off my feet.

Aeroplanes flew overhead regularly as aid trickled in to help us. We had received sponge mattresses, blankets and kitchen utensils. We had to line up for rations and cook meals with what we were given. At least we finally had the use of salt again.

Since we'd been living in the camp, I'd gotten used to the sound of the aeroplanes going overhead. It was still hard not to flinch, expecting a grenade. But we were in the free territory and away from enemy fire.

Life settled into a relatively basic routine of waking up, walking to the UN Headquarters, and checking the lists of refugees housed in refugee camps. The staff taped the lists to the corkboard on the main building, and as I used my finger to trace my way down, I noticed that most of the names were female. There were only a few male names, babies, or children that were too young to be separated from their mothers. I searched for the names of my father and brother, my grandfather, Ramo.

Edina had been collected by her daughter, who took her to Sarajevo. I had their contact details to call if Ramo returned.

"How's your Mum doing?" Belma asked. She checked the lists for her husband, brother-in-law Bilal, father-in-law Vahid, father Šerif, her brothers, and uncles.

"You saw her. She doesn't move from the tent if she doesn't have to." When we arrived to the free territory, my grandmother had been unconscious. We'd carried her from the bus to the free territory by foot, me and Luuk holding her up.

UN medics had placed her on a stretcher and taken her to Tuzla hospital. The doctors told us she was in a coma. She passed away early the next night, my mother and me by her side. We buried my grandmother in a cemetery in Tuzla. We were the only ones at the service, and after that, Mama had lain down in the tent and imitated a dead person.

We walked through Tuzla and next to the lake. The soothing sound of the wind rushed through the reeds, and I watched the calming glint of the sun on the water. I dreamed of throwing off my clothes and diving into the lake, but there were too many houses around.

We reached a cinderblock house, and Belma knocked on the door. Atifa, the Imam's wife, opened it. She was in her early twenties, her hair covered under a headscarf. Her eyebrows were dark, and she was plump, her pendulous breasts swinging as she walked in her *dimije*. Jealousy filled me. Those of us who survived in Srebrenica were skin and bones.

"He's with someone. He'll be with you in a minute." She offered us a seat in the kitchen and served us water.

The living room door opened, and she ushered a woman and her daughter out of the house, their eyes red-rimmed. She was another refugee who lived two tents up from us. She came from a family of twelve siblings, eight of them being male. All eight of her brothers and her numerous nephews and father were missing after Potočari.

"You may go in now." Atifa gestured for us to enter.

I followed Belma into the living room, and Imam Samed, a plump blonde-haired man with wispy hair that fluttered around his bald patch and wearing a green athletic suit, greeted us. Above the couch was a citation from the *Kuran* in a gold frame.

"And what is the name of your husband?" he asked Belma after we sat down.

"Nedjad Softić," Belma said softly.

Samed wrote his name and attached a number to every letter. He added the numbers together, then divided the sum first by twelve and then by a secret number. When he got to the last figure, Samed opened the *Kuran* and found a page and verse that apparently correlated to the number he had produced.

"Nedjad is tall, with brown hair and a scar on his eyebrow," Samed said.

Belma tensed with hope as she waited.

"He lived in a white-rendered house," Samed continued, staring down at the *Kuran*.

Belma nodded, tears pooling in her eyes.

"Did someone oppose the marriage?" he asked.

"My father. My father was against it."

"Nedjad is alive," Samed said with finality.

"But where is he? When will he find me?" Belma demanded.

"I can't say anymore," Semad said. "I need more information. You need to find a virgin. Someone who is not a relative, and who has blue eyes. She needs to recite the Arabic prayer El-Fatiha and sleep with a picture of Nedjad under her pillow." Semad returned the *Kuran* back to the shelf carefully and reverently. "Return in a few days and tell me what she has dreamed, and I will tell you more about Nedjad."

"Thank you, thank you." Belma blossomed with hope. She handed over half a kilo of flour that she had received from the UN rations as payment.

I looked at Semad's pot belly as he bent to receive the flour. He didn't need any more food. Belma, however, would go hungry again while she fed her son on the meagre food she had left.

"What about you, young lady?" Semad asked me.

"I have no questions," I said.

Death March-Day Two

The next day, the trek began again soon after dawn. He fell into a stupor, watching the feet of the men in front of him and following their pace. The chatter of the group quietened as they walked further and further, everyone needing to conserve their energy.

At first he thought he was hearing thunder, but the sky above him was cloudless and so blue it hurt his eyes. As the stupor cleared, he came to the realisation that it was the sound of heavy shelling. The Serbs were shooting at the column. The men behind pushed him forward in a panic, desperate to get out of the open. He surged forward and ran towards the woods, fear making him nimble. Men fell around him and he ran until he couldn't breathe anymore and the sound of gunfire was far, far behind him.

He didn't recognise any of the fields or woods around him. One man said he knew the area, had lived up the hill, and walked determinedly ahead. Lacking any better ideas, he followed.

They reached the edge of the forest. There was a small field to cross to reach the other side. He ran without realising his feet had received the command and the surrounding earth exploded with bullets, dirt and grass swirling around him. He reached the other side of the forest and fell to the ground, his strength leaving him.

"Come on, get up," a man urged him, lifting his arm.

Somehow, he found the strength to stand again and walked with those who had survived the clearing. As the sun set, the men he was with pointed and exclaimed with happiness. They had reached the front of the column where the scouts and fighters were.

He sat on the ground, his legs and feet sore, with sounds of artillery and guns on the other side of the hill. Thousands of people were sitting around with him, men, boys, and some women.

An elderly man sat beside him. He'd removed his shoes and his feet were red and sore, his blisters had broken and split, covering his soles with blood.

Bosnian fighters urged everyone to their feet. The Serbian army were attempting to lay a siege and surround them.

He offered his hand to help the elderly man stand.

"I can't make it," the old man said. "I'm going to surrender."

"Don't to do that." The Serbs were without honour. "I'll help you walk."

"Not on these feet. My journey is done, young man." The old man handed him his backpack. "Take this and go on. There's water and sugar. We thought Srebrenica was hell on earth, but we were wrong. We should have fought to the last man."

He took the backpack and watched as the old man sat straight, looking at the blue sky above him, calmly waiting for the Serbs to reach him.

He walked on, his feet sore and feeling like he was walking on glass. He focused on her face, each step getting him closer to her.

Free Territory

As we were leaving the Imam's house, I saw Kamila walking towards us. She glared at me, and I returned her stare, rage building within me.

"You go on ahead," I told Belma. "I need to speak with Kamila."

Kamila stopped, and we both waited for Belma to be out of earshot. "I gave the article to the UN officer, and he's passing it on to Alyssa," I lied.

Kamila tensed, her hands fisting together.

"I also included testimony about what you and Kinan tried doing to me." She averted her gaze. It seemed she still could feel shame about her attempted, cold-blooded murder. "If anything happens to me, Alyssa will write about it."

"Do you really think this is the time and place for such discussions?" Kamila demanded. "My father and brother are missing."

"So are mine," I said coldly. "You're no more victim than any other woman here. The only difference between us and you is that this is the first time your parasitic family is suffering the way the rest of us have."

"And you're naive if you think anyone cares what my family did during the war," she sneered. "Your Australian journalist won't write about us now that we're the victims of ethnic cleansing."

I felt like she'd punched me. She was right. I hadn't been able to give the letter to the UN officer, knowing in my heart of hearts that it didn't matter once the enclave fell. The news now was what had happened to our menfolk and what would happen to us.

"You will not get away with it," I spat out, enraged and impotent.

"I didn't get away with anything. None of us did," Kamila said coldly. She continued walking, and I watched her, stupefied, knowing that she was right.

Death March-Day Three

They walked through the night, stopping to rest along the way. He felt as if he were in a dream, walking and walking, but unable to move from his spot. Everything looked the same in the dark and the figures of the surrounding people blended into the shadows, so it seemed he was walking alone on the edge of the world.

A man behind him said they had only walked about 30 kilometres in three days. Only a third of the journey to Tuzla and the free territory.

Tears streamed down his cheeks. He didn't know how he was going to keep going. He'd been walking for three days and hadn't slept. A man behind him yelled a Serb tank was on the road.

Everyone fell to the ground and lay still as the sinister sound, like a chainsaw, grew in sound. The vibrations of the tank thrummed under his body as it rolled across the earth. Up, up, someone yelled, and they all ran across the now empty road. He heard the river before he saw it. They broke through the trees and the river Jadar was before them.

He raced down the banks and fell into the water. The current was strong, attempting to yank him away. It reached waist height and as he walked, his feet burned, the broken blisters stinging and burning from contact with the water. His boots dragged further onto the floor of the river, slapping his feet more and hurting them. He kicked off his boots and winced with each step.

When he reached the other side of the bank, the grass scraped across his skin. He looked at his soles and saw that the skin had peeled off completely. Removing his green chequered shirt, he tore it in half and used the pieces to wrap around his feet. He fell back on the ground, closing his eyes for a moment, drifting into blackness.

A man kicked him as he walked past. "Go to sleep now and you won't wake up."

He forced himself to his feet with a sigh, grimly continuing the trek to freedom.

He climbed the highest mountain and when he reached the top, a man pointed straight ahead and said that was the free territory near Tuzla. It didn't seem that far away. He held up his hand, touching the free territory in the distance. He knew she was there, waiting for him. For her sake, he had to make it.

Free Territory

When I returned to the tents, I found it in an uproar. Women were standing in the rows between the tents.

"Bilal Softić has arrived," one woman told us.

I went to my tent and roused my mother. "Please, he knows us," we demanded as we fought our way to Belma's tent, where she was living with her mother-in-law and her mother, her son and her younger siblings.

When we tore open the door, women who were naming their menfolk and holding up photos surrounded Bilal.

"Seka," Bilal said, gladly welcoming us in as his mother, Dželila, ushered out the other women. Belma's mother Aiša sat on her bed, her children gathered around her.

I hugged Bilal, taking comfort in his solid body. If Bilal was alive, then there was hope yet.

"What happened? How did you get out?" I asked.

"When I returned from the villages looking for food, Srebrenica was a ghost town. I took refuge in the forest during the day, and I scavenged for food at night. The only living things were the rats and dogs who sniffed the garbage and broke into houses. I broke into a house and had to fight off a starving dog. That's where I got this." Bilal held up his bandaged arm. "I walked to the hospital to treat the wound. The roof of the hospital was caving in one section where a mortar had struck it, making it appear abandoned and in disarray. I found supplies and returned to the woods. I realised I had to leave.

With the supplies I could gather, I made my way towards the free territory. Thankfully, I knew the way from my foraging days. It took me ten days." He looked ruefully at his feet. He had wrapped bandages around his feet. "My shoes didn't make it."

"Did you see Ramo?" I asked.

"What about Fadil and Emir?" Mama asked.

"Nedjad. Where is Nedjad?" Belma demanded, all of us clamouring at the same time.

Bilal held up his hands, hushing us. "I didn't see anyone, apart from a few men who were hiding in the woods."

"I'm sure that they are all right. You just have to have hope and pray," Dželila said. "I prayed every day, five times a day, and here he is, my treasure, my life, my Bilal." She hugged Bilal, kissing his face as if he were a two-year-old. Bilal bore her ministrations patiently. "I know Nedjad will join us soon too. He is still alive." She hugged Belma, who nodded, tears seeping down her face.

Belma told everyone that the Imam she went to see told her that Nedjad was alive. Mama listened intently as she shared the elaborate request for the virgin dream maker, her eyes blazing with hope.

"We have to believe," she said fervently.

Mama and I left their tent so Bilal could rest. The surrounding women asked about what had happened. Mama told them what Bilal had said. "He's sleeping now. Come back tomorrow and ask," Mama said.

The two of us trudged back to our tent. Mama sat on the sponge mattress and looked around for the first time as if she was awake from a nightmare.

"There is hope," she said. "There is hope that they survived."

"Maybe," I said.

She went to the communal bathroom and had a shower for the first time in a week. When she returned, she took her *abdest*, the Islamic ritual of washing herself before prayers. She prayed, and I joined her, lying prostrate as I begged to Allah to bring Ramo back to me.

When we'd arrived in the tent city, I had spent the first few days walking around in a daze, a heavy rock lodged on my chest, struggling to breathe. I had tossed and turned fitfully in the flapping tent only to dream I was under water, fighting to get to the surface, my chest getting tighter and tighter, the light above me disappearing as I sank deeper to the bottom, to wake up gasping for breath.

Until the night Aunt Adna appeared in my dream, Ramo beside her. "Don't worry, I am taking care of him."

"Remember, infinity." Ramo held up his ring.

I had woken up rubbing my finger absentmindedly, tears flowing down my face, sure it was an omen of Ramo's death.

Death March-Day Four

The column had thinned with less than a third of those who had started out. The men who arrived had wounds, their eyes filled with panic, and their clothes soaked in blood. They spoke of an ambush and massacre. The field littered with those dead.

One man with a wounded leg requested help from him. He was so tired and had little energy to carry himself along the fields and to the free territory. He looked into the stranger's blue eyes and knew that if he didn't try, the stranger was as good as dead.

He nodded and helped the stranger stand, placing his arm over his shoulder and slowly they hobbled. He saw many others helping the wounded walk. There were some on stretchers that they attempted carrying and dragging along.

As the bright sunlight lit up the sky, someone pointed to the road below where a column of men walked on the road, followed by a white UN armoured personnel carrier. A ripple of excitement that the UN soldiers were collecting wounded Bosnians to take them to safety.

A Bosnian man shouted through a megaphone towards the forests on the hills, calling to his menfolk to surrender. Shouting that they would be unharmed. He shouted through a megaphone towards the forests on the hills, assuring them that their wounds would be tended to. That they would be reunited with their womenfolk. Some men crept out of the woods close to the road and surrendered.

His feet burned and ached, his whole body trembled with fatigue. He didn't realise he'd taken a step to go downhill when a Bosnian fighter held up his binoculars and looked down. He told them the Serbs were wearing UN equipment and driving the UN truck, attempting to trick the Bosnians into surrendering. Those who surrendered had their hands tied.

He tasted the bitterness of defeat. There was no safety to be found. The Serbs seemed determined to round up every Bosnian man.

Free Territory

Mama and Belma spent the next few days scouring the tent city, searching for a blue-eyed virgin. The virgin dreamed Nedjad was walking in a forest. He came to a large field and found a pear tree that he ate from. Then a crow woke him up by pecking a fallen pear beside his head. Nedjad attempted to shoo the crow away, but other crows came to its aid, and he hurried off back to the woods, disappearing among the foliage.

"That sounds promising," Mama said. "I'll come with you to the Imam." She wrapped a scarf around her head before leaving the tent.

The Imam said that he was sure that Nedjad was alive. He'd told Mama that he saw an apparition, three men walking through a mist. Each of them wearing gold bands and searching for their wives. Then the mist lifted, and he saw they were in a wooden structure, a labour camp. He assured her and Belma that in six months or six years, a woman who would take her to him would contact them.

More and more women flocked to the Imam seeking visions and omens. As I overheard their conversations, the Imam could convince the women of his omens because he had detailed information about their physical appearance or family background. The more I listened, the more I formed a suspicion.

Death March-Day Five

Night fell and his eyes closed by themselves as he walked. Suddenly, the man who had been walking beside him for the past five hours looked at him like a stranger. "Who are you? You're a Serb," the man shouted and struck him to the ground.

He watched from the ground and at the chaos swirling around him. Bosnians attacked other Bosnians.

"There are Serbs dressed in civilian clothes. They are leading us to an ambush!" a man shouted and opened his grenade, hurling it into the crowd of Bosnians. The earth shook around him and dirt landed on his face and eyes. Screams of pain shattered the silence. A man screamed at the moon, his arm gushing blood on the surrounding ground.

He felt woozy and unwell. His eyes were blurry and unfocused. There were figures in white marching towards him. He crawled away, panting as panic built. He turned back, and the figures dissolved into the moonlight.

A man to his right began shouting, "We must surrender! We must surrender!" He threw down his gun and stripped off his uniform.

There was the sound of artillery weapons and then a voice demanded "Why are you crying Alija?"

The Serbs called Bosnians Alija, a slur using the first name of the Bosnian President. The Serbs had heard the commotion and were now attacking. He crawled across leaves and branches until the sound of screaming and artillery was far behind him and then he ran. Soon he was deep in the forest, and he saw the Bosnian fighter who had led them leaning against a tree.

"Are you all right?" he asked.

The Bosnian fighter panted. "I didn't breathe in much of the gas."

"Gas," he repeated, understanding why the men had lost their minds.

They walked further out of the woods and saw houses. They went in and drank water, found fruit in the orchard and broke open jars from the cooling room. He fell asleep on the couch, and in his dreams, he was on a mountain, and she was waiting for him, her arms stretched out, the wind blowing her dark hair back, her brown eyes sparkling with happiness.

Someone squeezed his shoulder, waking him. "We have to move," the Bosnian fighter told him.

He nodded and looked out the window. It was still night. He had slept perhaps an hour or two at the most. He rubbed his face as he stood and walked out of the house.

As dark fell, they reached a stream and had to stop. Heavy rain fell, the raindrops like needles on his skin.

Free Territory

I staked out the path leading to the Imam's house, watching as women passed to line up in front, noting the faces and names of those I knew. There had to be a repeat customer, someone who was a daily visitor. A woman passed by wearing a headscarf and it was only when she was in full profile to my hiding spot that I recognised Kamila. I peered out and watched her enter the house with others. She came out carrying two bags, and my arms broke out in goose pimples as I followed her back to her tent.

The next day I woke before dawn, my mother's dedication to morning prayer helping me. I went to the row near Kamila's tent and hid out of sight around the corner, watching the door. She exited early, and I followed her throughout the day as she completed her regular errands, checking the lists, getting provisions, chatting to different women. She returned to the Imam's house, and again exited with bags. When she exited, I followed her again.

The next day, I interviewed the women who she'd spoken to the day before. All of them went to see the Imam and were shocked by his accuracy in knowing about their families.

My stomach churned with nausea as I realised how the Imam was weaving his deception. I waited for Kamila on the third day, this time holding a large plank of wood I found. I stepped out when she was upon me. She gasped, stumbling and almost falling.

"What's in the bags?" I demanded.

"Nothing." She clutched them tighter to her chest.

"Drop it, or else." I motioned with the plank.

Her gaze narrowed with panic, and she looked around. I'd planned my ambush well. We were on a quiet path at the river, and there were no houses nearby. She dropped the bags, and I motioned for her to retreat before stepping forward. I opened up the first bag and found flour and sugar. In the second was coffee.

"You parasite!" I shouted.

"I'll share it with you," she blurted. "Half and half. No one needs to know but us."

For a moment, temptation overwhelmed me. All I had to do was make the deal and my mother's life would be immediately better. *But at what price, Seka*, Ramo's voice whispered in my ear.

I shook my head. "I will not be like you," I hissed. "Throw it in the river." I couldn't take the food and benefit from her evil deeds, and I couldn't let her have them either.

"No!" She threw herself forward and yanked the bags.

I swung the plank, and she just avoided it. With a maniacal laugh, I launched the bags into the water, enjoying the splash they made. "I'm going to tell everyone what you're doing. That you're working with the Imam and selling their private information."

She sobbed on her knees as she scratched at the ground, her desperate eyes searching the water.

"And I'll be waiting here every day, and you'll be throwing whatever food you stole into the river." I motioned for her to go.

Death March-Day Six

He crouched in the stream, shivering with cold, together with a couple of thousand others, hiding among the reeds as bullets whizzed overhead. They had reached the last Serb stronghold before the free territory, and their fighters were using the last of their ammunition to push them back. Suddenly, a hush descended, and the bullets stopped.

"Run, run!" someone screamed.

He sloshed out of the stream, relieved to feel the sun warming his skin. They walked through a valley and passed destroyed tanks and other military equipment.

"Not long now, comrades," the Bosnian fighter said.

Hours later, they arrived at a village. "We are free!" the fighter said.

He received food and drink, and that night he slept on the floor in the school building. After breakfast, the authorities guided him onto a bus with other refugees. When he woke up, the bus driver told him he was in Tuzla.

As he stepped out, women from Srebrenica surrounded him. He looked for her dark hair in the crowd while the women shouted the names of their menfolk, describing what they were wearing, asking him if he had seen them, desperation in their voices and eyes. He watched them mutely, unable to say the words they weren't ready to hear.

An hour later, everyone had claimed the men who had left the bus with him, and all the women were gone.

A widow and her young son watched him. "Do you have anywhere to go?"

He shook his head.

"Come home with me for a bit before you search for your kin."

Free territory

The next day, I told Belma, gaining her confidence, and we walked from tent to tent, telling all the women about the Imam's subterfuge and Kamila's hand in it. Some women shook their heads in disbelief, others outright accused me of lying.

"Then come with us," I implored. "We'll search her tent."

Soon, there was a crowd gathered behind me. When we reached Kamila's tent, she came out, her gaze widening in fear when she saw us.

"She's lying," she cried, trying to prevent us from coming in, but the crowd had a momentum of its own, and Belma and I, who were at the front of the line, were pushed in.

Her mother, Lebiba, was sitting at a table. "What is this ruckus?" she asked, standing to her full height and attempting to imbue her voice with authority.

I ignored her and headed for the crates that were stacked against the nylon wall. Lifting the blanket that covered it, I exclaimed with satisfaction and yanked out the provisions hidden within, throwing them on the bed. They had allocated so many provisions - two bags of flour, three bags of sugar, coffee, rice, noodles - that wouldn't have been given to just one person.

"You liar," Belma said, her gaze narrowing with disbelief.

"I had to." Kamila clutched her skirt. "My mother isn't well. I had to take care of her." Lebiba leaned her against Kamila's shoulders, trying to make herself pitiful.

"Neither is mine," I said. "You deserve nothing more than anyone else here." I waved towards the women who were now crowding into the tent.

One woman slapped Kamila so hard that she fell onto the floor. Everyone nearby snatched at all the provisions, and suddenly, the bed was empty.

I was the last to leave, smiling as I stared deep into Kamila's eyes as she wept. "I guess somebody cares."

Kamila and her mother left, going to Sarajevo to live with her aunt. The Imam's business took a downturn as women avoided him, but soon they found another mystic, an old woman who wrote out prayers in Arabic that they placed in a bottle of water. The women drank the water and then kneeled and prayed, and the old woman shared the visions they saw.

I found my mother searching through our meagre rations, taking the last of our flour. "No, you're not taking that." I snatched it back from her. "This woman is lying to you. She's just like the Imam, a faker."

"You don't know that," Mama argued, her gaze burning with the fervour of a believer. "She is a holy woman who knows."

I shook my head, holding the flour tighter against my chest.

Mama went to her bed and rifled under the mattress, taking out the gold necklace she'd worn when we escaped the enclave.

"No, don't trade that!" I implored. "Here," I said in defeat, returning the flour.

Mama left the tent, and I sat on my bed and cried.

"Torlak," Bilal's jovial voice called out. He lifted the tent flap and peered in.

I told him about the fight with my mother.

"You're fighting a lost cause," he said. "These women have nothing but their belief to sustain them."

I nodded, defeated. Who was I to take away their false hope?

Three weeks later

He arrived at Tuzla airport and saw the endless field of white tents stretching before him. He had spent two weeks in Tuzla with the widow, his feet bandaged and lifted up on the coffee table as the skin grew back on his soles.

Every day, the doorbell rang as more desperate womenfolk arrived and spoke the names of their missing menfolk; while he gave them her name, each side ended up disappointed and heartbroken.

He had already been to another refugee camp in a primary school in Kiseljak for three days searching for her, and then he'd taken a train and walked seven kilometres to reach the airport.

He approached the administration desk and told them his name, asking them to make an announcement. The administration desk repeated his name across the speakers, and a crowd gathered. Women holding photos, asking about their loved ones, begging him for answers.

"I'm sorry," he said, over and over.

He saw the crowd part as she shouted his name. Her dark hair flowing in the breeze, her brown eyes full of happiness.

"Emir, my son," she shouted as she engulfed him in a hug.

"Mama," he said, bending down to hug her tightly. He was finally home.

16-8,372

As I was walking to the headquarters, where they updated the lists of the missing, I heard a female voice cutting across the yard saying, "...Asian journalist..." I quickly ran to the headquarters and saw Alyssa Jones, her black glossy hair glinting in the sun.

I followed her to the administration building, intending to wait for her. Hearing her voice from inside the building, I walked around the corner and peered in the open window. She was talking to a UN soldier, holding a map in her hand. I quickly ducked back and stood quietly against the wall.

"So where did you see those remains?" she asked, holding up a map.

"Here at Konjević Polje." There was the sound of pen on paper. She must have been drawing on the map. "Also here on the hillside above Kravica. The bodies are rotting out into the sun. The bones scattered, skulls missing, and the clothes drying and rotting.

"How is it that the women outside know nothing about this?" Alyssa asked. "I've been interviewing all morning, and they keep talking about their men being prisoners in labour camps by Serbs. Even though they've been missing for eight months, they don't believe that they're dead."

"Nobody wants to tell them. No one in the Bosnian government wants to be the one to tell them that the world stood by as the Serbs created killing fields and were shooting them day and night for three nights until they killed everyone to a man. They don't have access to television or to newspapers. All they have are their fortune-tellers and their hope. And no one wants to be the one to tell them that the bodies are rotting because the Serbs won't have the bodies collected."

I leaned against the wall as I slowly and gently lowered myself to the ground, my legs trembling, covering my mouth to contain my moans of pain. When I heard Alyssa stepping out of the administration building, I finally returned to my body after losing time. I peered and saw she was speaking to Zaim, the interpreter from Potočari. He'd been able to leave Srebrenica because the Dutch had listed him as an employee. His family hadn't been so lucky. The Serbs took his mother, father, and brother, and now they were all missing. His wife Hedija had also been at Potočari, and they'd arrived together.

I had to see the fields, see if I could find Ramo.

I wiped my face and stood, taking deep breaths to give myself courage for the terrible deed I was about to commit. I ran to Zaim, who was standing by the cantina. "Zaim, Zaim," I said, sounding breathless. "It's Hedija." I grasped his jacket. "She's in pain. They think she might go into labour."

Zaim's face whitened. "Oh God, no, it's too early."

Guilt smashed into my stomach.

"It's okay. She's saying it's practice pain. That it's nothing. She didn't want me to come and worry you, but I thought you should know."

"I have to go." Zaim looked around frantically, searching for Alyssa.

"I'll tell them you'll be back soon. I'm sure they can wait for you." I nodded to the building as I tucked his identification in my pocket.

As soon as he was gone, I walked back to the side of the building and looked at the identification. We were both dark-haired and dark-eyed. I cut my hair soon after arriving, finding it frustrating attempting to keep it clean in the primitive camp-like conditions. I was tall and rangy, any feminine curves long vanished during the siege. It was an easy fix.

I found Bilal. "I need you to give me your jacket and hat."

"Why?" he asked, looking at me askance.

"I'm going to pretend to be Zaim so I can go with a UN convoy with a journalist."

"All right, Torlak. Don't tell me." Bilal took off his cap and placed it on my head. He put his cigarette in his mouth as he took off his jacket and handed it to me. I put on the jacket and snatched the cigarette from his mouth, taking a quick puff before returning it to him to settle my nerves.

"Hang on, are you telling the truth?" Bilal asked.

I gave him a quick smile and returned to the administration building.

Alyssa was standing outside, looking around with a concerned face.

"Do you remember me?" I asked in English. I'd been acting as an unofficial translator for all the desperate women who needed to speak to indifferent Red Cross volunteers, and my English had improved.

She frowned as she examined my face. It was two years since I saw her last.

"Yes, Srebrenica hospital," she said, placing me.

"That's right. Seka," I added.

"Of course, Seka." Alyssa's face cleared. "You and your family made it out okay?"

"Some of my family. Zaim had to go home because his wife is in labour. He asked me to take his place." I held up his ID badge.

Alyssa quickly glanced between the photo and me.

"Did you lose menfolk in Srebrenica?" she asked, her eyes narrowing.

"It's alright. I know," I said. "Zaim told me. I want to see it. I want to see if they're there."

Alyssa took a deep breath and nodded. "This is my interpreter, Zaim," she told the convoy, knowing that most of the non-Bosnians couldn't tell what a male or female name was.

When we drove through the Serb checkpoints, they gave my ID a cursory look and waved us through.

We arrived in Kravica, and I followed Alyssa up the hillside above the farmer's co-op. We reached the edge of the forest, and before us were corpses strewn across the earth. Skeletons rotting in the ground, the clothes stained and stiffened, infested with tiny grey flies and twisted around bones. The earth had bleached all the clothes of colour, blending them into the ground. The sight brought to mind a horror movie where a human body transformed into a wraith-like spirit, rising from the earth to attempt to drag others down. My soul was dragged to the depths of hell by the wispy spirits. There were holes in the clothing where bullets cut through. The bullets shot them where they stood, where they lay, as they crawled for a hiding place. Some corpses were headless or missing appendages, where animals had dragged off body parts.

Alyssa picked up a skull that was lying on the path and peered closer at the attached jawbone and the empty spaces among the teeth. "Someone has excavated teeth from this skull. There must have been a gold filling."

Serbs scavenged among the bones, searching for valuables. Those who were dead were denied the dignity of peace.

"This happened to my mother's people, too." She gently set the skull down on the ground again. "They had many enemies: the US, the Viet Cong all massacred them." She shuddered heavily, her dark eyes glistening. "When will we learn from our past?"

She gently squeezed my shoulder as she stood and waited respectfully a few steps until I gathered myself.

We walked further up the path and found bones ground into the earth, probably under the carriages of Serb families hauling wood. We entered the woods and saw bodies on stretchers made from wooden blankets and tree branches, their legs and arms still wrapped in blood-stained gauze.

I closed my eyes and focused my mind on my last image of Ramo. He'd been wearing his favourite t-shirt from his favourite band *Bijelo Dugme*, a bright blue t-shirt with a large white button on the front and the band's name. I searched for scraps of bright blue fabric in the field and saw a t-shirt that looked light. I bent down beside the corpse and, after steeling myself, wiped the dirt off the t-shirt, looking for a patch of white. There was only blue.

The jeep entered the refugee camp at Tuzla. I went to open the door when Alyssa stayed my hand.

"I was going to find you and give you this." She opened her satchel and took out an envelope. "I wanted to write an article about friendship during war." She handed me the envelope.

I glanced down and nearly dropped it when I saw Zora's name and her address in Australia.

"But after what we saw today, I can't bring myself to ask you for that." She patted my hand. "This is your letter. I'm just the courier."

I stumbled out of the jeep and watched it drive away. I went behind the headquarters and leaned on the wall, looking down at the envelope. I wanted so desperately to rip it open, to hear from Zora, to find out what her life was like.

I'd spent years dreaming of this moment and had never expected it would come like this. That I would hear from my Serb friend when the Serbs had killed so many people I loved. If I opened this letter and read what she wrote, then what? Write to her? What was the point of that? We weren't any longer those two innocent girls who had spent every day together. War had twisted me into someone dark and broken. I folded the letter and put it into my pocket, deferring my decision.

I returned to my tent and told my mother and brother about the remains scattered over the earth like they were God's fertiliser, that they stretched as far as the eye could see, and that our father was dead. Emir informed us that he hadn't seen him after the second day of the Death March when they were attacked and split up. If he hadn't been captured or killed, he would have returned to us by now.

"No, no," Mama cried, covering her ears. "Believe and pray. Your father will come back to us. You'll see," Mama said, her pupils wide and fixed, as she fervently believed. "Just like Emir came back to us."

My brother sat on the bed with his back bowed.

"Tell her Emir. Tell her he's dead," I begged.

He lifted his head, his blazing blue eyes resolute above his black beard. "We have to believe. I survived because it was divine will and so will our father."

Since returning from the Death March, Emir threw himself into religion: he abstained from alcohol and pork, prayed five times a day, and dressed modestly, with his arms and legs always covered, and grew a beard.

"No, he won't. They're all dead," I shouted, between tears.

"That's because your faith is weak." Emir stood and thundered. "They're slaughtering us because we're Muslim. We need to hold on to our faith and culture."

"I'm not Muslim, I'm Bosnian," I argued back.

"You're deluding yourself. You're a Muslim, Dževahira, and you will be to your dying day no matter what you do or say," he said.

He used my name as a weapon now and hardly ever called me Seka, even though he was the one who gave me the name.

In the past, I kept the peace by listening to him. Emir insisted we learn how to pray together and practised reciting Arabic prayers to each other. There was nothing much else to do, so I did. I learned the Arabic easier than he did, effortlessly being able to memorise prayers after a few passes, while he wrote out notes and read from them as he prayed. He'd say, "I have to work harder, but that's Allah's plan. To make me truly appreciate the effort to learn the faith," while I fought not to roll my eyes.

I'd placated him and my mother for months in their delusions, but I couldn't keep quiet any longer. "Stop believing in some magical entity that will save us. The existence of God is non-existent. There is no divine will. There is only what we can see and what we can touch. And our father is dead, and so is Ramo."

My mother gasped as I spoke. Emir turned towards me with rage in his eyes. For the first time in my life, I was afraid he would strike me. He walked over and gripped my shoulders. I flinched from the strength of his grip.

"All we have is faith. All we have is God's will. There is nothing else." He shook me so hard my teeth rattled against each other and then tossed me aside. I fell onto the bed. My mother cried as she watched, but didn't say a word in my defence.

I stood and ran out of the tent and into Bilal.

"You look like you saw a ghost, Torlak?" he said jocularly.

I stared at him with blank eyes.

"Woah," he placed his hands on my shoulders. "Are you all right?"

"They're all dead," I said, tears seeping from my eyes.

He quickly glanced around. We were in the middle of the row of tents. Passing women were looking at us curiously.

"Let's go for a walk." He put his arm over my shoulders and led me away from the tents and towards the forest behind the airport. He opened his jacket and took out a bottle of alcohol. "Here, take a sip."

I shook my head. I didn't drink any alcohol in the year since Emir returned from the Death March.

"Okay then." Bilal took a sip himself. "What did you see?"

I told him about what I'd seen and the argument with my mother and brother.

"Can you believe all these peasants?" he spat out. "They all think they're the chosen ones now."

"Don't you think it is Allah's will that you survived the killing fields?" I asked. Emir firmly believed that his survival was fated and a divine will, and he had to be devout to thank God.

"This world is fucking chaos. My survival was down to nothing more than sheer luck and rat cunning on my part. I knew when to hide and how to keep my head down," Bilal said, smoking feverishly.

"What about your Mum?" I asked.

"She was always a believer, and all this did was confirm her faith," Bilal said.

"But doesn't she expect you to do the same?" I asked.

Bilal shrugged. "I pray every once in a while, just for her sake, but I don't really give a shit. As long as I don't blaspheme, she leaves me alone. Plus, I tell her I'll marry a good Muslim girl, so that keeps her happy."

"My Mum and Emir are constantly on my back about it." I was bitter. It was like I didn't recognise my family. I'd lost everyone in my family already once, and it was like I was losing them again.

"That's because they're converts. There's nothing worse than someone who has converted. They're so self-righteous and overzealous. You know Torlak, you and I are very much alike. We don't buy into the bullshit that everyone else is peddling," Bilal said, his tongue thick as he blinked sleepily. "We should join forces."

He leaned over and attempted to kiss me. I let him for a moment. It was so long since someone touched me. Since the expulsion from Srebrenica, my family were strangers and there was no affection. I'd always had Ramo to hug and stroke and caress. It was nice to be hugged.

Bilal hugged me, and I curled into him, enjoying the feeling of a warm body and affection. He moved his mouth down and kissed me again. My eyes drifted closed, and I lay on the ground, feeling his hard body pressing me down. It was so nice to feel enveloped and safe. He nuzzled my neck, his hands on my breasts.

"Ramo," I whispered.

The warm body above froze, and Bilal lifted his head and looked at me. His face registered hurt.

"For fuck's sake, Torlak, you really know how to cockblock a guy," he said, sitting up.

"I'm sorry, I'm so sorry." I sat up, lifting my knees to my chest.

"I should have known better." Bilal lit another cigarette and stared up at the sky above us as he blew out the smoke. "You and Ramo had something special. He told me he would marry you, Seka Torlak. You were on his mind and his lips. I know that your name and face were the last thing he saw before he left this earth."

It was the first time someone told me openly Ramo was dead. Until now, everyone was constantly telling me to hope, to believe, while I was losing any hope.

"I miss him so much. He was my life, my everything. I don't know how to live without him." I cried deep, heart-wrenching sobs.

Bilal put his arm around my shoulders, holding me like a comrade. "You're going to have to find a way. You need to move on and get out of this shithole. He never wanted to stay in Bosnia. All he talked about during the siege was how the two of you would live a new life in Australia, where you didn't have to worry about all this bullshit. You do that, for him, for yourself. For me, because I'm going to be buried in this blood-soaked ground one day, my bones turning to dust, and I'll not have anything but this shit. You have a chance."

"But Emir and Mama don't want to go. They keep hoping that Babo and Ibrahim will come back. They don't want to make plans."

"Then fuck them. You move on and leave them behind. Take care of yourself if they're not going to."

11 July 1996

As I stitched his name, Ramo Muharemović, on the bright blue material, tears soaked into the fabric. It was the one-year anniversary of the massacre at Potočari, and the US Ambassador and Queen of Jordan had arranged a ceremony for the missing.

I took my place on the basketball stand, sitting between my mother and Belma. The stadium was hot, and I used the piece of paper I picked up off my seat to fan my face.

The translator repeated the words of the Ambassador after every few lines.

"And now we have a special videotaped presentation so that the world cannot deny what happened in Srebrenica a year ago and what happened to 8,372 of your menfolk."

There was a hushed tension in the room. The black screen turned on, and I saw the familiar white walls, which were a mosaic of windows and white panelling against the backdrop of the hills dotted with houses. Potočari. Women and men huddled beside the factory fence near the decrepit battery factory where I had spent three hellish days. Screaming filled my ears again. The odour of waste and blood filled my nostrils. I was back in hell. The screen changed and yet the screaming continued. The women in the basketball auditorium were screaming.

A shot of Ratko Mladić standing among the refugees, his face smiling and benevolent. *"We will evacuate anyone who wants to leave. Whether they are small, big, old or young, you will all be able to leave. Don't be afraid. Just slowly, let the women and children first. Thirty buses will arrive and they will transfer you to Kladanj. From there, Alija will transfer you to the territory they control. Just don't panic. Let the women and children go first and make sure you don't lose sight of any children."*

"Thank you, thank you," the women said.

"May you live long," a man called out.

Women screamed around me, their pain echoing in their unearthly screams as they saw the architect who was responsible for the death of their menfolk.

The picture changed, and Mladić was gone. Now, there were scenes of men on the plains near Kravica, surrounded by Serbs dressed in UN clothing. The camera panned out over the line of men kneeling on the ground. A close-up of a man's face screaming his son's name into the hills above him, asking him to surrender. On the ground behind him, a dark-haired man in a blue and chequered shirt, the unmistakable profile I'd seen every day of my life.

My mother screamed beside me. "That's my husband, Fadil, Fadil!" she screamed. I looked at her in slow motion. My veins froze as my mother screamed beside me. Her face showed anguish, and she yanked at her hair while crying before falling forward into a heap. Other women grabbed her, and a police officer carried her out.

I stood to follow, but couldn't look away from the screen. I searched as the frames changed, looking for a quick flash of blue, a white button, golden hair. Other women watched too. More screams followed, more women fainted. I stared so hard my head ached. There was nothing.

The screen stopped, and the US Ambassador stepped forward. She spoke about how she felt our pain, and she reached out to other women in the world to write letters we could read on our seats, but her words became white noise. I stumbled out of the basketball courts and towards my mother.

"He's gone, he's gone," she was swaying, holding the brightly coloured fabric that she'd sewed his name on.

"Yes, he is," I said.

Epilogue

March 1997

On the radio, the journalist announced the latest news. A team of twenty investigators and experts from the Office of the Prosecutor of the International Tribunal had exhumed the victims buried in a series of alleged mass grave sites in Bosnia and Herzegovina and Croatia on Sunday, 7 July 1996.

I took my mother's hand and held it tight as tears leaked from her eyes while Emir stared straight ahead, his hands fisted at his sides.

I picked up the duffel bag that contained my meagre belongings and got on the bus that was taking me to the airport. As we drove, I knew I should look out the window at my last glimpses of my homeland and attempt to record it in my retina for the future, but I just wanted to leave.

On the aeroplane, I looked as my homeland retreated. The verdant green forests that I had played in were now transformed into graveyards slipping from view. I felt relief.

I shifted, feeling the sharp edge of Zora's letter in my jeans pocket cutting into my skin. I didn't know if I would ever contact Zora, but I liked I had the option of a choice.

As the aeroplane moved away across Europe and the day vanished, I slid into sleep. Mama tucked my blanket around me, and Emir passed me his pillow.

In my dream, Ramo was sitting in the chair next to me. He took hold of my hand.

"We did it," he said, smiling as he peered out the window over my shoulder. *"We're leaving for our new world in Australia."* I looked down at our joined hands, our rings rubbing against each other. Our love would last for infinity. I held tighter onto his hand as we flew to our new life.

One year before–11 July 1996

Ramo stood in a field not far from Potočari, his hands tied behind his back, a blindfold over his eyes. He heard the angry sound of a bulldozer and then a gun shooting, shooting.

"Man, my trigger finger is sore," one of the Serbs spoke from somewhere in front of him. "Shooting this many Balija is giving me calluses."

A bottle sloshed, gulping sounds, a burp, and then breaking glass.

"We are doing God's work, cleansing the world of this filth."

Ramo let the darkness take him to Seka. In the blackness of his mind, they were sitting on an aeroplane, watching Bosnia recede from below them. They were moving into their new life.

Someone pushed him in his back, nudging him forward, and he left his dreamland and returned to hell. Someone ripped off the blindfold. He blinked, his eyes adjusting to the bright lights surrounding him. He was standing before a pit, a bulldozer on the edge of the pit across from him. Below him were the bodies of other Bosnian men he had spent days with on the soccer grounds, while the Serbs prepared for their final solution. The bodies looked like mannequins jumbled together in a tangle of limbs, blood seeping into the surrounding earth.

The Serb shooter stepped behind him, and the nozzle of the gun touched his scalp.

He closed his eyes and returned to the aeroplane. "We've made it," he told Seka and kissed her, taking hold of her hand and looking at their infinity rings side by side.

Note on the Novel

This novel is a work of historical fiction inspired by real events. To ensure authenticity and honour the experiences of those who lived through this period, I relied on first-hand accounts and survivor stories. These powerful narratives provided invaluable insight into the human cost of war and the resilience of those who endured it. The following books were instrumental in my research and served as essential resources for recreating the world and events depicted in this story. There were also numerous other sources that were used in the research of this novel. A more comprehensive bibliography is available in my book of essays *Fragments of History: The Essays Behind the Stories*.

Research Sources:

Clark, T. R. (2014). *The United Nations Peacekeepers and Local Population of the United Nations Safe Area Srebrenica: (De) Construction of Human Relationships*. Nova Gorica: University of Nova Gorica Graduate School.

Filipović, Zlata. (2006). *Zlata's Diary: A Child's Life in Wartime Sarajevo, Revised Edition*. New York: Penguin Books.

Fink, Sheri. (2003). *War Hospital: A True Story of Surgery and Survival*. New York: Public Affairs.

Hasanović, Hasan. (2016). *Surviving Srebrenica*. Aberdeenshire: Lumphanan Press.

Gutman, R. (1993a). *A witness to genocide: The first inside account of the horrors of "ethnic cleansing" in Bosnia*. Macmillan.

Leydesdorff, Selma. (2015). *Surviving the Bosnian Genocide: The Women of Srebrenica Speak*. Bloomington: Indiana University Press.

Nuhanović, Hasan. (2019). *The Last Refuge: A True Story of War, Survival and Life Under Siege in Srebrenica* (M. Evtov & A. Sluiter, Trans.). London: Peter Owen Publishers.

Rohde, David. (2012). *Endgame: The Betrayal and Fall of Srebrenica, Europe's Worst Massacre Since World War II*. New York: Penguin Books.

Sacco, Joe. (2018). *Safe Area Goražde: The War in Eastern Bosnia 1992–1995*. Seattle: Fantagraphics Books.

Sekulić, Midhat. (2014). *Srebrenica: Massacre on School Playground*. DW. Retrieved March 25, 2019, from .

Sells, M. A. (1996). *The bridge betrayed: Religion and genocide in Bosnia*. University of California Press.

Sudetić, Chuck. (1998). *Blood and Vengeance: One Family's Story of the War in Bosnia* (1st ed.). New York: W. W. Norton & Co.

Suljagić, Emir. (2005). *Postcards from the Grave*. London: Saqi Books.

Willem, J., & Both, N. (1996). *Srebrenica: Record of a war crime*. London: Penguin Books.

Fragments of History: The Essays Behind the Stories

If you're interested in learning more about the historical context of Srebrenica and the research that informed this novel, I have compiled a companion collection of essays titled *Fragments of History: The Essays Behind the Stories.*

This book is not commercially available and is offered exclusively to my newsletter subscribers. You can sign up at www.amrapajalic.com

Acknowledgment

I would like to express my deepest gratitude to the survivors who have shared their stories, both in books and through interviews. Their courage in recounting such painful memories has allowed future generations to bear witness to the truth and understand the enduring impact of these events. This novel is dedicated to them, as well as to all those who were silenced by war and genocide.

BONUS CONTENT

A powerful reckoning with memory, identity, and survival.

Fragments of History uncovers the hidden truths behind the Srebrenica genocide—from the silencing of Muslim identity to the weaponisation of Islamophobia and the myth of Yugoslav unity. Through deeply personal and sharply analytical essays, it honours the resilience of Bosniak women and preserves the voices history tried to erase.

Only available to email subscribers and not commercially sold

https://www.amrapajalic.com/seka-torlak-series.html

Seka Torlak Series

0.5: The Tree That Stood Still

Srebrenica 1992

In a town shattered by prejudice, two girls forge a friendship that defies the ravages of war...

Seka and Zora have been inseparable, growing up as neighbours and best friends in the once peaceful town of Srebrenica. But as Yugoslavia begins to splinter and nationalism sweeps through the region, their town is torn apart by prejudice and violence. Suddenly, Seka and Zora find themselves on opposite sides of a brutal conflict, their friendship strained by the rising tide of hatred.

As the horrors of war descend upon Srebrenica, Seka and Zora's bond is tested like never before. With nationalist propaganda fuelling distrust andf ear, the streets they once played in become battlegrounds. Amidst the chaos, they must navigate a world where friends can become enemies overnight. Will their friendship endure the storm of war and prejudice, or will it be shattered by the forces tearing their town apart?

Book 1: Time Kneels Between Mountains

Srebrenica, 1992

In a town where survival is a daily battle, there are those who seek justice...

Overnight, Seka Torlak's life as a regular teenager is upended as Srebrenica, her once peaceful town, falls under siege and she faces starvation, shelling, and sniper attacks. When desperately needed antibiotics and food disappear and are sold on the black market, Seka vows to investigate the corruption and bring the culprits to justice.

As the war ravages Srebrenica, Seka's resilience is tested as she navigates loss, fear, and the harsh realities of war. Yet, amidst the devastation, she finds a glimmer of hope as her relationship with Ramo blossoms from friendship to love. But as she fights for justice and love, will Seka triumph, or will the brutal war tear everything she holds dear apart?

Bonus Short Story: Belma's Liberation

In a village shadowed by abuse, there are those with courage who fight for liberation...

Sign up to my newsletter and read *Belma's Liberation* to find out how Seka saved her friend from her abusive father

Book 2: Ghosts Among the Gumtrees

Melbourne, 1997

In a city where the guilty roam free, there are those who seek retribution...

After surviving the brutal siege of Srebrenica, Seka Torlak is trying to rebuild her life as a refugee in Melbourne, 1997. But her fragile peace is shattered when she spots a war criminal responsible for her father's death walking freely in the city. Determined to uncover his true identity and bring him to justice, Seka delves into an investigation that reveals a sinister underbelly of suburbia, where genocide deniers hide in plain sight.

Haunted by memories of war and loss, Seka grapples with the raging conflict within her: the pursuit of justice versus the thirst for retribution. As she navigates this perilous path, she must decide what she is willing to sacrifice for the truth. Will Seka find her salvation, or will she lose her soul in the process?

Bonus Short Story: Zora's Story

In the ruins of war, there are those who cling to memories of friendship...

Sign up to my newsletter and read *Zora's Story* to find out her story in escaping the war

Book 3: Mad Dawn Winter

Riverwood, 1998

In a town submerged with secrets and corruption, there are those who seek the truth...

Seka Torlak, now a journalism cadet, relocates to the tranquil town of Riverwood in 1998, seeking a fresh start. However, her peace is short-lived when she stumbles upon a cold case involving the murder of a formerVietnam Vet. Driven by a grieving mother's plea for justice, Seka begins to uncover a web of secrets that this seemingly idyllic town has buried deep.

In her quest for truth, Seka befriends Dawn Winter, a fellow Bosnian woman haunted by the loss of a friend and ostracized by the townspeople for her tributes to the fallen. As Seka digs deeper, she finds herself entangled in a dangerous game of deceit and loyalty, facing ghosts of the past and present. Will she unravel the truth and deliver justice before it's too late, or will the town's dark secrets consume her?

Bonus Short Story: Art's War

In a time of loss and grief, there are those who pursue the truth...

Sign up to my newsletter and read *Art's Fall* to find out about his investigation first-hand

Bonus Short Story: The Regrets of Ben Hayes

In a war where fear reigns, love remains unspoken...

Sign up to my newsletter and read *The Regrets of Ben Hayes* to find out about his first love during his service as a National Serviceman.

BONUS CONTENT

SHORT STORY
HISTORICAL RESEARCH ESSAYS
TEACHING RESOURCES

https://www.amrapajalic.com/seka-torlak-series.html

About the author

Amra Pajalic is an award-winning Australian author, educator, and indie publisher known for crafting compelling stories that blend heart, humour, and heritage. Her work explores themes of identity, belonging, and resilience, often drawing from her Bosnian background.

She won the 2009 Melbourne Prize for Literature's Civic Choice Award for her debut novel *The Good Daughter*, re-released as *Sabiha's Dilemma* (PishukinPress, 2022). The anthology she co-edited, *Growing up Muslim in Australia* (Allen and Unwin, 2014), was shortlisted for the 2015 Children's Book Council of the year awards and her memoir *Things Nobody Knows But Me* (Transit Lounge, 2019) was shortlisted for the 2020 National Biography Award. Her short story collection *The Cuckoo's Song* (Pishukin Press) features previously published and prize-winning stories.

Amra is the author of the Sassy Saints series, a young adult contemporary trilogy set in Melbourne's western suburbs. These stories feature smart-mouthed teens, love triangles, fake friends, and fierce girl power, offering a refreshing take on multicultural Australian life.

She is also the creator of the gripping Seka Torlak crime mystery series. Forged on the war-torn streets of Srebrenica, Seka Torlak fights for justice, retribution and truth.

Amra is committed to accessibility and inclusion in publishing. Through her micro-press, PishukinPress, she releases her titles in a wide range of formats—including audiobook, large print, dyslexic font, paperback, ebook, and hardback—to ensure all readers can experience her stories.

When she's not writing, Amra is podcasting on *Amra's Armchair Anecdotes*, mentoring emerging writers, and delivering workshops across Australia on self-publishing, writing craft, and creative resilience.

Amra Pajalić publishes her dark fiction using pen name A. P. Pajalic. She also publishes romance novels under pen name Mae Archer.

goodreads.com/author/show/3310015.Amra_Pajalic

facebook.com/AmraPajalicAuthor/

instagram.com/amrapajalicauthor/

https://twitter.com/AmraPajalic

tiktok.com/@amrapajalic

youtube.com/c/AmraPajalicAuthor

SIGN UP FOR AMRA'S AUTHOR NEWSLETTER
For news, giveaways, bonus material, and sneak peeks, please sign up to her newsletter below.

www.amrapajalic.com

Help Bring the *Seka Torlak* Series to Life—Your Reviews Matter!

Dear Reader,

Thank you for reading *Time Kneels Between Mountains*, the first novel in the *Seka Torlak* series—a gripping story of justice, survival, and resilience set against the backdrop of war. This series is deeply personal, shaped by years of research and a passion for shedding light on untold histories.

Now, I need *your* help. Reviews are the lifeblood of independent authors like me. They help spread the word, connect the right readers with the book, and ensure this series reaches as many people as possible. If you've read *Time Kneels Between Mountains*, I'd love to hear your thoughts!

A few sentences about what resonated with you—whether it's Seka's journey, the historical depth, or the emotional impact—can make a world of difference. You can leave your rating and/or review on the website you purchased the book from.

Your support means everything. Thank you for being part of this journey with me.

Hvala lijepo/Much thanks,
Amra Pajalić

Also by

Seka Torlak Series
The Tree That Stood Still
Time Kneels Between Mountains
Ghosts Among the Gumtrees
Mad Dawn Winter

Memoir
Things Nobody Knows But Me
Growing up Muslim in Australia

Sassy Saints Series
Sabiha's Dilemma
Alma's Loyalty
Jesse's Triumph

Young Adult
The Cuckoo's Song
The Climb

Romance as Mae Archer
Return to Me
Hollywood Dreams

Vintage Dreams

Dark Fiction/Horror as A.P. Pajalic
Woman on the Edge

www.ingramcontent.com/pod-product-compliance
Lightning Source LLC
Chambersburg PA
CBHW030535190726

48283CB00006B/1922